HOT SEAL TARGET

HOT SEAL Team - Book 6

LYNN RAYE HARRIS

The Hostile Operations Team® and Lynn Raye Harris® are trademarks of H.O.T. Publishing, LLC.

Printed in the United States of America

First Printing, 2018

For rights inquires, visit www.LynnRayeHarris.com

HOT SEAL Target
Copyright © 2018 by Lynn Raye Harris
Cover Design Copyright © 2018 Croco Designs

ISBN: 978-1-941002-38-4

Chapter One

ADAM "BLADE" GARRISON SAT IN A CONFERENCE room at HOT HQ and waited for someone to tell him what the hell was going on. An hour ago, he'd been at a housewarming party for one of his teammates. Shortly after he left the gathering, he'd gotten a call from Colonel John "Viper" Mendez ordering him to come in to work. So here he was, still wondering what the CO had meant by his cryptic comments about an assignment and a woman.

The door swung open and Mendez entered. His second-in-command, Alex "Ghost" Bishop, followed. A third man strode inside, and Blade's gut tightened. If Ian Black was involved, you could be sure this assignment was going to be sketchy as fuck.

Blade got to his feet, but Mendez waved him off. "As you were."

He sank onto the seat again, his gaze darting between the three men.

"You speak Mandarin," Black said casually.

"Yes, sir. I also speak Cantonese." Blade answered automatically before his brain processed the fact that Black had spoken in Mandarin. "My parents were international bankers," he continued in Chinese. "I basically grew up in Hong Kong. I learned Cantonese because that's the primary dialect there. But Mandarin is more useful in general."

"That it is."

Ghost and Mendez watched them with interest, but Blade was pretty certain neither man spoke Chinese. Though scratch that, because with those two you just never knew. They wouldn't reveal a skill unless they had to.

Black switched back to English. "Mandarin is a necessary skill for this assignment. Though Cantonese is certainly useful."

Ghost dragged out a keyboard and called up a slide show. Blade stared at the man pictured on the first slide. He was older, probably about fifty, with graying temples and an arrogant expression that spoke to an infallible belief in his own superiority.

"Hunter Halliday," Mendez said. "He owns Halliday Tech Solutions. Made a mint selling microchips for the personal computer market. He has strong ties to Chinese technology companies. He just signed a contract with the US government to supply computer mainframes to the military for their operations centers."

"I take it there's a problem somewhere," Blade stated. It wasn't a question.

"Hunter Halliday has a lot of ties to China, some of which aren't quite as lily-white as he'd like us to believe," Ian Black said. "I'm not willing to trust any Halliday products near military assets, quite frankly, but it wasn't my decision to make."

Blade frowned. "So if you don't get the evidence to prove he's up to something, the military will soon be relying on his equipment in their ops control centers." Which was like taking over the brain in order to control the body.

"Bingo," Black said.

Blade slewed his gaze to Mendez and Ghost. Mendez was as cool and unreadable as always. Ghost was only slightly less so. If they were both here, on a weekend, then this was a seriously big deal.

"So where do I come in?" Blade asked the three of them.

"Mrs. Halliday," Mendez said as the slide flipped to a picture of a woman.

Blade's gut tightened. She looked familiar. He knew her, but how? She was gorgeous, and he didn't think he would have forgotten a woman like that.

And then it hit him like a ton of bricks. *Impossible.*

It couldn't be her. Could it?

"There's been a mistake."

"No mistake," Mendez said. "Quinn Evans married Hunter Halliday two years ago."

Quinn Evans.

The woman on the screen was beautiful. Incredibly so. The Quinn Evans he'd known had been terminally shy and extremely overweight. He'd met her when his parents moved to London during his junior year of high school. Some kids were bullying her in the hallway, calling her fat and telling her to be careful or she'd fall through the floor when she took a step. They hooted and howled and called her a pig. Tears had been streaming down her chubby face— and Blade had snapped.

He didn't know why he'd cared, but there was no way in fuck he was letting those assholes break her down any more than they already had. He'd grown up in Hong Kong, learning to fight and participating in mixed martial arts bouts that sprang up in the meaner districts of the city. So when he'd turned his anger on those punks, they'd scattered.

And they'd never bothered Quinn again. She'd taken to following him around shyly, and he'd mostly ignored her. He'd had big plans for himself, and he wasn't going to get bogged down in relationships— friendly ones *or* romantic ones—that made leaving hard when the time came.

When he'd finally realized Quinn wasn't going to stop following him, he'd sighed and turned and started talking to her. They'd become friends in spite of his self-limiting beliefs. Quinn was funny and smart and pretty in her own way. He'd encouraged her to believe in herself even when she didn't want to. He'd never thought of her romantically, but he'd cared for her more than he'd cared for anyone during that time.

They'd been friends for nearly two years when they graduated and went their separate ways. They'd stayed in touch for the first couple of years, but gradually they'd stopped communicating. Or maybe he had. It was hard to be in touch regularly when you were a SEAL.

"Mrs. Halliday was a fitness blogger and a model," Mendez said as Ghost clicked over to a montage of a very slender and toned Quinn posing in a bikini.

A fucking bikini! Whoa…

"She moved to New York, where she met Hunter. They dated on and off for a few months before they married. Immediately afterward, she stopped working. No more blogging or photo shoots, though her blog was very popular at the time. Millions of people wanted her advice on losing weight."

"She married a billionaire. She probably didn't need the money," Blade said wryly. He let his gaze drift over the photos. Holy shit, what a transformation. He was proud of her. Not because she was thin but because she'd made up her mind and gone after her goal. She'd always said she wanted to walk into a store and buy something off the rack instead of needing to go to a special store and pray they had something big enough to fit. And by God, she'd done it. She'd really done it.

Ghost flicked to a new slide. This one was more

recent. Blade could tell because her expression wasn't the same as in the earlier photos. It was less... happy. Yeah, that was the word. She'd looked free and proud in the pictures of her fitness modeling. She looked troubled in this photo. Like a dark cloud had settled over her life and wasn't budging.

"I knew Quinn a long time ago. If you think she's going to tell me all about the dirty dealings of her husband, I think you're mistaken," Blade said to the other men.

Ian Black lifted an eyebrow. "Quite frankly, we don't know if she's in on it with him. So no, I don't expect her to confess to you. There are rumors she's tried to leave him but he won't let her go." Black shrugged. "Could just be gossip to try to deflect any suspicion from her."

Blade was still trying to process the possibility that Quinn was guilty of conspiracy. Her mother was British, but her father was American. She'd been born in Atlanta, Georgia, and she had dual citizenship. He liked to think she'd care at least a little bit about her country. Enough to not betray it, at any rate.

Then again, he'd met a lot of people over the years who didn't give a shit one way or the other. Money was a powerful motivator. And there was no doubt Quinn was living a life far removed from the one she'd led when he knew her. Her parents hadn't been dirt poor or anything, but they certainly hadn't been rich. Her mother worked in the same bank as his parents. Her father had been a businessman of some sort. Not banking though. A manager in a retail store or something. If Quinn left her husband, what kind of life would she lead? Not the kind she currently had, that's for sure.

"Then what do you want from me?" Blade asked. Because he was thoroughly confused about the entire situation. It was clear they'd brought him here because of his past relationship with Quinn. And because he could speak Chinese.

The three men exchanged glances. It was Ian Black who spoke. "You know I run a mercenary outfit," he said. "I'm the guy people call when they want stuff done. I'm a fixer, a man willing to work for anyone, the kind of guy who'll take anybody's money so long as it spends. Including Hunter Halliday's."

Blade didn't believe it for a second. He'd been involved in more than one operation where Black was clearly on the right side of the situation. The man was a patriot regardless of how he operated. In fact, his operations were nothing more than a cover for the important work he did in protecting the country from traitors and terrorists. He worked for the same reasons HOT did, even if he did it differently.

"Mrs. Halliday needs a protector. Her husband asked me to find one for her."

Blade's hackles rose. "Is she in danger?"

"Hunter is a collector," Black said. "He likes beautiful things. Mrs. Halliday is a possession, a one-of-a-kind object he intends to protect—or imprison. Not sure which. But if she's in danger, he's the one who put her there."

"How so?"

"We think the microchips in his processors have backdoor coding that will allow him to spy on American military technology and movements. There are a lot of people who would kill for that ability, and Halliday is busily playing them against one another. The Chinese mafia, Beijing." He frowned. "No matter what she might know, Quinn Halliday is a pawn in his game. If someone thinks it will gain them access to Halliday's machines, they won't hesitate to use Quinn as a bargaining chip."

Blade's head was spinning. "It sounds like a *Mission Impossible* movie."

"Yeah, kinda."

"What do you want me to do?"

"Go in as her protector. Infiltrate Halliday's network and find out who he's working with. We don't know that the backdoor coding is really there, but we'd like to find out before the computers are in use."

"I'm not a programmer."

"No, but you have other skills."

"And what about Quinn? She'll know me."

"That might work to our advantage."

Blade didn't like the sound of that. "You want me to lean on our former friendship to see what she knows?"

"That's precisely what we want, sailor," Mendez

said. "The security of this nation might depend on it."

All he could picture was Quinn's tearful face that day when he'd beat the hell out of those boys for teasing her. She'd looked at him like he was magical. Like he could do no wrong. And now he was going to approach her like she was the enemy.

Because she could be. "Then I guess I have no choice."

Ian Black reached into the leather case he'd brought with him and pulled out a folder. He tossed it on the table.

"Memorize the contents before leaving this room. Halliday's in Hong Kong on business. He has a home and an office there, so he could be there for a few weeks. You're on the noon flight tomorrow."

Blade reached for the folder with two fingers and pulled it toward him. He looked at the three men. "Will I have backup?"

Mendez's expression didn't change. "You'll have a contact in Ian's outfit. HOT can't be involved in this operation. In fact, you aren't HOT at the moment—you're a mercenary in Black Defense International. Otherwise known as Black's Bandits."

Ian Black gave him a sugary-sweet grin. "Smile, pumpkin. We're gonna have a good time. Promise."

Chapter Two

WHEN THE PLANE LANDED IN HONG KONG, BLADE grabbed his carry-on bag from the overhead compartment and made his way to the exit. It was early morning and he'd been flying for what seemed like a week but was really only about twenty-four hours, give or take.

He'd gone over Ian Black's dossier on Halliday a million times before he walked out of HOT HQ. Everything they knew about Halliday's business was in there. Hunter was dirty, no doubt about it, but he was also smart. Nothing seemed to stick to him. He could walk through a rain of shit and come out smelling like a bouquet of roses.

Why had Quinn married a man like that? Was it the money? Blade frowned. Had to be. What else?

It was odd to think he was going to be her protector. Halliday didn't have a personal bodyguard, but he wanted one for his wife. He had security at his business, and there was security at his residence, but he didn't travel with anyone. His wife, however, wasn't allowed out of the house without protection—or, to be more accurate, someone to control her movements.

A chauffeur waited at the curb, standing beside a Rolls Royce and holding a sign with Blade's name on it. Blade walked over and spoke to the man in Cantonese. He and Ian had considered obscuring the fact he spoke the language, but Quinn would know he could.

The chauffeur took Blade's bag and placed it in the car. Blade climbed into the back seat, and they were soon gliding away from the airport and toward Kowloon and Halliday's apartment.

Once they finally reached the building, another man met the car, opening the door and smiling. "Mr. Garrison?"

"Yes."

"Mr. Halliday would like you to go straight up, sir."

Blade exited the car and waited for his bags, but the man shook his head. "Your bags will be sent up. Please," he said, waving his arm toward the entrance. "Mr. Halliday awaits."

Blade dug a few bills from his pocket and handed them to the man. He knew his bags would be thoroughly searched before they arrived, which was one of the reasons he had no surveillance equipment on him. If he tried to smuggle bugs into Halliday's home, he'd be busted before he ever got inside. And the mission would be over.

He headed for the elevator that would take him to the top of the tower. Once he reached the suite, he was shown inside by a butler in white gloves who bowed and spoke softly.

A man stood on the balcony overlooking the harbor, holding a glass of whiskey and barking orders into a phone. He looked just like his photos. Fiftyish, a little paunchy, with graying hair and a manner that said he was the shit and he knew it. Blade disliked him on sight.

Halliday turned and saw Blade standing there. He motioned for Blade to come outside while he continued to talk on the phone. Blade did so, glancing around in case Quinn was nearby. She'd be surprised to see him, but that was nothing he couldn't handle.

"Yeah, yeah. I hear you, but that's not the way this is going to go," Hunter said. "Get me my price or I'm done." He pocketed the phone and turned a toothy smile on Blade. "If you don't tell these people what you want, they'll dick you over every time."

Blade didn't answer since an answer didn't seem required.

"You're Adam Garrison?"

"Yes, sir."

"You come highly recommended," he said, clinking his ice before sipping the whiskey. "Mr. Black says you were a Navy SEAL."

"I was."

"Why'd you quit?"

"Quit?" Blade shook his head. "You don't quit being a SEAL, sir. You simply take your skills elsewhere. And I did so because I like to get paid. If I'm risking my ass, that is."

Hunter laughed. "That's fair. What did Black tell you about this job?"

"That your wife needs protecting."

"That's true. She's a hot little piece, make no mistake, but that's not the entire reason." Hunter sighed and motioned toward the door. They returned to the suite, and he strode over and sank into a chair that faced the view.

Spectacular fucking view of the harbor and Hong Kong laid out in the foreground with mountains soaring in the background. Blade hadn't been to Hong Kong in years now. He'd almost forgotten how beautiful it was. And how amazing. He'd missed it.

He sat when Hunter waved his hand toward a chair. The butler appeared.

"Get me a cigar, Li-Wu. Mr. Garrison?"

"Call me Blade. I'll have a whiskey."

"Cigar and two whiskies, Li-Wu."

The man bowed and strode away.

Hunter leaned back against the cushions and took a slug of his drink. The apartment was opulent, with floor-to-ceiling windows—truly impressive because the ceilings were about eighteen or so feet tall—rich furnishings, including a grand piano, and multiple rooms leading off the main seating area. What Blade assumed was priceless art graced the walls.

Hunter followed his gaze. "You ever collect art, Blade?"

Blade settled his gaze on Hunter. "No, sir. Can't say as I have."

"But you've been to museums? Seen the great masters?" He pointed at one of the paintings. "That's a Picasso. Ever see one of those before?"

"Been to the Prado in Madrid once. Can't say as they had any Picassos there." He tilted his head. "There was another museum though. Had a big fucking painting by Picasso. Took up an entire room."

Hunter's eyes gleamed. "*Guernica*. His master-work." He swigged the remainder of the whiskey in his glass. "When something is truly beautiful and one of a kind, you want to own it. And then you need to protect your property from others who might try to steal it away. Because they will try. Do you understand what I'm talking about?"

Blade's gut tightened. He understood far too much, unfortunately. Aided by the dossier, he knew what kind of man he was dealing with. Halliday was implying that Quinn was his property. That he owned her. She wasn't the first woman he'd treated like a possession—but she was only the second he'd married. His first wife had died in a skiing accident in Chamonix five years ago. Her family despised Hunter and blamed him for her death even though he'd been on business in Paris at the time.

He had not, however, been too broken up by the loss.

"I think so, sir," Blade replied, bringing his mind back to the conversation at hand.

"My wife is a beautiful woman, Blade. There are people who would take advantage of that. I won't allow it."

Anger began to flare deep inside. "Have there been any threats to her safety? Or is this more of a general protection detail?"

"There are always threats. I'm a powerful man, and there are people who would use any method they can think of to get to me. I don't want Quinn talking to anyone you don't talk to first. No private conversations. No private meetings. You will accompany her everywhere and you will let no one get near her without you. And you'll clear her schedule with me. No exceptions."

Blade didn't like this man. At all. But then again, he hadn't thought he would. The wariness in Quinn's eyes had told him that much. She might be involved in Hunter's schemes, but she still wasn't a happy woman.

"It would help if I had a better idea of what you're trying to prevent, Mr. Halliday."

"I just told you." His eyes were steely. "Any questions?"

Fuck yeah. But Blade managed not to lose his cool. "Not at the moment."

"Good."

Li-Wu returned with a tray containing whiskeys and a cigar. Once he passed them out, Hunter lit the cigar and stood. "Li-Wu will show you to your room. We're dining out tonight, and I'll expect you to accompany Quinn while I do business."

"Yes, sir." Blade set the whiskey down without touching it. Hunter didn't even blink.

"And Blade?"

"Yes, sir?"

"My wife is a beautiful woman. You may be tempted. Don't." There was true malice in the man's eyes.

Blade nodded. "I'm a professional, Mr. Halliday."

"Ian Black said so."

"He wasn't wrong."

"I hope not. I won't hesitate to have you thrown off that balcony out there if you prove otherwise."

Blade picked up the whiskey and downed it. *Fucker.*

"Noted, sir."

————

QUINN WAS TRAPPED. She gazed out at the lights flickering in the darkness and felt like she should be able to disappear in a city this size. Except she couldn't disappear at all. Hunter would find her. He had too much money, and too many people were willing to be bought. No one would protect her from him.

She turned and went into the bathroom so she could apply her makeup. There was a business dinner tonight, and Hunter had decreed that she was going. She hated attending these things, but she had no choice. If she feigned sickness, he wouldn't believe her.

He never believed her.

She brushed on mascara, let her hair down from the hot rollers and finger combed it, then pulled on her little black dress and smoothed it over her curves. She'd fought for those curves. She still fought for them, truth be known. Losing over one hundred pounds hadn't been easy—the constant exercise and dieting, the surgeries to remove excess skin and lift her breasts, the fight to maintain her weight—but she'd never go back to the girl she'd been before.

One last look in the mirror and she turned on her heel and strode from the palatial bathroom to the bedroom she shared with Hunter. Not that she really shared it with him since he never spent the night there these days. He worked long hours when they were in Hong Kong, though he also went to parties where he indulged in hookers and God only knew what else. When he came home late, he slept in one of the guest rooms.

She was relieved, to be honest. Quinn held no illusions when it came to the man she'd married. Not anymore, anyway. He wanted a beautiful trophy on his arm, but he wanted something far different in his bed. There he wanted someone he paid, someone who asked no questions and did anything they were told to do, no matter how degrading.

He hadn't touched her in six months now. She didn't know what she'd do if he tried—though she always expected it, especially when he was drinking or angry.

Quinn slipped on a pair of strappy designer heels, gathered her wrap and clutch, and made her way toward the living room where Hunter was waiting for her. He sat in a chair facing the hallway. There was another man with him, but this one's back was to her. She hesitated only a moment before striding forward under the possessive eye of Hunter. He made her shudder with revulsion, but she kept going.

Once, she'd thought he was charming and wonderful. And he had been, so long as he'd been trying to win her. He'd been tender, attentive. He'd made her feel special. After she'd married him, he'd stopped the pretense of being a decent human being. He'd gotten his prize and there was no longer any reason to pretend. She could still recall with brutal clarity the first time he'd backhanded her. They'd been married a week.

"Here is Mrs. Halliday now," Hunter said, and the man sitting in the chair stood. He didn't turn immediately. She had an impression of strength and size—and then he turned and Quinn halted. Blinked.

Her heart sped up and her tongue stuck to the roof of her mouth. But Hunter was watching, and the last thing she would ever do was show him that she was stunned. Because he'd want to know why, and then he might send Adam away once he knew.

Adam Garrison! She had so many questions, none of which she could ask with Hunter standing by.

"Mrs. Halliday," Adam said, and her heart throbbed as her brain raced to figure out the situation. Why was he here? What was going on? Was this an elaborate setup? Was Hunter doing this to punish her?

"This is your new bodyguard, Quinn," Hunter said. "You can call him Blade."

Blade?

Quinn took a deep breath. She couldn't show any emotion until she figured this out. She forced a polite yet distant smile to her lips. She was good at that. So good. She'd had to learn since the man she'd married looked for any signs of partiality or affection toward anyone—or any creature—on her part. Then he ruthlessly cut them from her life. She'd learned the hard way when she'd come home one day and her cat was gone.

After she'd sobbed and begged him to give Tigger back, he'd said it was too late. Tigger had been taken to a shelter and adopted by a family with a little girl who adored the cat. Did she really want to ruin a little girl's happiness that way?

Yes, she did, but she knew it wasn't going to happen. Hunter wasn't going to get Tigger back no matter how she begged. She'd called the shelter when

Hunter wasn't around and verified that her cat was really okay. Once she knew that, she'd stopped asking for his return. But she still missed him. So damn much.

Quinn swallowed a knot of unhappiness as she looked at the man standing in front of her. He was still tall, still handsome. But so much more intimidating than he had been when she'd last seen him. When was that? Eight years ago?

Only eight years. She felt as if she'd aged fifty years since then.

She held out her hand for a polite shake. She was trembling, but she hoped he didn't notice.

"Blade? Well, that certainly sounds intimidating."

"I hope so, ma'am." His gaze searched hers as he took her hand briefly, but she didn't give in to even an ounce of reaction. So far as he was concerned, she had no idea who he was. It was better that way. Better for them both.

Li-Wu walked into the room and announced the car was ready. Hunter strode away, utterly unconcerned about her. Adam—Blade—stepped aside and motioned for her to precede him.

There was a lump in her throat as she followed Hunter's retreating form. Tears gathered in the corners of her eyes. She dragged in a breath and told herself in no uncertain terms that she couldn't indulge them. Not now. Not here.

Not ever. Tears were weak. And Quinn couldn't

afford weakness. Not if she wanted to survive the hell she currently lived in. There would come a day when she could walk away without consequences.

But that day wasn't today.

Chapter Three

BLADE KEPT AN EYE ON THE PEOPLE AROUND QUINN. They were attending a house party at the home of one of Hong Kong's premier businessmen. His rooftop apartment was even more spectacular than Hunter Halliday's, complete with a pool and grass and a band. Waiters circulated between the guests, offering trays of appetizers and glasses of wine and champagne.

Hunter held court with a group over in one corner of the yard, smoking cigars and howling with laughter. Quinn was with a different group. She didn't talk much, but she stood politely and nodded, adding to the conversation when required.

Blade stayed behind her, just within reach, not saying a word, not drinking alcohol or eating any of the food. Instead, he sized people up, watched those who stared at Quinn until they caught him looking and turned away.

He hadn't had a moment alone with her yet, and he wasn't trying to get one. It would happen naturally, and he'd let her lead the conversation when it did. He knew she'd recognized him, no matter that she'd played it cool.

He was curious about that coolness. About why she hadn't admitted she knew him. It should be a harmless thing to do, and yet it clearly wasn't. Still didn't mean she wasn't guilty of being involved in Hunter's dirty deals. She might know all about them even if she wasn't actively a part of it.

The ride over here had been interesting. Hunter was already in the Rolls when Quinn and Blade walked out of the building. Blade held the door for her, and she climbed into the car. He'd gotten into the front with the chauffeur, and they'd glided away from the building. Hunter made phone calls and talked the entire way. Quinn didn't say a word, and Hunter didn't talk to her.

When they arrived at the venue, Hunter left her in the car. Blade was the one who waited for her. The chauffeur held the door but didn't offer a hand. Blade did. She took it, her fingers closing into his palm, an electrical sizzle skimming through his veins at that slight touch.

It surprised him more than anything. If she felt it too, she didn't give it away by word or look. She simply emerged from the car, one creamy leg after the other, then stood and straightened her dress before walking after her husband.

Now she excused herself from the others and turned to give him a look. "I have to go to the restroom," she said in her soft British accent. "Are you following me there too?"

"Yes, Mrs. Halliday. Those are my orders."

Her mouth tightened at the corners. God, he couldn't get over how she'd changed. She was still Quinn. Still the girl with the pretty green eyes and the long russet hair, but she wasn't the Quinn he'd known. Her face was thin. Her features were well-defined. Her eyes were no longer lost in her face. They were prominent, as were her cheekbones and her nose and chin.

"Then I guess we'd better go." She spun on her heel and marched into the apartment, heading straight for the restroom. The door was locked when she got there and she halted, squaring her shoulders before turning to face him again.

There was no one else waiting to use the facilities and they were far enough away from the other guests to finally be alone. Sort of.

Blade gazed down at her, studying her. "You look good, Quinn," he said softly.

Her brows drew low and she dropped her lashes. "You might have known if you hadn't disappeared on me. What's it been—eight years?"

"Yeah."

Her gaze speared into, eyes blazing. "You dropped off the face of the earth. But we weren't really friends, were we? I was just some fat girl you felt sorry for when we were in high school."

Guilt pricked him. "I *was* your friend. Life just got in the way after high school. I joined the Navy and I didn't have a lot of time for texting or posting updates on social media."

That was an understatement. Not that he had time for it now either. Social media was not only a time suck, it was also pretty dangerous considering what he did. So he avoided it.

"Why are you here now? How did Hunter find you?"

"I'm in private security. He contacted my boss. This is a coincidence."

She was frowning hard. "He doesn't know that you know me?"

"No."

"Then don't tell him. Whatever you do, don't tell him. He won't like it."

Blade wanted to punch Hunter Halliday square in the mouth. "I'm not afraid of him."

Her lip trembled, and a stone formed in his gut. "You should be, Adam. Hunter is not a nice man. And if he has any idea that you were once important to me—well, it won't be pretty."

He was angry. Fucking pissed as hell. She was scared for him. And he didn't like it. "Call me Blade or he'll suspect something." He sucked in a breath. He could be cool about this. He *would* be cool for her.

Because she was afraid. Though a little voice niggled at him, wondering if this was all an act.

We don't know that she's not involved.

"I won't tell him, Quinn. I'm here to protect you."

"Protect me?" She laughed bitterly. "No, you're here to imprison me."

The bathroom opened and a woman walked out. Blade didn't get a chance to say anything else before Quinn went inside and locked the door.

———

HOW WAS she supposed to do this? Quinn stood in the bathroom and sucked in deep breaths, willing herself not to scream. She had to act normal or Hunter would suspect something. Worse, what if Adam—Blade—decided this whole situation was too crazy for him and quit? She'd be alone. Even with a new bodyguard, she'd be alone. Because at least Blade was someone she shared a history with.

She couldn't decide if that was a good thing or not. It certainly made her emotions more chaotic. She'd had the hots for Adam Garrison in high school. Who hadn't? He was beautiful, and that hadn't changed. He'd grown older, tougher, bigger. But he was still the boy who'd whipped asses for her. He'd stood in the circle of those bullies and he'd warned them what was going to happen if they didn't apologize and walk away.

They'd laughed louder. Until he'd mopped the

floor with them. She'd never seen arms and legs move like that before. He'd just moved to London from Hong Kong. He had martial arts training and he wasn't afraid to use it.

Nobody at that school ever bothered her again. Not with Blade in her corner. He hadn't even minded that she followed him around like a lovesick puppy. He'd ignored her for a few days, and then he'd started talking to her.

She'd loved his cute American accent. She had a British accent because she'd spent most of her life in London, though she was an American too. They'd had some things in common. Blade listened to her, and he encouraged her. She'd begun to believe that she could do anything if she tried hard enough. It had still taken her a few years to actually do it, but she had.

She washed her hands and fluffed her hair. Reapplied her lipstick. She had to go back out there and not let emotion get the best of her. Blade wasn't her friend anymore. He'd graduated and moved away, and then he'd stopped answering her texts. She'd stopped messaging after a while, but she'd never forgotten him. Or the way she'd felt for those couple of years she'd known him, when she'd wanted him to be her boyfriend but she'd known he never would be. Because he was beautiful and she wasn't.

She was now. She knew she was. She'd worked hard to get there. But being beautiful hadn't done her any good. It had brought her attention she didn't know how to handle, and it had brought her Hunter. She definitely hadn't been prepared for him.

Quinn unlocked the door and stepped out. Blade was waiting, a silent, hulking shape standing against the wall. He wore a suit, and she knew beneath that suit he'd have a gun. He wasn't her first bodyguard. The last one had been sent packing when Hunter found out he'd taken her to see an attorney when they were still in Texas. She'd had to beg the man not to report that trip, but someone had. Someone always did.

"Blade," a voice said, and she jerked to see Hunter striding toward them, face florid from drink, a smelly cloud of cigar smoke rolling off him. Richard Jenkins, the man he'd brought from Texas to take over the Hong Kong operations, stood a few feet away, waiting for him to return. She liked Richard, but his devotion to Hunter had cost him his marriage not too long ago. "Take Mrs. Halliday home, would you? I'm going to be here a while."

"Yes, sir," Blade said. "Any instructions?"

"Take her straight home. No stops. No side trips. No phone calls."

If Blade found that instruction odd, he didn't let it show. He simply inclined his head. "Understood."

Hunter gripped her arm, put his face down into hers. "Be a good girl, Quinn," he said, his cigar-drenched breath disgusting in her face. "And I'll buy you something nice."

She refrained from jerking her arm away, but only

barely. "I'm always good, Hunter," she said from between clenched teeth.

He snorted. "Not always. But you're learning." He stepped back, waved at someone on the terrace. "Don't wait up, darling," he added before he laughed and walked away.

"I won't," she said under her breath. She tossed her hair and glared at Blade, who was watching her with a neutral expression. "You heard the man. Take me home and lock me up. I prefer it there anyway."

He motioned for her to go ahead of him. She made her way to the hostess, the wife of some government official Hunter was schmoozing for his company, and thanked her for the lovely evening. The woman inclined her head politely as Quinn expressed her thanks. When it was over, she headed for the door.

Blade reached out to stop her before she could open it. "Wait until I call the car, Mrs. Halliday."

She folded her arms over her chest and huffed.

A moment later, he put his phone away and nodded at her. "Let's go."

He opened the door. But instead of letting her go first, he led the way onto the elevator and down to the circular drive in front of the building. The Rolls was there, the chauffeur bounding from the car to open the rear door.

Blade handed her in and then he got in beside her. She'd expected him to go up front, so it surprised her when he sank onto the seat next to her. But she didn't say anything. Neither did he.

The trip back home took nearly half an hour because of traffic, but eventually they reached the building. Still she didn't say anything—and neither did Blade—as they walked toward the elevator. But once they were inside and the doors slid closed with a soft whoosh, his brows drew down, his expression hardening.

"Jesus, Quinn—what the fuck did you marry that guy for?"

Chapter Four

Blade didn't understand it. Quinn had been a sensible girl when he knew her—or so he'd thought. And then she'd accomplished so much on her own, before Hunter Halliday came into her life, that it was hard to imagine how the fuck she'd fallen for him in the first place.

She looked furious, but then her expression collapsed. She didn't cry, but he thought she might want to. Her nostrils flared, her chest heaving as her breasts pushed against the satin fabric of her dress, emphasizing her cleavage, and Blade clamped down ruthlessly on his reaction. He didn't have time to get worked up by a pair of tits, no matter how fabulous they might be.

She tossed her mane of silky red hair and stuck her nose in the air. "I married him for the money. Why else?"

He wasn't sure he believed that. It was possible,

sure—hell, he'd said so himself back in DC—but she didn't exactly seem to be enjoying the money and privilege that came with being Mrs. Halliday.

"And has it been worth the price so far?"

He could see her trembling. See the tremor running through her, vibrating her body where she stood.

"Nothing is worth this price," she said softly.

The elevator bumped to a halt and the doors whooshed silently open into the Halliday penthouse. Li-Wu stood quietly in the foyer, as if he expected orders of one sort or another.

Quinn emerged, her heels tapping on the floor. Blade followed. She stopped in front of Li-Wu.

"Thank you, Li-Wu. I don't need anything. Please feel free to retire for the evening."

Li-Wu gave a formal nod. "Yes, madam."

He melted silently away as Quinn strode over to the bar and opened the wine refrigerator. She held up a bottle. "Wine?"

Blade shook his head. "I'm on the job."

She shrugged and reached for a glass with slender, elegant hands, her manicured nails clinking the side of the crystal for a second. She set the glass down, took the stopper out of the bottle, and poured. Then she took a healthy swig.

"I met Hunter at a party. My fitness blog was gaining in popularity and I'd been doing some modeling. I had a transformation story that people were amazed by. I'd lost a hundred and twenty pounds, and somehow there was a pretty face under all that fat. People were mesmerized."

"You were always pretty, Quinn."

She waved the glass as if to shush him. "No, I wasn't. But I appreciate your saying so." She took a sip of her wine. "Hunter blew me away. He was larger than life, so successful, and he seemed to know just what to do and say. He quite literally swept me off my feet. I'd never met anyone like him before. And he was good to my parents. My dad had cancer and Hunter paid for an experimental treatment. Dad made a full recovery, by the way."

"I'm relieved to hear it."

"I owed him so much." She swiped at her eyes. "I married him happily. I thought I was the luckiest woman alive."

"So what happened?" Blade asked, thinking back to the way she'd cringed at the sight of her husband earlier. And the way Hunter referred to her as a possession. There was no caring in their relationship, not anymore.

"Hunter likes to win," she said. "And once he's won something, he loses interest." She shrugged. "I don't know why he took it as far as marriage, but once we walked down the aisle… things changed."

Blade tried to process it all. There was so much he wanted to know, but he didn't want to push her too far. "So why don't you leave?"

She snorted softly. "He won't let me. I've tried."

"He can't force you to stay," Blade ground out,

even while a part of him knew he was wrong. Rich people? They didn't always play by the same rules as everyone else. Not to mention the fact Hunter was involved in criminal operations. If he'd do that, he'd have no qualms about doing whatever it took to keep a woman by his side.

Quinn shook her head. "You don't know Hunter." She took another gulp of wine. "You have no idea how glad I was to see you today. Or how shocked. But once I got over that—well, I felt like maybe God had answered my prayers somehow."

His throat was tight. "What prayers were those?"

She didn't speak for a long moment. When she did, her voice was low and measured. "I'm tired of being alone. A friend would be nice, but Hunter won't let me have any of those. And then you showed up, and he has no idea." A small smile curled the corners of her lips. "I'm not alone now that you're here."

Fuck. He didn't know how long he'd be here, not really. He had an assignment, one that didn't concern her at all except as a way to get him into this house. That made him feel like a shithead, but there was nothing he could do about it.

"Aren't you worried he's recording this conversation?" Because Halliday seemed like the type of man who would do such a thing.

"He has cameras, but they don't pick up sound. Not here anyway. He's afraid of foreign governments listening in on his conversations, so as much as he might like to record what I'm saying, he doesn't. For fear they'll pick up something he says that he doesn't want anyone to know."

Blade's senses prickled. "What kind of things?"

"You think I know?"

"You might have heard something."

"I hear things occasionally. I don't know how important they are."

He wanted to urge her to tell him, but he couldn't be too eager. He'd give away the game if he did that. And what if she was playing him? What if this whole thing was an elaborate act?

His gut clenched at that thought while his instincts told him it wasn't the case. There was no way she was happy with Halliday. No way she'd protect his ass if she thought something she knew could get him locked up.

But that didn't mean Blade didn't need to proceed carefully with her.

"If you don't want to tell me, that's cool," he said. "But if you do, I'm here."

She studied him. "Why do you care?"

Be cool. "About what he's doing? I don't. I only care if you're upset about it."

She chewed her lip. "Did you know when you took this job that it was me?"

Fuck. "Not at first, no. But when I did—well, I couldn't say no."

"Why not? We aren't friends anymore."

"That's my fault," he told her truthfully. "I dropped off the face of the earth. But I still think of you as a friend. So, yeah, I took the job because it was you."

Her brows drew low. She swigged her wine and seemed to be thinking. And then she closed her eyes for a moment. When she opened them again, they lanced into him. "I don't really *know* anything. Mostly he goes outside to talk. Or he spends his time in meetings elsewhere. He's always focused on the business, but right now he's more uptight than usual. He's got a deal with the US government to supply computer terminals to the military. He's not as happy about that as he should be. I don't know why."

She twirled the wineglass in her hand, her gaze fixed on the red liquid. "A man came here three days ago. He wasn't anyone I recognized. He and Hunter went into the study and didn't come out for an hour. When the man left, Hunter seemed shaken. He poured whiskey and drank it all at once, which isn't like him. He's a sipper, not a gulper. He drank another after that, the same way. Then he called for the car and I didn't see him again until the next day. He was back to being his usual self by then."

Blade thought back to the dossier he'd read. Ian Black was having Halliday watched and they knew that a man who was reputed to be an enforcer for a Hong Kong triad, or mafia gang, had come to see him. The triad was involved in drug trafficking as well as counterfeiting money and goods. What they wanted with Hunter Halliday was a bit of a mystery, though clearly there was something going on if Halliday had been rattled by the meeting. But did it have anything to do with the microchips in his computers, or was it peripheral?

"What do you think it means?" he asked.

She shrugged. "Honestly, I have no idea. Probably that he's made a bad investment somewhere and he's worried he'll lose money. That's the only thing he cares about." She glanced up at the ceiling. He didn't follow her gaze because he knew she was looking at a camera. He'd pegged them all when he'd entered earlier today. There was one in each room he'd been in, though he didn't yet know where the control room was or what the cameras recorded. Except she'd told him they didn't record sound, though he'd have to verify that for himself.

She stood and grabbed the wine bottle. "I need to go to bed now. If I talk to you for too long... Well, Hunter will have questions. Good night, Adam— Blade. I'm glad for whatever remarkable set of circumstances brought you here. You make me feel safe, even if it isn't true."

"You are safe. That much I promise you." He didn't want to let her walk away just yet. But he couldn't endanger his mission here by doing anything Hunter would find suspicious. And talking to Quinn for an hour would be super suspicious. "Good night, Quinn. It's good to see you again. I'm stoked as hell that you reached your goal, by the way. You look amazing—but you were always an amazing girl to me."

It was true, though he'd probably never told her that before. He'd always been amazed by her spirit in the face of so much adversity. Yeah, he'd stood up for her back then—but she'd endured so much before he'd even arrived and she hadn't caved.

She smiled. "But not a pretty girl to you. Which was too damned bad because I seriously wanted you back then. If only you'd been into fat chicks."

His heart throbbed. Yeah, he knew what this sounded like. And what his attraction to her now said about him back then. "I was a bit of an idiot."

"Yes, you definitely were. I'm the same person I was, though I find that most people like this package better than the previous one."

"I'd apologize for being shallow, but there is no excuse."

She tipped her head. "No, there's not. Night, Blade."

He watched her tight ass sashay away from him until the hallway swallowed her up. Then he slanted a glance at the camera out of the corner of his eye. He was going to need to find a way to disable those motherfuckers if he wanted to get a good look at the apartment. But first he had to make contact with Black's outfit and get some surveillance gear to smuggle inside. Then he'd go after Halliday's spy cameras. He owed Quinn that much.

———

QUINN WOKE the next morning alone. She hadn't expected otherwise, but there was always the possibility that Hunter would return in the night and come to their room. Just because he hadn't in months didn't mean he wouldn't one of these nights.

She showered and dressed and then went to the dining room, knowing that Li-Wu would have breakfast ready. Her heart was lighter than usual as she contemplated the fact that Blade would be there.

Blade. It suited him. In high school, he'd been deadly with his hands and legs. He'd been a blade, striking with precision and lethal skill. When he'd beat those bullies up for harassing her—well, it had been a thing of beauty. She'd watched as he'd cut his way through them, arms and legs moving so fast she couldn't tell what he'd done until none were left standing.

He'd gotten in trouble for it, but he hadn't been repentant. She'd asked him about it. About what he'd done. He'd told her he'd grown up in Hong Kong, learning martial arts and fighting in street gangs. She'd thought he was the baddest man she'd known.

It was incredible that he was here now, but it wasn't unbelievable. He'd gone into the US Navy. She remembered that from the messages she'd gotten before they'd ended. That he was in private security now, and that Hunter would hire him from a firm, wasn't as surprising as it was amazing.

This wasn't the first time she'd been to Hong Kong, and it wasn't the first time she'd thought of

Blade. She'd gone to the markets and shops, and she'd wondered if he'd been to the same places. She'd been kind of homesick, and she'd wondered where he was. If he was still alive, if he ever thought of her the way she thought of him.

She'd searched on Facebook, but the only Adam Garrisons that were there looked nothing like him. So she'd imagined him living somewhere with a wife and kids, too busy and too happy to be on Facebook. She'd been glad for him.

And then he'd turned up here, in her living room, shocking the absolute hell out of her. Now she couldn't imagine him doing anything *but* working as a bodyguard.

She dressed in her gym clothes and headed for the dedicated workout room she'd talked Hunter into putting into the apartment. It wasn't large, but there were a couple of treadmills and a weight machine as well as a bench and some free weights. It was enough to get in a good workout. She was kind of obsessive about it, in fact. She never wanted to be so out of control of herself that she let the weight creep back on. She'd briefly considered letting herself gain weight again as an escape mechanism, but she'd realized that Hunter wouldn't let her get away with it so easily. The moment he thought she was getting too plump, he'd hire some insane exercise guru to work her to exhaustion.

Didn't matter that he could stand to lose a few pounds himself. He was a hypocrite when it came to weight, and he'd ride her into the ground if that's what it took to keep her at trophy weight.

Well, it wasn't going to take that. Quinn was in charge of her body and she was going to stay in shape for her own satisfaction, not his. She grabbed a bottle of water from the kitchen and then went into the gym, expecting to find herself alone.

She wasn't.

Blade jogged steadily on a treadmill, his gaze fixed on the fog wreathing the mountains surrounding Hong Kong. He glanced over as she approached, but he didn't break his stride. She got up on the machine, set her water in the slot, queued up her audiobook about a woman finding love with a military man, and started walking briskly.

After five minutes, she broke into a slow jog. It was all she could do to jog at a steady pace for thirty minutes while beside her Blade sprinted as if the hounds of hell were on his heels. She cut her glance at him a few times, admiring the hardness of his physique. His breathing was deep and steady but not labored. There was a fine sheen of sweat on his skin as he ran. He wore headphones, so she couldn't talk to him—as if she could find the breath anyway.

She wound down her workout, not as pleased as she usually was, and walked briskly as she started her cooldown. Beside her, Blade was still sprinting, and annoyance flared in her belly. She was just about to end her walk when he punched the button to slow down and ripped the headphones from his ears.

His breathing was brisk but not labored. Sweat trickled down his brow and over his muscled chest and tattooed forearms. His shirt was wet. Quinn huffed as she walked, determined not to look at him.

"Morning, Quinn," he said.

"Morning."

"You sleep all right?"

"Well enough. You?"

"Jet lag," he told her. "But I'm working on it."

She didn't look at him, though she could see his reflection in the window. Which meant he could see hers too.

"Where did you come from?"

"DC."

"Washington?"

"You know of another one?"

"No. Just checking."

"I got the call for the assignment and had to hop on a plane within hours. Otherwise I'd have acclimated myself better."

"What was your assignment before this one?"

"The one I can tell you about is this one: rescuing a woman from a human trafficking gang. They kidnapped her and we had to go get her."

"We?"

"Buddies. We all either work for the US government or we go into private contracting. It was a private assignment."

"Did you get the woman back?"

He snorted. "Of course."

"And then?"

He hesitated. "Some stuff I can't talk about."

"Why not?"

"Just can't."

She drew in a breath. "Okay. How are your parents?"

"Divorced," he said without missing a beat.

Quinn nearly stumbled on the treadmill. But she didn't. Jeez, Mr. and Mrs. Garrison had seemed so perfect to her. Unlike her parents, who'd argued about everything.

"I'm sorry."

"Don't be. Shit happens."

"When did it happen?"

"Five years ago. Dad was having an affair with his secretary. Midlife crisis, I guess. Mom told him to shove it."

"My parents divorced too. Mom was the one who cheated."

"Sorry to hear that."

"It was inevitable. They always argued."

"I remember."

"Dad went back to Georgia. Mom is still in London. They don't speak."

"Did they come to your wedding?"

Quinn frowned. It wasn't a pleasant memory. "They did. Mom with her new husband, Dad all alone and recovering from his cancer. He walked me down the aisle, but Mom was pissed about it. Like she thought I was going to choose her new husband to

43

join him or something."

"I'm sorry, Quinn."

She shrugged as she punched the button to stop. "It's life, right? It's what happens."

"Yeah, it happens. My dad remarried last year. Mom has a boyfriend. They're friendly with each other. It's kind of odd, really. I don't know why they try. I mean, I'm out of the house and there are no other kids, so why bother?"

Her heart pinched. Maybe because the Garrisons were decent people? "I don't know, but thank your lucky stars. It's far preferable to having them at each other's throats."

He stopped the treadmill. He wasn't even breathing hard. Bastard. "Yeah, I guess you're right. I spend time with both of them when I can, and they don't give me a hard time about anything. Hell, we all had Thanksgiving together last year. Me, Dad, his new wife, Mom and her boyfriend. If it was awkward, they didn't let on."

Her heart swelled. "That's the way it's should be. You're lucky."

He got off the treadmill and picked up a towel, wrapping it around his neck. "I should shower. I'll be ready in twenty minutes if you want to discuss your day."

She couldn't help but gape at the muscles of his biceps as he gripped the ends of the towel that hung around his neck. His shirt clung to him, soaked with sweat. She wanted to peel it off and press herself to him.

Not a good idea, Quinn.

"I don't have any plans," she said. "I'm not allowed to leave the apartment without permission."

His eyes went dark and hard a moment. "As you wish, Mrs. Halliday."

Her throat was tight. She didn't want to be called Mrs. Halliday. She didn't want to *be* Mrs. Halliday. But she had no choice. Hunter had made certain of that.

"It's not what I wish," she said in a low voice. "It's my reality."

His eyes flashed. "Tell me where you want to go. I'll make it happen."

Her heart stuttered in her chest. "Honestly? Anywhere so long as it's far away from here. But even you can't work that kind of miracle."

"Not yet," he said. "But give me time."

Chapter Five

WHAT THE FUCK HAD HE SAID THAT FOR? HE WASN'T here to promise her the moon. He was simply here to find out what her husband was up to. And if she was involved. Nothing more, nothing less.

He couldn't get involved in Quinn Halliday's drama, no matter how much he might want to rescue her. And yet the hope flaring in her eyes made his heart swell with determination.

Goddammit, stop.

Her gaze dropped. Her face was red with exertion. Her russet hair was wound up in a messy bun on top of her head, and beads of sweat glistened on her skin. His gaze dropped to the neon-turquoise workout bra covering her breasts, the smooth flat plane of her abdomen, and the formfitting black workout pants that clung to her shapely ass. Geez, Quinn had changed.

"Don't make promises you can't keep," she said

softly. "I appreciate the sentiment, really. But Hunter has too much money and too many resources. I shouldn't have said I wanted to go far away. It's not up to you to make it happen, so don't worry that I expect it."

He wanted to tip her chin up and force her to look at him. But there was a camera, and he hadn't yet gotten what he needed in order to redirect them. So he stood there like an asshole with his hands gripping the towel, staring down at the top of her head.

"If it can be done, I'll do it. I promise you that," he said before turning on his heel and striding from the room.

He didn't look back in case Hunter viewed the footage, and he didn't break stride until he was in his quarters, stripping the wet workout clothes and dropping them on the floor. He'd cased his room until he found the camera hidden behind the mirror of the dresser, then he'd unplugged the fucker. If Halliday didn't like that he'd done that, Blade didn't care. There were some things he wasn't going to accept, and someone watching him dress and sleep was over the line.

Blade went into the bathroom and turned on the shower. Then he stepped under the hot spray and stood there with it pounding down on his back for long minutes. He kept hearing the resignation in Quinn's voice when she'd said she was never getting free. Halliday was one of those rich assholes who thought he could buy and sell people. He'd bought Quinn, and he intended to keep her.

Well, fuck him. Blade was going to find a way to break Hunter's hold on her. First he had to figure out what the man was up to, and then he had to find a way to take him down. Only then would Quinn be free.

Blade finished showering, pulled on jeans and a button-down shirt, slipped his Glocks into their respective holsters, then went to find something to eat. Li-Wu had asked this morning if he had specific requirements. The man had been shocked when Blade answered in Cantonese and told him that whatever the household ate was fine with him.

There was a buffet in the dining room. Blade grabbed a plate and pulled off the cover of the closest chafing dish. There were fluffy scrambled eggs, so he took a heap of them. Next were sausages. He only took two. After that, potatoes. He grabbed a big scoop of those, continuing down the line with fruit and a big glass of milk.

He sat at the table and began to eat. Copies of the *Wall Street Journal*, the *New York Times*, and the *South China Morning Post* lay folded neatly, presumably for Hunter or Quinn. Blade didn't touch them. Instead, he asked Li-Wu for a copy of the *Headline Daily*, a Chinese language paper. Li-Wu brought it with a smile on his face.

"Where did you learn to speak Chinese?"

"I grew up in Hong Kong," he answered. "My parents were in international finance."

Li-Wu nodded. "You speak without an accent. I wondered how that was possible."

"I was three when they took the job here. I had a Chinese nanny. She taught me both Cantonese and Mandarin."

"You live in Hong Kong now?"

"Not anymore. Not for many years. But it's good to be back."

Li-Wu nodded. "Yes, it is a wonderful place to live."

Blade ate a bite of eggs while Li-Wu busied himself at the buffet. "How long have you worked for the Hallidays?"

Li-Wu looked up. "I don't actually work for them. I am with a service that sends staff when required. I work for many different part-time residents. But this is my second stint working for the Hallidays while they are in town."

Which meant Li-Wu probably didn't know anything about Hunter or his business. Blade nodded. "It must be interesting to work for different clients."

"Yes. There is never a chance to get very bored. People are so different."

Quinn entered the room then, dressed in a pair of black trousers and a silky tank top. She had on low heels, and her hair fell in a silky curtain to her ass. Blade had to work to keep his jaw from dropping. Li-Wu poured a cup of coffee and brought it to her.

"The usual, madam?"

"I can get it, Li-Wu," she said softly.

"It is my pleasure to serve, madam," he said, smiling.

Quinn shot Blade a look as if he would judge her for allowing Li-Wu to serve her, but then nodded. "Thank you, Li-Wu. That is very kind."

She took a seat and Li-Wu went to fix her a plate. He returned with a small helping of eggs and two slices of plain wheat toast with a side of jam. Then he brought her a glass of water.

"Is there anything else, madam?"

"No. Thank you again, Li-Wu."

He brought over a pot of coffee and set it nearby, then bowed and retreated from the room. Quinn put her fork into her eggs and took a dainty bite. Blade kept eating too. But he also watched Quinn. She took measured bites of everything, sipping her water and her coffee frequently, as if filling herself with liquid so she wouldn't eat too much.

"How's your jet lag?" she asked.

"Oh, I'm sure it'll kick my ass again soon. But I'll power through it."

"I'm sure you will. I doubt Hunter will return for a few hours, so you've got time to nap if you need to."

"I'll keep that in mind." He took a drink of his milk. "Does he often stay out all night?"

Her eyes flashed as she met his. "He sleeps elsewhere whenever the mood strikes."

"Does it strike often?"

"Often enough." She set her coffee down. "He has a suite at the Peninsula Hotel. He thinks I don't know about it."

"What's he doing there that he can't do here?"

Quinn snorted. "Fucking whores, I imagine."

Blade nearly choked on a potato. He took a drink to dislodge it. "Jesus, Quinn."

She shrugged. "It's true. Why hide it? My husband likes blind adoration. I've stopped giving it to him."

"And he won't let you leave?" Blade shook his head. "That doesn't make a lot of fucking sense."

"It does to Hunter. He doesn't like to lose. If he lets me leave, it's losing of a sort."

"Not if he's the one to initiate it."

"He won't. He likes his life just the way it is. A trophy wife at home and whores and groupies everywhere else."

"I don't think I like your husband."

"Welcome to the club," she said with a fake smile. "There are a lot of people who don't like Hunter. It's a wonder nobody's taken a shot at him yet."

Blade's gut tightened. "Don't say stuff like that, Quinn."

"Why not? It's the truth."

"Because if it ever does happen, you'll be on the suspect list. Best not to have shit like that floating around. Somebody will know you said it and they won't keep quiet."

She frowned. "That's kind of a stretch, isn't it?

You're assuming that it won't be obvious who did it, if it were to happen."

He couldn't tell her that in his world he was trained to think of all possibilities, no matter how unlikely. It was a big part of being prepared.

"Might be a stretch, sure, but just keep those kinds of comments to yourself, okay? You never know."

She sighed. "Look, I despise him but I'd never hurt him—or anyone. I would hope most people who know me know that."

"If your husband ever ends up dead under suspicious circumstances, it won't matter what people *think* they know about you. They'll be quick to imagine they didn't know you nearly as well as they thought they did."

She didn't break eye contact. "Do we ever really know anyone?"

"No, I don't think we do."

———

HUNTER RETURNED AROUND NOON. He had his phone to his ear, as he always did, giving somebody on the other end hell. When he hung up, he turned his ire on Quinn. She was sitting on one of the overstuffed couches in the living room, reading a novel, her mind still on Blade and how her body sizzled with energy whenever he was near. Just having someone to talk to, someone she knew from before, made her life more exciting. It was sad, but she didn't care so long as he was here.

Hunter glared at her. "Why are you lounging around doing nothing?"

Quinn's belly tightened into a knot. "Because you haven't approved any outings and my new bodyguard refuses to take me anywhere until you do."

Hunter looked mollified for a second. But then he got angry again. "We're having an important function here in three days. Do you think you could do something about that?"

Quinn's heart raced, but she forced herself to be calm. To speak slow and measured. Like soothing a damned bull. "Li-Wu has arranged the caterers. I've approved the menu. If you allow me to go out for a bit, I'll shop for the flower arrangements and decorations."

Hunter's expression didn't ease, but he waved a hand as if to dismiss her. "Fine. Go. Where's your bodyguard?"

"I believe he's in his room, though I don't know for certain. I can send Li-Wu to get him."

"I'll do it," Hunter growled before stalking off down the hallway.

Quinn sat quietly, listening for any sound. She heard a distant pounding as Hunter rapped on Blade's door in the staff quarters. She didn't hear anything else for a very long while but finally Hunter returned, looking pleased with himself. He went to the bar and poured a whiskey, then sank onto a chair and picked up his phone again. Soon he was on a call, barking orders at Richard Jenkins.

Fifteen minutes later, Blade emerged. His expression was carefully neutral, but she could feel the hostile energy rolling from him.

Hunter didn't notice as he ended his call with a terse "Get it done, Jenkins" and waved absently in Blade's direction. "Take Mrs. Halliday shopping. Have her back in two hours."

"It will take longer than that," Quinn interrupted. "Traffic."

Hunter dragged in a breath and then blew it out. "Fine." He slanted his gaze to Blade. "Can I trust you to keep her out of trouble?"

"Absolutely, sir."

Hunter's eyes narrowed. He liked to intimidate people, and that's all this was. He'd done it with every single staff member they'd ever had and all the protection people he'd hired. Her last bodyguard hadn't taken it very well, which was part of why he was no longer here.

Blade didn't bat an eyelash. He simply stood and waited. Finally Hunter turned away and made a new call.

Quinn stood and smoothed her trousers. "I'll get my purse."

Blade tipped his head. "I'll arrange for the car."

Quinn strode to the bedroom, her heart racing at the idea she would be alone with Blade for the next few hours. No cameras. No one watching or listening.

She could talk freely. Laugh if she felt like it. Touch him, though she'd have to be careful about that since there was no reason for her to do so.

The thrill ricocheting through her at the idea of a free afternoon was no surprise. But worry followed hard on its heels, threatening to steal any joy she might find in the outing. If she wasn't careful, Hunter would fire Blade and then she'd be right back where she'd been before his arrival.

Alone.

Chapter Six

BLADE WAS HAVING A HARDER TIME DEALING WITH THIS assignment than he'd expected. He'd been here just about twenty-four hours now, and he despised Hunter Halliday in a way he usually reserved for proven traitors and terrorists. But the man was a walking piece of shit. A bully who took pleasure in browbeating those around him.

When Blade had answered his door earlier, he'd been catching up on sleep. Hunter had been standing there, puffed up like a rooster. Without missing a beat, the man had started berating him. Then he'd ordered Blade to get dressed and get out to the living room.

Blade thought that when he got Ian Black on the phone again, he was going to cuss that motherfucker up one side and down the other. And maybe Colonel Mendez too. They'd specifically chosen him because he spoke Chinese and he knew Quinn. But they hadn't warned him strongly enough that Hunter Halliday was a major fucking dick.

Yeah, he'd read the dossier on the man. But it didn't go into a lot of detail about the way Hunter treated his wife—or his subordinates. *Total* dick.

Blade waited for Quinn at the elevator. She strode toward him, wearing a pale yellow jacket over her silk tank and carrying a small purse. She had a pair of sunglasses in her hand and she slipped them on, hiding her eyes. They stepped into the elevator. Hunter walked up and down, his attention on his phone, gesticulating wildly as he yelled at someone named Jenkins on the other end.

Blade would have liked to listen to the conversation, but so far there'd been nothing of substance. The man was yelling about projections and suppliers, but that was it.

The elevator doors closed and the car started to move.

Quinn exhaled slowly. "I almost expected him to change his mind."

"Does he do that often?"

"It's a control issue. So yes, he does. He likes to keep everyone in a state of uncertainty. It's his superpower."

He hated that he couldn't see her eyes. "And you had no clue about any of this before you married him?"

"Nope. He's actually quite charming when he wants to be. I kept thinking there had to be a mistake, actually. Why was he interested in *me?* He's rich, he could have anyone. So why me?"

"And what conclusion have you come to?"

"That I was profoundly unlucky to attract his attention in the first place. And vulnerable. He wouldn't have succeeded had I not been in a certain frame of mind."

He didn't have to ask what she meant. He knew Quinn, and he knew that even with her weight loss and success, the same uncertain girl had probably lurked within. Her parents had never given her much encouragement, and they'd always harped on her weight. So to meet a man who doted on her? Yeah, it was no wonder Halliday had succeeded.

"Do you have a prenup?"

She snorted. "Of course. I mean I'd get a substantial amount, at least I think so, but I have no claim on his businesses or the majority of his fortune."

"He has a son with his previous wife."

"He does. Darrin. He just graduated college a few months ago, and Hunter brought him into the company. But he has no authority over anything. He's mostly a glorified mail boy right now, I think."

"And how does he feel about you?"

"I don't really know. He's polite when we meet for events. But not overly so. Truthfully, I'm not sure he's a fan of his father. He doesn't go out of his way to come home for holidays or any of that."

"He's the heir?"

"I assume so. Hunter hired him so he could teach

him the business, though I don't think he's taught him much of anything just yet."

The elevator came to a stop and the doors slid open. Blade preceded Quinn out of the car, assessing their surroundings. There was security in the building, but his job was to be suspicious. Nothing was out of place, however, and they walked toward the exit and the car that was waiting there.

Blade handed her inside and then got in beside her.

The driver turned to them. "Where to, madam?"

"The Landmark," she said, naming a large designer shopping mall.

Blade didn't like the idea of going to such a big place, but it was upscale and very public. Two hours would have never been enough if they'd had to stick to Hunter's original timeline.

The car merged into traffic, and she pressed a button to make the glass slide up between them and the driver. Blade turned to her.

"Is that a good idea?"

"I'm not sure, but I'm not going to have him spying on me while I talk to you."

"Fair enough." Except that Hunter was unpre-dictable as hell. If the driver told him she'd put the window up, he might explode. Or he might not give a fuck, so long as there was nothing else to report.

"I'm glad you're here," she said, glasses still on her face. Still obscuring her eyes. He wanted to tear them off but he wouldn't. That would certainly give the driver something to talk about.

"I'm glad we met up again."

"I wish you'd stayed in touch."

"Yeah, me too."

"I texted you a few times and you never answered."

"I'm sorry. I lost my phone. I didn't have anything backed up, and I lost your number. I could have searched Facebook, I know, but I just never got around to it." He sighed. "My job is kinda intense, Quinn. I'm gone a lot. I never know where I'll be next, so it's hard to stay in touch with anyone. Still, I'm sorry I didn't try better to keep up with you."

He kind of thought maybe, if he'd still been in her life, she wouldn't have married Hunter Halliday. Though that was probably just a certain kind of arrogance on his part, because why wouldn't she? It wasn't like the two of them had ever been an item. He'd never even thought about it.

But she had. He'd known it in high school, but he hadn't felt the same way. And not just because she was chubby. She'd been like a little sister to him back then. He'd felt protective of her, nothing more.

Besides, he hadn't been interested in any relationships that might tie him to one place. He'd gone out with girls, but never more than a couple of times. He didn't want to get stuck. It'd been an odd way to feel, maybe, but his parents always told him to be careful—don't get a girl pregnant, don't fall for your high school sweetheart, and don't think you've got your life figured out before you even reach adulthood.

"I appreciate that. I wish you'd been around when I started working out. You were my best friend. My only friend really. And you weren't there to share the journey with."

"You started a fitness blog."

She turned her head. "Yes, I did. I had to document my journey somewhere."

"You brought hope to people going through the same thing."

"How do you know that?"

"I read some of it. I wanted to know who you'd become."

She snorted. "I became a ghost, Adam. Nothing but a ghost."

"After you married Halliday. Not before."

Her chin quivered. "Maybe I was always a ghost. I never felt like much else." She shook her head suddenly. "You know what? Don't listen to me. I shouldn't be complaining, right? I'm married to a man who's richer than God. Even if he's an asshole, I've got more money and privilege than most people will ever have. And maybe if I tried harder…"

His blood boiled. "No. Fucking *no*. That's what abused women say, Quinn. If I'd tried harder, been better, done things differently. He may not hit you, but that doesn't mean you aren't abused."

She turned her head away. Her shoulders started

to shake, and then she went stiff. "No," she hissed. "No, I won't cry."

A horrible thought occurred to him then. Because her reaction was so extreme. "*Does* he hit you?" He tried to keep his voice soft, but the lump in his throat made it hoarse instead. His brain ached. His chest hurt. His heart careened like it was out of control on a slalom course.

She didn't face him. Her entire body trembled. He could see the quivering all along the lines of her form. He wanted to crush Hunter Halliday between his fists. He wanted to hit and punch and jab and kick.

"Sometimes. Not often. I've learned not to provoke him." She spun around, her damned eyes still behind the glasses. "He never punched me or anything. Just a slap here or there, when he was angry. It's not like I'm a battered wife."

Fucking motherfucker. Blade squeezed his eyes closed for a second. Clenched his jaw. Fixed her with a hard stare. "Quinn," he whispered, his throat so damned tight it hurt to talk. "Honey. Jesus. If the man hits you, you're battered. Do you understand me? There are no degrees of abuse. *Anyone* who thinks it's okay to slap you around a little bit when he's angry with you is a wife-beating motherfucker, okay? It's not your fault, and there's nothing you did to cause it. It's his fault for being an abusive dick, understand?"

She nodded slowly, sucking in a breath, her nostrils flaring. "I…" She swallowed. "I want to cry right now but I won't. I can't. The driver. Hunter pays him to spy on me. If I get hysterical, and I will if I let the first tear fall, he'll tell Hunter."

"I hate that you're in this situation. Fucking hate it." He wanted to kill Ian Black and Colonel Mendez, and he wanted to thank them too. He was here and he hated this shit, but he had to know.

And he had to save Quinn. There was no doubt in his mind now. He was getting the information they wanted and then he was leaving. But he wasn't leaving without Quinn. Consequences be damned.

————

QUINN SUCKED in a few deep breaths, willing herself not to cry. She'd felt more in the past few hours with Blade—she had to think of him that way so she didn't screw up and call him Adam in front of Hunter—than she'd let herself feel in months. Maybe longer. Quinn kept her eyes on the colorful sights of Hong Kong and worked to find her calm place again. She'd repressed so much for so long, and now she was having a hard time keeping her emotions inside.

She'd confessed that Hunter slapped her sometimes. She'd honestly convinced herself that it was her fault, that if she'd been more careful or less mouthy or something, it wouldn't have happened. She knew he was a volatile man, so why didn't she work harder to be less annoying to him?

But then Blade said what he had and something inside her broke free. She'd known—*known*—that what Hunter did to her was wrong. But she'd convinced herself that she was the one who was incorrect, the one who needed to be careful what she said or did. He was an asshole and she knew that, so why push him to the point he physically retaliated?

A smarter woman wouldn't let it happen. That's what she told herself. And it made her feel so stupid and inconsequential when she thought those things. She'd been convincing herself she was at fault, but Blade was right—she wasn't. It was Hunter's moral failing that was the problem, not hers.

They didn't speak for the rest of the journey. Because she couldn't. She had to get herself together before they arrived at the mall, and then she had to keep herself together for the rest of the afternoon. Hell, for longer than that.

Because she wasn't free to be herself, and she didn't know if she would be ever again. She was stuck, and yet Blade gave her hope. Just by being here, he gave her hope. He'd saved her in high school—could he save her again? *Would* he?

That was the million-dollar question. She didn't know the answer. He was a different person now, a bodyguard in the hire of her husband, so who knew what he might do?

Except that he'd been so angry just now, when she'd confessed what Hunter did to her, that she had to believe he cared. A little bit anyway.

They reached the mall and the driver let them out near the main entrance before going to park somewhere and wait for a call to retrieve them. Blade escorted her inside, his hand against the small of her back as they went through the doors. The contact was light, but it burned into her. It was persistent, and she could do nothing but focus on his touch. It was impersonal, yet still. It made her blood sing and her heart soar and her brain hope. So damned much hope.

He stayed close to her as they walked, but he let his hand drop when they reached the more public areas of the mall. "Are you okay?" he asked softly as she tucked her sunglasses into her purse with trembling hands.

"I'm fine."

"You're shaking."

"I'm nervous."

He frowned. "Why? I'll protect you from harm. Swear to God."

"I know you will. It's not that. It's just—" Her eyes searched his. They were so serious. So concerned. Her heart skipped and flipped and her stomach fluttered. "I can't afford to hope, Blade. I can't think I'm going to escape somehow, that you're going to get me out of this. I can't want that because…" She sucked in a breath. "Because if it doesn't happen, I think I'll die."

He reached for her hand. Squeezed it in his larger one. His skin was warm, rough in spots. "If you want out, I'll get you out."

Her heart skipped. And then her stomach dropped because what if he meant something drastic…? "I don't want you to hurt him," she said quickly. "I just want a divorce. My own life back. Somewhere far away from him."

His eyes widened. Then he laughed. "Quinn, I'm not a hit man. I won't touch a hair on Hunter Halliday's worthless head—okay, fuck, that's a lie. If he gives me an excuse, I'll punch him in the damn face. But I won't kill him. It's not what I do."

The relief rolling through her was palpable. "I'm glad to hear it. And I'm sorry if I thought you might, but Adam—Blade—I remember what you did to those boys that day. They weren't in school for a week."

"They deserved it for the shit they said to you." He shook his head. "You hear me? They *said* ugly things to you and I beat their asses. Hunter Halliday hit you—you think I don't want to fucking beat him into a pulp? I'd like to throw him off that balcony he threatened to throw me off."

"What? He did that? Why?"

Blade laughed. "Don't worry about it, Quinn. He said he'd throw me off if I took a shine to you."

He heart stuttered. "Oh God. You need to be careful, Blade. If he thinks you're getting too close to me—he'll do something drastic."

Blade put his hands on her arms, squeezed. She loved that he was touching her, and it also terrified her. What if someone was watching?

"Hunter Halliday is no match for me, sweetheart. None at all."

She frowned. Then she broke free of his grasp and socked him in the arm. Lightly, but enough to get his attention. "You listen to me, you big jerk. You're my friend. Probably my best friend ever in spite of the fact you ghosted me, and I don't want Hunter to know anything about it. I don't want to give him any reason to take you away from me—so don't you go glaring at him or threatening him or anything. Just find a way to get me away from him, okay?"

His brows drew low. He looked angry and frustrated all at once. His nostrils flared. Then he nodded. "I promise you, Quinn. I won't do anything suspicious, I won't get myself fired—and I'm getting you out of here if it's the last thing I do. I've got your back. Same as always."

She wanted to throw her arms around him and hug him tight. But she didn't. She took another step back, just in case, her heart hammering and her throat aching. "Let's go shopping then. Help me find what I need for this stupid party. Then we can get back and pretend not to know one another."

"You got it."

Chapter Seven

BLADE KEPT A CLOSE EYE ON QUINN AND THEIR surroundings, but when she was safely in a store and talking with the salesperson about what she needed, he retreated a few steps and made a call.

Ian Black answered on the second ring. "Whatcha got, pumpkin?"

Blade rolled his eyes. Black loved to push as far as he could. The man was acerbic as hell. "Nothing much. I need to disable some cameras, or tap in and redirect them. Whatever you can give me. I can't search the premises until we do that."

"All right. Can you put the system to sleep or take it down first? I'll send a technician and we'll get the job done."

"I'm sure I can. But I'll need the recordings reset or he'll see that it was me."

"No problem. How soon you need it?"

"I can probably get in there tonight."

"We've got a bug on Halliday's phone. I'll make sure the service call is routed where we need it to go. You take it down temporarily and I'll get control of it."

"I'll ping you when it's done."

"How's it going so far?"

Blade watched Quinn talking to the salesgirls as they helped her choose decorations for the party. She was elegant, graceful. She'd always been graceful, even when she was overweight. She moved with a fluidity that he'd always found fascinating. She hadn't lost it. If anything, it was more apparent now that she'd shed the extra weight. Not that a woman needed to be thin to be beautiful. She only needed to be comfortable in her own skin. Quinn hadn't been. Now she was, and it was an awesome sight to see.

"Challenging."

"Not sure I like the sound of that."

Blade frowned, his gut churning as he thought about his conversation with Quinn. "Did you know that Halliday hits her? That she's basically a prisoner in his house?"

There was silence on the other end for a long moment. Blade didn't quite know what to make of that.

"I knew he wasn't letting her go, but no, I didn't know he hit her. Motherfucker." The man sounded vicious. Blade liked that because it was exactly how he felt.

"Yeah, exactly."

"You okay?"

"Not entirely. Quinn was my friend. Like a little sister to me. She doesn't deserve what she got when she married Halliday."

"Is she still like a little sister to you?"

Hardly. "We lost touch, but that doesn't mean I don't care about her."

"Hmm. So she doesn't know what her hubby is up to?"

Blade hesitated. Did he think she had a clue? No, he didn't. He'd considered that she could be playing him, but there was no way she was that good an actress. His Quinn had always worn her heart on her sleeve. Besides, she was too uncertain of herself to be that diabolical. She just didn't have the confidence. Never had.

"My gut says no."

"But you don't know for certain?"

"No. But I trust my gut."

"You're compromised by your feelings for this girl."

Blade wanted to lash out and punch something. "Maybe I am—so why the fuck did you send me? You knew what could happen."

"Because I don't have time for someone else to gain her trust. You are the logical choice. Don't fuck this up, Garrison."

"Jesus, I won't. But I'm telling you Quinn isn't involved. She hates that asshole. If she knew he was committing treason, she'd spill the details just so she could be free of him."

"I hope you're right."

"I am."

"Then get the goods and get the fuck out as soon as you can. We'll arrest his ass and she'll be free."

She'd be free before that if he had anything to say about it. "Copy that."

"Garrison," Ian Black said before he could hang up.

"Yeah?"

"Don't let your heart overrule your head. Be the fucking SEAL you are and get this done."

"I will."

The call ended and Blade pocketed his phone. Quinn was standing in front of a display featuring fairy lanterns and flowers and gauzy fabric that made the whole thing look ethereal. She turned to him as he walked up, frowning.

"Not elegant enough, right?"

"Are you going for elegant?"

"That's what Hunter will want."

Fuck Hunter Halliday and his pretentious ass. Except that Blade didn't want Quinn to do anything that might piss her husband off. "Then maybe something else, huh? Looks like something you'd find at a summer garden party."

She gaped at him for a second, then she laughed. "A summer garden party? Do you throw many of those?"

He couldn't help but grin. "In my copious spare time, yeah, I plan garden parties. I keep inviting the queen, but she won't come."

Quinn's smile was a thing of beauty. He found himself wanting to kiss her suddenly. And that was so shocking that he didn't hear a word she said.

"What? Sorry, I was thinking about something," he added when she appeared to be waiting for an answer.

She shook her head. "I asked what you like to serve at these garden parties. It was a joke, obviously."

"A joke?" He pretended to be shocked. "I take my garden parties very seriously, Quinn."

She rolled her eyes. "I'm sure you do." She turned back to the display and shook her head. "This won't work. I need something that says *Look at me, I'm so bloody rich I shit gold bricks.*"

Blade laughed. It was funny, but Quinn's proper British accent made it even funnier. He turned to the salesgirl, who seemed to be somewhat confused at their rapid-fire English conversation as well as, no doubt, a few words she wasn't familiar with. He told her in Chinese what Quinn wanted—without the vulgarities.

The lines between her brow eased and she nodded enthusiastically. "Yes, I understand. This way please." She turned to walk away.

Quinn was watching him. "What did you say?"

"I told her what you want." He held out a hand, indicating she should go first. "After you."

She started walking, but then she threw him a glance over her shoulder. "I didn't think this would be fun. But it is. Thanks, Blade."

He didn't know what to say. Guilt speared into him when he thought about what he was really here for. Except he wasn't leaving her to deal with Hunter Halliday alone, so that was something of a comfort. "It's part of the service, babe."

She stopped and turned. "Babe? Really? What am I, some random woman whose name you forgot?"

He put a hand against her back and pushed her forward gently. "I could never forget you, Quinn. Not in a million years."

———

SHE DIDN'T WANT to go home. Quinn thought about returning to the luxury apartment she shared with Hunter and didn't want to go. It was more fun to hang out with Blade. Walking through the mall, stopping in shops and picking out things for the party. And things for her. She needed a new outfit, so she'd gone into a few boutiques and tried things on.

Blade stood like a hulk outside the dressing rooms, arms crossed in front him, scowl on his face, ready to deter anyone who might think to attack her. Not that anyone would, but it was nice to have Blade at the ready. Even if what he was really meant to do was prevent her from running.

He was, but Hunter didn't know they had a prior

relationship and that Blade was more likely to favor her than he was Hunter. If push came to shove, she knew Blade was in her corner.

She tried on a deep blue gown that clung to her curves and had a slit that went halfway up her thigh. It was sexy and clingy and just the sort of thing Hunter would approve of. She knew that, and yet she wanted to know if Blade approved. Not because she needed his approval, but because she craved it. How sad was that?

"Can you give me an opinion on this one?" she asked from behind the dressing room door, her heart beating fast.

He grunted. "Sure. But I'm not Tim Gunn, you know."

Quinn snorted. Of course she knew he wasn't the *Project Runway* judge. "How do you even know who that is?"

She could feel his hesitation. "You know, I have no fucking idea. It's disturbing now that you mention it."

She laughed. Then she drew in a deep breath and pushed the door open, smoothing the shiny fabric as she did so.

Blade's gaze dropped to her feet, then slowly made its way up her calves, her thighs, her torso, her chest, her shoulders, finally landing on her face. He was scowling. Hard. Her heart skipped.

"Is something wrong?"

He sucked in a breath. "No. Not at all. You look amazing, Quinn."

She ran her hands nervously down her waist and over her hips. "Are you sure?"

Because, though she thought she looked beautiful, there was that little voice in her head that insisted she could still lose a few pounds. That she had rolls of fat and she shouldn't wear something so clingy. She hadn't put on any weight since she'd stopped fitness modeling, but that didn't mean she hadn't gone to fat in areas since she no longer worked out as intensely as she once had.

It was ridiculous, and yet the voice was there. Chipping away at her self-confidence like a relentless waterfall of negativity.

"I'm sure," Blade said. "Seriously, that dress should be illegal. It gives a man ideas."

Her heart soared and she lifted her head, her eyes locking with his. Her throat went dry. "Don't say that unless you mean it."

"I mean it."

She couldn't breathe. "Does it give *you* ideas, Adam?"

His stare didn't waver. "Yeah. It gives me ideas. Does that scare you?"

"Are you kidding me? It's pretty much my childhood fantasy come true. Adam Garrison, the hottest American in school, fantasizing about *me*."

"I was the only American in school," he said, his voice containing a healthy dose of amusement.

"Details," she said softly. "Mere details."

"Quinn, you kill me."

"I always did. You couldn't help but laugh at my jokes."

"True." He jerked his chin at her. "You just about done? We need to get going."

Her heart fell. "Yes, I think so. This is the one. Unless you tell me otherwise."

"Oh no, it's definitely the one. Sexy as fuck."

She went back into the dressing room, exhilaration rushing through her, and changed into her clothing, thinking about the deep timbre of his voice as he'd said the dress was sexy as fuck. She returned it to the hanger and emerged a few moments later to hand it to the salesgirl who appeared. The dress was designer and expensive, but she didn't care.

"This one, please," she said.

The girl beamed. "Yes, madam."

She didn't even need to produce a credit card. That was one of the benefits of being superrich and well known in the shops. Her account would be automatically charged.

The girl zipped the dress into a bag. "Thank you, madam. Will you take it now or should I send it over?"

"Send it, please." Because why carry a garment bag around when you didn't need to? Especially for a dress that cost so much.

They left the shop, and Quinn started to feel the weight of duty pressing down on her. She'd found the decorations. Picked a dress. There was nothing left to do.

"You hungry?" Blade asked.

She swung around to look at him, grasping at the straw he offered. The opportunity to stay out a little while longer. "I could eat."

He put his hand against the small of her back again. Her skin tingled. "I know some good places—or at least they were good when I lived here. We'd have to venture out a bit though. What do you say?"

She gazed into his dark eyes and her heart skipped. "How far?"

"Tai Po."

That was a little far from Kowloon, but she didn't really care. The longer she got to stay away from home, the better. "Let's go."

———

MAYBE HE WAS an idiot for venturing out so far, but he didn't want to take Quinn home just yet. She didn't want to go either. That much was clear. They made their way back to the entrance. He'd called the chauffeur, who rolled up as they emerged. He didn't get out of the car, but Blade opened the door and held it for Quinn. Then he followed her inside.

The driver waited expectantly. Blade gave him a direction in Chinese. The man merely nodded, then pressed the gas pedal and they were on the way. It took almost an hour, but soon they were pulling up in front of a market on a street in Tai Po. It was the kind of place where you had to walk in and find what you wanted. The chauffeur looked up and nodded at Blade. Blade swung the door open and held out a hand for Quinn. She took it and he helped her stand. Then he bent down and told the driver to pull around to a parking garage and wait.

But then he thought better of it and asked the man if he wanted to join them instead of waiting.

Dark eyes met Blade's in the mirror. "Yes, that would be nice."

"Then park and meet us in the alley."

"Thank you, sir."

"Not sir. Just Blade."

"Blade."

He drove away and Quinn stood in the street, gazing up at Blade. "What was that all about?"

"I asked him to join us."

Her jaw dropped open. "But why?"

"Because it's the right thing to do. He might be reporting to Hunter, but he won't be reporting this. Because if he does, he'll have to admit he joined us."

She shook her head. "He can lie. He doesn't have to admit it at all."

"He's not that kind of man, Quinn. He has a family. He has honor. He does what he does for pay, nothing more."

She gaped at him. "How do you know that?"

"Experience." It was true. He'd seen it a million times before. Men who did things they didn't like because they needed the money. But they had honor and integrity anyway. He knew it because he'd read

the dossier, which included Hunter Halliday's employees, as much as was known about them. Li-Wu had an
impeccable background. The chauffeur, Fai Kwan,
wasn't quite impeccable, but he had nothing major to
condemn him. He'd been a part of a triad once, a bit
player who had no influence and made no money.

He also had a family—a wife, three sons, and
hefty bills to support them all. He'd left the triad and
gotten legitimate work. But spying for Hunter Halliday was too much of an incentive to be ignored.
When Halliday wasn't in town, Fai Kwan drove for
other rich men. None of those seemed to pay him as
much as Halliday did.

"I hope you're right," she said, wringing her
hands. "He could cause me a lot of trouble."

"He won't. He's coming to eat with us. Breaking
bread with people is an important step."

She sighed. "God, I hope you're right."

A few minutes later, Fai Kwan joined them. Blade
led them into the market, deep into the alleys, until he
found the food stand he was looking for. A man and
woman ran the place, cooking dishes they'd learned
from countless ancestors. The fire was hot and
sizzling, the stools around the tables packed, and the
atmosphere was nothing to write home about. But the
food was definitely the star.

Blade walked up to the counter and stood there.
The woman turned and barked at him. *What do
you want?*

Blade replied that he wanted the best damned

shrimp and chicken dumplings in all of China. The woman gasped and dropped the knife she'd been wielding. Then she came over and hugged him tight, throwing a stream of Cantonese at him. It was so rapid and intense that he thought someone who wasn't raised in Hong Kong might have missed it all.

Quinn stood by smiling but not understanding a word. Fai Kwan blinked rapidly as he took in the scene. Hui Yin, the female proprietor, showed them to a table nearby. Then she hugged Blade tight and admonished him for disappearing for so long.

"Sit, sit. I'll bring food quickly."

Blade held out a seat for Quinn, then took his own. Fai Kwan sat opposite them, his eyes wide as they roamed the street.

"You ever come here?" Blade asked.

"No. I'm from Yuen Long. I haven't been here."

It would have been odd except that so many people could live within a couple of miles of interesting stuff and never get there, no matter where they lived in the world. It was the nature of people that they stuck to their grooves.

"Then prepare for the best dumpling you've ever had," Blade said.

Fai Kwan suddenly grinned. "I won't tell my grandmother you said that."

The food arrived shortly after and they dug in. For Blade, it was like being transported back to childhood. He'd spent many hours roaming the streets, exploring, and eating as many varieties of dishes as he could find. But this stall had the best dumplings he'd ever tasted.

And it still did. The food was perfectly prepared, flavorful, and delicious. Quinn looked happy as she ate, though he noted that she was careful how much she consumed. Fai Kwan looked stunned at first and then pleased. Blade was just pleased. Hui Yin came over to talk when she could. Her husband had always been taciturn and focused on business, but even he stopped to say hello.

"Where have you been, boy?" Hui Yin asked.

"Everywhere. I joined the US Navy, and I travel a lot."

"You find dumplings as good as mine in your travels?" Her eyes gleamed and he laughed.

"No, ma'am," he said. "Not possible."

She squeezed his arm. "Good answer."

"So you came here often, I take it," Quinn said when Hui Yin walked away.

Blade nodded. "I did. My parents were busy, and when I was about ten, I started going places on my own. I think I found this food stall when I was around twelve."

"You really did have an amazing childhood."

"Yeah, I think so." But also a lonely one in some ways. His parents were never home, always working, and he had no siblings. Quinn didn't have any siblings either, which was part of the reason they'd bonded as teenagers. He'd had friends in Hong Kong, but he was always the outsider.

He'd been the outsider in London as well, but so had Quinn. Not quite British enough, not American enough. And then there was her weight.

"Did you miss this?" she asked, waving her chopsticks at their surroundings. The market was busy, colorful with people and a variety of food and goods for sale. It was loud too, but that was part of the charm.

"Yeah, I did. I've been through Hong Kong a couple of times, but always on the way to somewhere else. I've never had the chance to stop and explore the old stomping grounds until now."

Quinn smiled. "I'm glad you brought me here." Her green eyes were warm, and he found himself smiling in return in spite of Fai Kwan's presence. The man understood some English, but their conversation was vague enough that it would be impossible to know they'd met before yesterday.

"Me too."

They finished the food, then Blade glanced at his watch and frowned. "We should get back."

Quinn's contented expression clouded. He hated seeing it, but there wasn't much choice. "I know." She sighed.

Blade asked Fai Kwan to get the car and meet them at one of the market entrances. The man nodded and melted away into the crowd. Blade studied their surroundings, because that was his habit, and then after a goodbye hug to Hui Yin and a promise to return, he led Quinn through the crowded market.

They were almost to the outside again when Quinn grabbed his arm. He stopped and turned, but before he could ask her what she wanted, she flung her arms around him and stood on tiptoe. He should have stopped her—*could* have stopped her—but he didn't. Instead, he caught her around the waist and held her as she pressed her lips to his.

It wasn't a sexy kiss, not really, and yet every nerve ending in his body blazed to life. Her lips were soft, warm, and he suddenly wanted more. Much, much more.

Chapter Eight

QUINN'S HEART THREATENED TO POUND RIGHT OUT OF her chest as she stood in Blade's arms and kissed him. She hadn't intended to do it, but as they'd neared the exit to the market, she'd needed an outlet for the feelings swelling up inside before she exploded.

So she'd grabbed him and kissed him. She'd only meant to kiss him quick and thank him for making her life bearable again, but as his hands tightened on her, she knew it wasn't enough. This one quick kiss would never be enough.

She prepared herself for his rejection, for the moment when he thrust her away—but he didn't. His grip on her tightened, and then his head slanted side-ways and his tongue slipped between her lips. Stroked against her tongue.

Quinn's body went up in flames. She hadn't been touched in so long that she was like dry tinder. Blade was the match. No, Blade was the flame thrower. Because she was going up in smoke here.

His mouth claimed, demanded, devoured. She clung to him, let him lead her, enthralled by the power and passion his kiss created.

This was what it meant to *want*. To need. To desire.

She clung to him, wanting more, wanting everything.

She felt the moment it all changed, felt him stiffen and drag in a breath. Then he growled low in his throat and pushed her away. Gently, but it was still a rejection.

His eyes flashed hot and her stomach twisted into knots. "Don't do that again," he said hoarsely. "It's too dangerous."

She didn't bother to protest or tell him what her initial plan had been—just a quick kiss of thanks—because it didn't matter. They'd crossed a line with that kiss. A line that was never going to be the same again in her heart. Or maybe in his either.

"I'm sorry. I shouldn't have…," she began. But she didn't regret it. Not at all.

He shook his head. "I shouldn't have either. It wasn't just you."

She touched her lips. They still tingled and stung from the kiss—but it was a delicious feeling. One she wanted more of.

"But it was amazing, right? Tell me it wasn't just me."

He frowned hard. And then he shook his head. "It wasn't just you."

Tears pricked at her eyes. Anger flared. "Dammit, why couldn't you have kissed me like that years ago?"

"I should have. I wish I would have."

She searched his gaze. "Do you actually mean that or are you just saying it to make me feel good?"

He gripped her shoulders, his touch sending lightning bolts flashing through her. His face lowered until they were nearly eye level. "Listen to me, Quinn. I know you were overweight and you hated your body back then, but you were still pretty. Losing weight didn't magically make you into someone else. You're still the sweetest girl I ever knew—and yeah, I wish I'd realized all this years ago. But I was an idiot, and I was selfish. Neither of which were your fault."

He stepped back and glanced over his shoulder. Fai Kwan was pulling the car up to the curb. "You okay to go now or you need a minute?"

Quinn swallowed the knot in her throat. How could she possibly unpack all he'd just said? "I'm okay... Blade?" she asked when he turned away.

He focused on her again, his gaze hot and troubled at the same time. "Yeah?"

"I wish things were different." Her heart hurt. Just hurt.

"I do too. Because I wouldn't have stopped at that kiss, believe me."

Her body trembled at that statement. Because what did it mean? What would have happened if she wasn't married to Hunter? Would he have taken her to bed? Made love to her?

And how would she have handled it if he had? They'd been friends first, but she'd be lying if she said she hadn't wanted more all along. It was a cruel trick of fate that he was here now and they'd just shared their first kiss.

"You don't have to stop," she blurted.

He turned to stare at her, his brows drawn together. "I do, Quinn. You're married and your husband is my boss."

"He hates me. And I hate him. We can find a way."

He shook his head. "It's not that easy."

No, it wasn't. Her shoulders sagged as he opened the door to the Rolls. She stared at the interior of the car, the rich creamy leather, and hated her life so much in that moment.

"Get in," he said softly.

Quinn sank onto the plush seat and closed her eyes. Trapped. Always trapped.

———

BLADE DIDN'T SLEEP WELL. It was part jet lag, part obsession over that kiss he'd shared with Quinn. He hadn't known what the fuck she was up to, but if he'd been in battle and she'd been an enemy combatant, she would have killed him dead.

Because she'd thrown her arms around him and

kissed him for all she was worth, and he hadn't seen it coming. Why hadn't he?

He wasn't sure, but he lay awake for hours, thinking about the kiss and the way he'd responded— not to mention the things she'd said about finding a way—and his resolve to get her the hell out of there hardened.

He had to get those cameras stopped first, however. It would have been easier if Hunter Halliday had gone out again, but he stayed in the apartment that night, drinking whiskey and talking on his phone until the late hours. When he finally retired, he didn't go to the room where Quinn lay. Instead, he went to another room. Blade only knew that because he listened and then he followed, staying in the shadows as he did so. Halliday went to a different room and closed the door behind him. Then a television came to life, the sound leaking through the walls.

Blade stood there and frowned for a moment, then he melted in the opposite direction, searching for the room where the cameras were controlled. He finally found it. It was the only room that was locked. He picked the locks and let himself in quietly, walking over to the console and sitting down to study the setup. It wasn't very sophisticated, but it was the kind of basic shit a novice with a Napoleon complex could handle. Hunter Halliday could sit in here and view his videos—good-quality videos—with the glee of a petty god.

There was no sound, as Quinn had said, but that

wasn't because the system wasn't able. It had every-thing to do with Halliday's paranoia, no doubt. The man didn't want his *own* utterances recorded. Though he could record conversations while sitting here, which meant that Quinn wasn't really safe from her husband's spying if he wanted to listen in on some-thing she was saying.

The camera displays were on the screens in front of him. Nothing, predictably, in the room where Hunter had retreated. But the cameras were every-where else—the living areas, the kitchen, the hallways and bathrooms. And, yes, the bedroom where Quinn lay sleeping now.

Except she wasn't sleeping. She was lying in bed and reading a book. She was covered head to toe in sleepwear—a button-down pajama shirt and pants—and she flipped through her book at regular intervals.

He couldn't read the title, though it looked like a romance novel if the cover was anything to go by. A shirtless dude with tanned muscles. Quinn's hair was piled on top of her head in a messy bun, and her face was makeup free.

Blade shook himself and searched for the controls to the system. There was an alarm system for the apartment, which had an outgoing line to the alarm company. But the cameras were not monitored remotely. They were for Hunter's use, and for use in case of a break-in when they would presumably be studied by the police. Once he shut them down, they had no notification system to the alarm company.

LYNN RAYE HARRIS

Hunter might get a notice on his phone, and he might make a call immediately. Otherwise, it would be morning by the time it happened.

Which meant Blade could search Hunter's office tonight if he wanted. But it was safer to wait until Ian Black had control of the camera system, so he'd chill until then.

Blade used a simple command to shut the cameras down. It wouldn't hold if Hunter did a full diagnostic, but they were counting on the fact he was the kind of man who'd call someone to fix it for him.

Blade let himself out of the control room, locked the door, and made his way back to the small room where he was staying. Then he pulled out his phone and sent a text to Ian Black. "It's done."

The ping came back a couple of moments later. "Got it. Don't worry your pretty head."

Blade sat in the darkness and stared at the phone's screen. It wasn't lost on him that he could go to Quinn now. That Halliday wouldn't know. Unless the man got a hankering to go to her room himself, which seemed doubtful if what Quinn had said was anything to go by.

But Blade wasn't going to do that. There was no way, even though he wanted to, that he would go and do all the dirty things he imagined to Quinn while in the same house with her husband. While she was *married* to her husband.

He wasn't that kind of guy. Even if she was unhappy and her marriage was a sham, he wasn't taking advantage of that. Besides, they were friends first, no matter that they'd shared that kiss today. Yeah, it had been a hot kiss that gave him all kinds of ideas, but moving beyond it wasn't a good idea.

He'd get Quinn out of her situation, but he wouldn't take advantage of her emotional turmoil. That's not what friends did. Even if he couldn't stop thinking about the way her tongue felt in his mouth—or the way his body responded at the thought.

"Down, boy," he murmured as his cock got in on the trip down memory lane. "Not happening."

But sleep was a long time coming. And when it did, Quinn was featured front and center in all his dreams.

———

WHEN QUINN GOT DRESSED and went to breakfast the next morning, Hunter was sitting at the table, frowning hard and yelling into his phone as usual. He glared at her as she sat. Li-Wu brought her coffee and fixed her plate. Blade wasn't there. Probably avoiding Hunter.

She took a dainty bite of toast and chewed slowly, though her food tasted like sawdust in spite of the jam she'd slathered on. When Hunter was in a bad mood, he took it out on everyone. And he'd been in a bad mood since they'd arrived in Hong Kong a couple of weeks ago.

He finished the call and threw the phone down.

Quinn hated the tension knotting her stomach, but she was used to it by now.

"Did you fuck with my security cameras, Quinn?"

Quinn blinked, toast hovering in the air as she processed his question. "What? No! How could I? You keep that room locked."

He had always been obsessed with security, which was his primary reason for having the system—or so he said—but she'd never been inside the control room. She wasn't allowed.

He snarled. "I've called a technician. He'll be out in an hour. I'm going to the office, but make sure he doesn't leave until the damned thing is fixed."

"Would you like me to stand over him, or would you prefer I send Li-Wu?"

"Send that damned bodyguard of yours. He needs to do something to earn his pay."

Frustration hammered her. "You're the one who thinks I need a bodyguard, Hunter. If you don't want to pay him, then send him away."

Her heart thumped. She didn't want Blade to leave, but she also didn't want Hunter to know that. So she shrugged and tried to look nonchalant about the whole thing.

"Nice try. He stays."

Hunter threw down his napkin and got to his feet before pocketing his phone. He stopped beside her chair and glared down at her. Quinn's pulse raced. She didn't stare, because he wouldn't like it, but she glanced up at him. He gripped her chin and forced her to meet his gaze head-on.

"Don't eat so much you bloat before the party. My wife is supposed to outshine all the other wives. It's why I keep you."

His words rained down like poison darts on the insecure girl lurking inside her. That girl never wanted to be made fun of again. She feared failure more than death. It wasn't logical, but there it was.

Quinn swallowed. "I know. I will."

He let her go and straightened. "You can be replaced, Quinn. Never forget it."

Chapter Nine

BLADE FINISHED HIS WORKOUT, THEN WENT BACK TO his room and showered. A text came in while he was standing beneath the spray. He checked it after he'd dried off.

It was Ian Black. *Call intercepted. Man on the way.*

Blade acknowledged the text with a thumbs-up before sauntering into the bedroom and dragging on jeans and a button-down shirt. He holstered his weapons—one concealed at his back, one concealed over his hip—and headed for the dining room. If Hunter Halliday was there, he wouldn't stay.

But Halliday wasn't. It was only Quinn, and she sat at the table with her head bowed, a plate of food barely touched in front of her. She looked up when he entered. Her eyes flashed with hurt and pain, but she quickly covered it up with a broad smile.

"Morning," she said. "You sleep well?"

"Jet lag is improving, so yeah, not too bad." He grabbed a plate and loaded it up. He didn't usually get such a late start, but he was still adjusting to the time. If he was here for much longer, he'd start rising before dawn and get his workout and breakfast out of the way before Quinn or Halliday showed up at all.

"You should know that Hunter's cameras are on the fritz," Quinn said brightly. "It's too much to hope they'll stay that way, of course. A technician is coming out. Hunter wants you to supervise."

Blade raised an eyebrow. "Me?"

"He doesn't trust me, and Li-Wu has enough to do —that leaves you. He thinks you need to earn your pay."

Blade snorted. "No problem. I'm happy to watch a technician fix a security system." He took a bite of sausage and chewed. "Any idea what happened?"

"None whatsoever. And I don't care either. I wish they'd stay broken, but they won't."

They would, in fact, but he couldn't tell her that. "Well, maybe he'll have to order a part or something."

"Not likely. Hunter would offer somebody a million bucks to turn Hong Kong upside down and find the part before he'd go without his cameras for even a day."

Yeah, the rich bastard probably would. The man had a superiority complex that made him think his needs were more important than anyone else's.

Quinn moved food around on her plate with her fork. But she didn't eat it. Blade nodded at the plate. "Second helping?"

He knew it wasn't, but the way she toyed with it told him she had no plans to eat it.

She lifted her gaze from her eggs. "What?"

"You aren't eating because you're full, right? You went back for seconds?"

She bit her lower lip. "I didn't go back for seconds. But yes, I'm full."

"Bullshit."

She looked surprised. He didn't let her offer an excuse.

"You aren't eating because your asshole of a husband put you off, right? What did he do?"

Her skin turned pink. One thing about being a redhead with pale skin—it was easy to tell when she was affected. Which confirmed his suspicions.

"Nothing. It's nothing."

"Quinn."

She dropped the fork with a clatter and folded her arms over her chest as she leaned back in the chair. "Jesus, it's *nothing!* I'm just not hungry."

"I don't fucking believe you," he growled. "Tell me what he did or so help me God I'm walking out of here."

He wasn't and it wasn't a fair thing to say, but her lip quivered. *Bingo.*

"I know better, all right?" she blurted. "But he said something about my being bloated for the party if I ate too much, and my damned brain won't let it go."

Blade's gut churned. He literally wanted to smash Hunter Halliday in his smug face. Then he wanted to tell the bastard what a tool he was before sweeping Quinn up and taking her far away from this place.

"Quinn," he said, his throat tight. "You have to eat. Fuck him and his narcissistic bullshit. Is he the picture of fitness? Does he have a trim waistline? Or does he wear a fucking man girdle beneath his trousers so he doesn't have to order bigger pants?"

"He has high blood pressure and he needs to drop thirty pounds."

"Then who the fuck is he to talk about bloat? Eat what you want. A real man doesn't care how much you weigh—he only cares how you *feel* about yourself. If you feel like a million bucks, then it doesn't matter what you eat. Be healthy, but don't starve yourself for some idiot's ideal of the perfect woman."

Her eyes glistened. She sniffed. Then she shook her head as if clearing it. "If I gained all that weight back, would you care?"

"Yeah, I would."

Her gaze fell. "Of course you would."

Anger flared deep inside. "Not for the reason you think, Quinn. I'd care because *you* wouldn't like it. I knew you back then. If you'd been happy in your skin, it wouldn't matter. But you weren't. You were miserable and you hated yourself."

She dropped her head and turned away from him.

Her hands clenched into fists on the table. "Sometimes I still hate myself," she said softly.

His heart ached for her. He shoved back from the table and went around to her chair. Then he dropped to his knees and put a hand to her cheek, turning her toward him. She came reluctantly, but she came. Her gaze was defiant.

"Quinn. Baby. I failed you as a friend. I didn't stay in touch. I wasn't there for you. I should have been. Because if I had been, I'd have told you I was proud of you. That you're one of the sweetest people I know. You can hate yourself if you want, though it hurts me to hear you say it. Because I don't hate you. I never have. I've always, always cared about you. From the first moment I saw you crying when those bullies were teasing you, I cared. I couldn't help myself. And I care now." He sucked in a breath. She trembled beneath his touch. "Eat breakfast, Quinn. You don't have to gorge yourself, but eat what you like. Don't let that asshole dictate what you do."

Her hand came up and wrapped around his wrist. Her fingers were cold. "You have no idea how happy I am you're here—but no matter what you think, you won't stay. He'll fire you or you'll get sick of his shit and leave. But I'm stuck, and I have to think about that every day."

"Madam," Li-Wu called from the hallway as he approached. "There is a man to fix the security system."

Blade stood quickly and moved away from Quinn as the butler entered the room. His gaze flickered over Blade but didn't linger. Quinn swiped beneath her eyes and stood. "Yes, Mr. Halliday said there would be. Did you show him to the room?"

"I did, madam."

She sucked in a breath. "Mr. Garrison will supervise him."

Li-Wu bowed. "Of course." His gaze flicked to her plate. "Your breakfast is cold. Would you like me to fix another plate?"

Quinn dragged in a breath. She didn't meet Blade's gaze. But she raised her chin and nodded. "I would. Thank you, Li-Wu."

"It's my pleasure, madam. Let me refresh your coffee as well."

"Thank you."

Blade drew in a breath, thankful that she seemed to be willing to eat after all. He couldn't stay to verify it, however. He quickly made a sandwich with toast and a fried egg since he wouldn't be able to eat what was on his plate.

Li-Wu handed him a fresh, steaming cup of black coffee. "I will bring you more coffee in fifteen minutes if you wish."

Blade could have kissed the man. "That would be great. Thanks."

He waited until Li-Wu was busy fixing a new plate for Quinn. She looked up at him as he stopped by her chair. He didn't know what made him do it—it was madness to do it—but he bent down and placed a swift kiss on her mouth while Li-Wu's back was turned.

Her eyes popped as she gaped up at him. "Are you crazy?" she hissed out.

"Yep. Now eat—and fuck anyone who tells you not to," he growled for her ears only. He started to walk away, but she reached out and caught his wrist, stopping him.

He frowned down at her pretty face. At her green eyes that were so wide and innocent, her high cheekbones and pert nose. Her mouth that begged for someone to kiss it. She squeezed his wrist before dropping it.

"For what it's worth," she said softly. "I've always cared about you too."

———

BLADE STOOD in the control room with Ian Black's technician—he hoped to God it was Ian Black's technician anyway—and watched the man work on the system. It wasn't until he turned and winked at Blade that he finally knew this was the guy Black had sent. He didn't know any of Black's people, so he hadn't been certain.

"Jace Kaiser," the guy said as he finished screwing the control panel back together and then plopped down and inserted a flash drive into the USB port on the keyboard.

"Blade."

"That's what I heard," Jace said, grinning. "Welcome to the team."

"Thanks."

He tapped some keys and brought up a diagnostic program. "When I finish this, you'll be able to control the cameras from your phone. You can turn them off when you need to, only they won't show as off. They'll loop footage showing an empty room or hallway—or whatever you choose to show. You can control that through the app."

That would certainly be handy when he was ready to start searching Hunter Halliday's office.

"You'll be able to view the footage and activate the sound controls as well. Same as Halliday can—except you'll get a notice when he sends the command and then you can block it. He'll get white noise."

"Which means he'll be pissed and calling you back to fix it."

"Get what you need quickly and it won't matter. But yeah, if he calls for service, we'll pretend to do the work." Jace grinned. "Man, I love this job."

Blade drank his coffee. He'd finished the sandwich already and he was about due for that fresh cup from Li-Wu. "What'd you do before this?"

"I could tell you, but then I'd have to kill you," Jace said, grin still firmly in place.

Blade rolled his eyes, but he was humored. "CIA's my guess. You've got a military bearing, but not quite enough of one to indicate you ever did more than a couple of years."

"You're close, but not quite." He tapped some keys when the program prodded him to do so, then hit Enter. A command line scrolled across the screen. He turned and held out his hand. "Give me your phone."

Blade fished it from his pocket and handed it over. It wasn't his personal phone anyway. That was back in DC, safely stowed at his house. This one had been furnished by Ian.

Jace took it, then handed it back. "Lock screen."

Blade grinned as he unlocked the phone. "Should have said so in the first place."

Jace brought up the keyboard and started typing. A few seconds later a program downloaded. "Just configuring the app now. Won't take too long."

When he handed the phone back to Blade, he pointed at the app. "Tap that."

Blade did so. A control screen showed him all the cameras in the house. He scanned the various tabs. "Seems straightforward enough."

"It is. But now is the time to ask questions."

"Can we do a dry run?"

"Yep, just let me finish the command sequence on the main panel."

Blade heard approaching footsteps. He turned to see Li-Wu coming down the hall with a tray containing a silver pot of coffee, fresh cups, and cream and sugar.

"For you both," Li-Wu said politely.

"Thank you," Blade replied. "You're a godsend."

"May I?" Li-Wu asked, indicating the door and the table just inside the room.

"Certainly."

The man walked into the room and placed the tray on the table. Then he proceeded to pour a new cup for Blade and hand it to him. "Sir?" he asked Jace.

"Yes, thank you," Jace replied. "Just black."

Li-Wu completed the task, handed over the coffee, and fixed Blade with a serene look. "Mrs. Halliday has finished her breakfast. She is in the sunroom, reading newspapers."

"Did she eat everything?"

"Most of it, sir. Is there anything else I can get you?"

"No, Li-Wu. Thank you."

After the man disappeared again, Jace frowned over his cup of steaming coffee. "What's up with the missus? She sick?"

"Not sick. Just married to a misogynist jerk."

Jace didn't ask any other questions. He finished running his diagnostic program and started to pack up his tools. Then he turned to Blade. "You ready for the run-through?"

"Yep. Sooner I get this figured out, sooner this job is over."

And the sooner he could get Quinn out of this nightmare she was leading.

But then what?

He shook himself. That was the part he didn't know…

Chapter Ten

BLADE WOKE IN THE MIDDLE OF THE NIGHT. HE rolled over and checked his phone, then lay there blinking for a few moments. The apartment had been busy with contractors, caterers, and cleaners all day. Quinn and Li-Wu were in battle mode for the upcoming party that Hunter was throwing.

Blade had been able to get a quick look at the guest list. It was a veritable who's who of Chinese government officials and technology titans. There were others as well. Men from international finance and a couple of guys who were certainly connected to a triad. But which triad? He'd texted the names to Ian Black, but there'd been silence on that end other than a terse "Got it."

He sat up and dragged on a T-shirt and a pair of shorts over his briefs. He tucked a Glock into his waistband, just in case, and grabbed his phone. Hunter was here tonight, ensconced in his room separate from Quinn, but there'd been no noise from that quarter in hours.

Blade called up the app that Jace had installed and killed the cameras for all the public rooms. He could see Quinn in her bed, sleeping, the covers thrown back and one bare leg thrown free. The bed was king-sized, but she only took up one side. She looked small and alone there.

He could also see Hunter. There was a camera in that room, but Hunter had disabled it because he so often spent the night there. Jace had reenabled it while also removing it from Hunter's feed, which meant the rich bastard wouldn't even know it was on. But Blade did.

Hunter was asleep, his body sprawled across the king-sized bed. There were papers at his side and a laptop computer near his head. The lights were still on, which told Blade that Hunter had been burning the midnight oil. He'd gone as far as he could apparently, and now he was done.

Li-Wu wasn't spared from the cameras. He was asleep too, lying on his back, looking as cool and regal in sleep as he did in his daily life, hands folded neatly on his chest, face serene. The man was the perfect butler even when passed out.

Blade kept his eye on the cameras as he slipped from his room and padded down the hallway, heading for the office where Hunter Halliday did his business at home. Blade had wondered why the camera control room wasn't also in the office, but Hunter's office answered that question. It was super neat, minimalistic. There was a desk, a computer, and a phone. Papers were nowhere to be seen. There was a television on the wall. It was still on, the sound muted, the screen showing a crawl of the world stock exchanges. The New York Stock Exchange was still open, and the crawl displayed what was happening on Wall Street at that moment.

Blade opened drawers, searching for anything that might stand out. The files were neat and sparse. He powered up the computer, encountering a password request.

"Shit," he mumbled. What would a narcissist like Halliday use as a password? Not his wife's name. Not his son's. Not even his own.

There was no fucking way Blade was going to figure it out. He could restart in Safe Mode and reset the password, but Halliday would know. Blade started opening drawers and looking for a notebook or piece of paper where Halliday might keep his password.

And then, because people were predictable as hell, he found a small address book at the back of a drawer. Inside were websites and passwords rather than addresses. Blade flipped to the entry that said Desktop and snorted. Of course.

IamtheChamp!@#.

He typed it in and the computer welcomed him like he was an old friend. There were documents on the desktop, but nothing suspicious.

He kept looking, kept opening files. Kept checking

the cameras to make sure people were still sleeping. And then, when he was beginning to think there was nothing at all, he decided to check the trash—and, bingo, there it was. Purchase orders from Chinese companies that detailed the number of processors, the equipment numbers they would be supplied in, and the specs for the processors.

Asia Sun was the supplier. Blade didn't know anything about them, but he'd get that info to Ian Black. He inserted a flash drive and downloaded all the documents. Then he kept poking around, searching for more, but there was nothing else. He ejected the disk, put the desktop back the way he'd found it—complete with files still in the trash—and shut everything down.

One last look at the office and then he was heading back to his own room, checking the cameras on his phone. Quinn was still hanging out of the covers, but her silky top had slipped up to reveal more leg and hip. He wished he had time to look at that, but he had to get back to his bed first. Hunter was sprawled in the same position as before. Li-Wu was on his side, one arm flung out.

Blade slipped into his room and closed the door. He turned the cameras back on, excluding the one in his room—yeah, he'd been pissed to find one there that he'd missed. That one was hidden inside the vent, and very cleverly too because he'd done a preliminary search and missed it. Now he'd put it on a loop of him in bed, and he wasn't inclined to change it. He would in the morning, but not right now. Hunter Halliday wasn't going to be interested in him sleeping anyway.

Blade stripped off the T-shirt and shorts and climbed back into bed. He grabbed an adapter for his phone, inserted the USB drive, and uploaded everything to a shared online folder for Ian Black. Once he was certain it all went through, he sent the contents of the folder to a covert HOT email address and then erased the USB for safety reasons. It wouldn't do to get caught with Halliday's files.

After the USB was clean, he cleared out his sent folder and all traces of the HOT email. He also erased the texts with Ian Black. The number was in his contacts, but he'd added no names.

He brought up the cameras again and chose the one he wanted. Yeah, maybe it was wrong of him to spy, but he wanted to see Quinn again. She was still in the same position, her little silk top slipping off her shoulder now. She was wearing sleep shorts, so there was no chance he was getting a peek at anything he might be interested in.

He put the screen to sleep and lay back against the pillows. Morning would come soon enough, and he'd see her again. He only had to hope that whatever was in those files was enough to put a stop to Halliday's scheme. And to break Quinn free of the bastard forever.

QUINN WORKED hard for the next couple of days, getting everything ready for Hunter's party. He liked to entertain, and when he did he wanted everything as big and sparkly and fancy as possible. No expense was to be spared. Of course they hired people to cater and serve and clean, but it was Quinn's job to select everything and make sure it was all done to perfection.

Well, hers and Li-Wu's. Li-Wu was wonderful, of course, but Quinn didn't feel right leaving everything to him. So she spent time going over the menu with the caterers, double-checking the guest list, approving seating arrangements, and generally checking that all the arrangements were running smoothly.

The day of the party dawned. Hunter went to the office that morning and left Quinn with strict instructions to dazzle. She had a stylist and makeup artist booked for late afternoon, so she wasn't particularly worried. When they arrived, she was bathed and ready for the pampering and primping.

She closed her eyes and thought of Blade as one girl worked on her nails while another styled her hair. The makeup would come later, once her hair was done.

She wondered what Blade would think. They'd talked quite a bit over the past couple of days—about life, about high school when no one was listening, about what they'd each been doing since graduation.

Not that they didn't already know those things, but they went into more detail—about his travel, about her weight loss and surgeries and fitness modeling. She wanted to understand how he'd come to be here, working for Hunter, but he was vague on details.

"I left the Navy and went into private contracting" was all he'd say.

"But why did you leave the Navy?" she asked. Because he'd sounded like he really loved it when they'd been talking.

"This pays better." He said it in a way that invited no further commentary.

She didn't really know him anymore. That was apparent. But she wanted to. The crush she'd had on him in school was as big as ever. She told herself it was because she was desperately unhappy and there was no guarantee she'd be happy with Blade even if he did return her feelings. She'd made the mistake of thinking a man adored her once before and look where that had gotten her.

Desperate-for-love Quinn had fallen for the wrong guy, and he'd wasted no time in smashing all her illusions about him. That was one thing she would never understand, because if he'd kept on the way he'd started, she'd probably still adore Hunter in spite of his caustic personality. She'd be his biggest cheerleader.

It took a couple of hours, but Quinn was dressed and ready for the arrival of their guests. She wore the deep blue gown with the slit up her thigh. Her red hair was styled in great chunky waves hanging over her shoulders and down her back. Her makeup was sheer perfection, highlighting her green eyes and making her face look like she'd stepped out of the pages of a magazine.

It never ceased to amaze her how beautiful she looked with the right makeup. She'd worked hard to lose weight and transform her life, but there were things about her appearance she'd never liked. Her nose was a little too big for her liking. Her eyes weren't wide enough. Her lips were too full.

But add the right shading and coloring and she looked like a million bucks. Precisely what Hunter wanted.

The stylist and her girls departed, and Quinn glided from her room into the main living areas of the apartment. It was still light outside, the setting sun sparkling on the harbor and throwing warm light into the depths of their dwelling.

Blade looked up from where he stood with Hunter on the terrace as she emerged onto the marble tile. His eyes widened and he blinked rapidly before frowning hard. Hunter didn't see it though. He glanced up as her heels clicked over the tile.

"Ah, Quinn." His gaze raked over her approvingly. "Yes, that's what I wanted." He held out his arm, inviting her into the circle of it. She cringed at the thought of going, but she wouldn't anger him. Not when he seemed in a good mood.

She stepped into his embrace, and he tightened his arm around her, turning her to face Blade. "Look at this woman," he urged.

Blade did so, blanking his expression into one of cool impassivity. "She's very lovely."

Hunter dragged her closer and pressed a dry kiss to her cheek. "She's not merely lovely. She's exquisite. The most beautiful woman in all of Hong Kong."

Red-hot embarrassment flooded her, but she didn't dare argue with him.

"I believe you're right, sir," Blade replied.

"Damn straight I'm right. These bastards tonight will envy me. They'll want what I have instead of the tired old nags they've got. You mark my words."

Quinn wanted to disappear. She hated when Hunter talked that way. She hated that he *thought* that way. But he put more stock into appearances than into loving relationships.

Worse, when he was this pleased with himself for choosing her, he could start feeling amorous. What if he decided tonight was the night to end his absence from her bed?

Just a few days ago, she could have borne it. But now that Blade was here, in her life? Now that she'd kissed him and felt what it was like to really, truly want someone?

Oh God, how would she survive it?

"Yes, sir," Blade said.

"Keep an eye on her tonight, boy. I want them to know it's impossible to have her. She's mine."

Hunter's arm tightened around her waist and he dropped in to kiss her again. Only this time he aimed

LYNN RAYE HARRIS

for her mouth. Her heart throbbed as she ducked her head just in time.

"Lipstick," she whispered as his eyes hardened. "It will stain your mouth." She stepped up on tiptoe and touched her cheek to his, hoping that would appease him.

His arm slipped from her waist, but not before his fingers brushed the underside of her breast. "You can suck my dick instead, Quinn. Nobody will see the lipstick there."

He grasped her hand as if he planned to tug her toward the bedroom. She wanted to protest, but her voice stuck in her throat. She shot a look at Blade, who clenched and unclenched his fists at his sides. She wanted him to do something, and yet she didn't.

Because if he did, if he said anything, he'd be on the next plane back to the States. And that she couldn't handle at all.

Li-Wu appeared in the entry and bowed. "Sir, the Chens are here," he said, standing back to allow a couple to enter the room.

"Ji," Hunter exclaimed, letting her hand go and throwing his arms wide in welcome as he approached the man and his wife. "Welcome."

The man held out his hand and the two shook. "Thank you, Hunter. We are happy to be here."

Quinn pressed a hand to her chest, breathing in and out steadily. Calming herself. She glanced at Blade. His mouth was set in a flat, hard line.

"You remember my wife?" Hunter asked, turning

114

to indicate Quinn. "Darling," he urged, his eyes flashing. "Say hello to Ji and his lovely wife."

Quinn immediately morphed into hostess mode, hurrying forward to shake hands and kiss cheeks. "Welcome. It's so nice to see you again, how are you?"

She didn't dare look back at Blade. But she could feel the angry heat rolling from him. She prayed he was still here at the end of the night—and that she went to bed alone.

Chapter Eleven

BLADE GOT A TEXT FROM IAN BLACK ABOUT AN HOUR into the party.

It's good intel. Not a smoking gun, but good. Need more.

Blade clenched the phone in his hand and gritted his teeth. Then he shot a text back. *Working on it.*

Except what the fuck was he working on? Working on not losing his goddamn mind when Hunter Halliday tried to drag Quinn away for a quick blow job, which she clearly didn't want to give, before their guests arrived.

Hell, it wasn't so much the idea of Quinn sucking the man's dick—though he didn't like it—as it was the idea the bastard had said it in front of him. Totally disrespecting his wife, as if she were a whore he paid for her services and not the woman he'd married.

Sex was personal and private. It wasn't the kind of thing you talked about in front of someone who was supposed to be an employee—and a stranger. He was fucking pissed that the man had done that to her. She deserved respect and dignity, and Halliday didn't allow her either one.

And then there'd been the look in her eyes. That frightened, disgusted, panicked look that said she didn't want to be alone with her husband under any circumstances.

What the hell was Blade supposed to do about that? There wasn't *anything* he could do. He'd stood there and told himself not to drag the motherfucker off her and disable him—and he'd told himself he had no choice, that he couldn't let her be abused that way.

Thank God for Li-Wu and the Chens. Because he would have gone to her defense in about three point two seconds, and then the shit really would have hit the fan.

But it hadn't, and the moment had passed. He needed to get over it and do the work he was here to do.

Blade stayed in the shadows, observing the guests. He sipped club soda with lime and made mental notes about the people here. They looked like your typical rich people. Richard Jenkins came about a half an hour after the party started. Blade knew from the dossier that the man had recently moved to Hong Kong to take over Halliday's operations here. He had an ex-wife and a twenty-year-old daughter who'd been in college but dropped out a few months ago. The divorce was fairly recent as well, and it hadn't gone smoothly. The ex blamed Jenkins's work for causing them to grow apart.

Blade's parents had worked together for years, and it hadn't stopped them from falling apart, so maybe there was something else at work in Jenkins's marriage as well. Not that Blade cared, but Jenkins seemed to watch his boss quite a lot when the other man wasn't looking. Like maybe there was some resentment there. Or maybe it was just the general dislike that Hunter Halliday seemed to provoke from those who knew him well.

Eventually Blade's attention moved on. When a new man entered the gathering, four other men following him, the mood in the room shifted. Blade perked up at that.

Now this man—*this man*—was somebody to be reckoned with. He didn't smile. He didn't look pleased. When a server approached him, he waved her off. He didn't drink, didn't eat. He glared.

Hunter Halliday seemed to sense the man's presence because his head lifted from where he held court with a group at one end of the room. A moment later he was moving toward the newly arrived men. He smiled and held out his hand. The other man took it, but not with any great pleasure. The four men with him didn't offer their hands at all.

Blade recognized a triad kingpin when he saw one. But which triad? Or did it matter?

Hunter ushered the man away from the party, toward his office, talking the whole time. Blade slipped from the shadows, casually, and followed. One of the men shut the office door as soon as they passed inside. Blade pulled out his phone, calling up the camera inside Hunter's office.

He could see Halliday, the four men who were clearly the hired help, and the boss. He turned on the sound and listened.

"Where is my money, Halliday?"

"It's coming, Mr. Shan. As soon as I get my share. I told you that."

"You borrowed a lot of money to make this happen. The interest is compounding as we speak."

"I know—and I'll pay it all back. But first I have to sell these terminals to the US military. Once they're in place, the money will flow."

Blade frowned. Money would flow? Why? The deal with the military was already done, but Halliday wouldn't have received payment yet. The promise of payment, however, should have been enough to loosen any credit problems he had. The US government didn't typically rescind contracts once they'd been awarded. Not without gross misconduct on the part of the contractor.

"Only if the information is worthwhile," Shan said.

"It will be. It's the US fucking military."

"Asia Sun is unproven. And so are you."

"Yes, but Beijing approves of the partnership."

"But Beijing hasn't provided the money for your operation. I have. And I'm beginning to have doubts.

Especially since you missed your first interest payment."

Halliday held out both hands in a placating gesture. "Shan, I'll get the money. I swear."

"When?"

"In a few weeks."

Shan shook his head emphatically. "No, not a few weeks. Tonight. You will transfer the money tonight."

Halliday was still trying to make a deal. The fucker was stupid. "A week."

"Tonight. Or your lovely wife could be the first casualty."

Blade's gut twisted.

Halliday shrugged. "Kill her then. It won't get your money any quicker."

Shan frowned. "You seriously goad me?"

"I'm not goading you. I just don't have the money yet."

Shan snorted. "Fucking American billionaire. Such a joke. You can't even touch your money—how can you be a billionaire?"

Halliday puffed up. "I am. *Forbes* ranked me. But I don't keep my money in cash. I keep it in assets—and I need time to liquidate."

Shan made a circuit of the room. Casually. Coolly. He stopped and tapped his fingers on the desk. "And how much are you worth dead, Mr. Halliday?"

Hunter straightened. Indignant. "If you kill me, you won't get anything."

"Nothing except the satisfaction of killing you."

"But is that satisfaction worth more than cash?"

Shan lifted an eyebrow. "Sometimes. Maybe not this time." He jerked his head at one of the enforcers he'd brought with him. The man stalked forward as Hunter looked puzzled. And then he put his hand on Hunter's shoulder, so friendly like, before hauling back and punching the man in the gut.

Halliday doubled over, wheezing and coughing, and the man turned to kick him in the kidney. He collapsed onto the floor, too out of breath to scream, too much in pain to defend himself. Blade didn't move a muscle to help—it wouldn't do any good anyway, plus he didn't like the man. Hunter Halliday was an arrogant son of a bitch who could use a good ass kicking.

The man bent and inserted a piece of paper into Halliday's fist.

"You will send the money tonight," Shan said. "The information is in your hand. Send it, or you will not see the sunrise."

———

QUINN STOOD in the bathroom in her underwear, her gown hung neatly on a hanger, and stared at her body in the mirror. She'd had such a love/hate relationship with this body over the years. It had been so lovely and flexible when she'd been a kid. In her teenage years, it hadn't stopped growing and she hadn't figured out how to make it. She'd been painfully shy and she'd eaten for comfort.

As a young woman, she'd been so unhappy that she'd finally decided to do something about it. She'd viewed enough television shows on drastic weight loss to believe she could do it too. Of course she'd done her research and started off exercising and trying to eat better. She'd fallen off the wagon many times, but she'd always gotten back on.

It had taken finding a gym that encouraged her as well as a lot of hard workouts and struggling, but she'd ended up with this body here. The one that was thin and muscled and felt like it could do anything.

And yet she still let Hunter make her feel like shit. Why did she do that?

She reached in to turn on the shower, but a knock at her door sent her heart diving to the floor. Was it Hunter? Was he back so soon? Before the party had even ended, he'd left the building. A meeting, he'd told her. A very important meeting.

He'd only told her so she could disseminate the information to their guests, not because he truly cared if she knew where he was going. But appearances were everything to Hunter and he'd want their guests to know he was such an important man he had to dash out for a meeting.

Even if it wasn't true.

Quinn hadn't known if it was true or not, but she'd been relieved that he was going. If he had other things to do, he wouldn't remember his threat to her earlier.

The knock sounded again, more insistent this time, and her heart crashed into her ribs. Maybe he'd remembered after all. She dragged on her robe and called out, "Just a minute!"

Then she hurried to the door, which she'd locked out of habit, and sucked in a breath. "Who is it?"

"It's Blade." His voice was low, urgent, and she tugged the door open to meet his hard, dark eyes. He was fully dressed in jeans and a T-shirt with a light jacket and a backpack slung over one arm.

Her stomach dropped. "You're leaving?"

He pushed into the room, past her, and closed the door. Then he dropped the backpack on the floor. "Yes. And so are you. Get dressed, Quinn. There's no time to waste."

Her feet wouldn't move as her brain rushed through all the possibilities. He was leaving and he wanted her to go with him. She wanted to go with him too. But what was this? Why was he running in the middle of the night, and was it the best way to go? Couldn't they simply go to the airport in the middle of the day when they were on an approved outing?

"Quinn. Now," he ordered.

"But... why?"

He came over and put his hands on her shoulders, squeezed. "Listen to me, honey. Hunter has gotten involved with some very bad people. People who have no qualms threatening *your* life in order to get what they want from him. We have to go because they're coming for you. I'm trying to save your life. I need you to do what I say."

Her throat had gone utterly dry. She blinked up at him, both terrified and certain she was safe so long as he was around. "Okay," she whispered.

He let her go and she stumbled over to her drawers, dragging out fresh underwear. She went to the closet and pushed the door to, quickly stripping out of the underwear that went beneath the gown and putting on her everyday stuff. Then she grabbed a pair of black leggings and a long-sleeved, lightweight jersey T-shirt, dragging it over her head. She also grabbed a jacket; then she snatched a pair of cross-trainers for her feet.

"Do I need to take anything else?" she asked as she hurried over to sit on a chair near the bed so she could put the shoes on.

"If you have a small tote or a backpack, grab a couple of shirts and some underwear and toiletries. Anything you can grab quick, okay?"

She nodded, her throat tight. She grabbed a Louis Vuitton tote that she stuffed with socks, panties, a sports bra, and some lightweight T-shirts and more leggings. She also rushed to the bathroom to grab a toothbrush and paste. Her purse with her phone and ID were beside the bed, so she shouldered it and slung the tote over her other shoulder.

"What now?"

"Now we go."

"What about Li-Wu? I should say goodbye to him."

"No. It's not safe. If he knows you're leaving, he could inform someone."

"He wouldn't," she gasped.

"I like him too, Quinn, but the truth is you don't know what anyone's motivations are or where their choke points are. He might because he has to. And he might because someone forces him, so it's better if he doesn't know."

It hurt to think such a thing, but she understood. "Okay."

Blade switched off the light, plunging them into darkness. It took a few moments for things to start to resolve in her line of vision. He pulled the door open and stood there, listening. Then he turned back to her.

"Follow me. Hold my jacket and don't say a word. Whatever I tell you to do, you do it. Understand?"

"Yes."

The apartment was dark and still as they ghosted through. The party had only been over for about an hour now. The caterers had cleaned up, the servers were gone, and everything was back to normal. In the morning, there wouldn't be anything to even indicate there'd been a party. That was the way Hunter liked it. Throw a shindig and then clean it all up and put everything back to normal the moment it was over.

Unlike the parties she'd attended in college, where

drunken students still sprawled on couches and floors the next morning and beer bottles were everywhere.

Blade led her to the elevator. When the doors whooshed open, the light was a shock compared to the darkness they'd been moving in. She squinted as she followed him onto the elevator.

She was surprised when the elevator opened onto the garage level. As if sensing her confusion, he held up a set of keys.

"You're stealing the Rolls?" she whispered.

He put a finger to his lips. "No."

She stayed behind him, close behind him, as they traversed the sea of automobiles. Finally one chirped, and she realized he'd pressed the button to unlock it. It was a Toyota. Definitely not one of Hunter's vehicles.

They got inside and Blade started the car as she fastened her seat belt.

"Whose car is this?" she asked.

He glanced at her. "A friend's."

"You didn't steal it from Li-Wu did you?" Not that she even knew if Li-Wu had a car since he stayed in the apartment while they were in residence.

"Of course not." He paused. "But I would if it was the only way out."

"What's going on, Blade?" she asked as he eased out of the spot and put the car into Drive.

"I told you. Your husband is involved with some bad people. He made a deal with the mafia, and they're leaning on him because he hasn't paid up yet."

Shock throbbed through her system. "The mafia? But why? He's a rich man. He doesn't need the mafia."

"How do you think he got rich in the first place? Hunter Halliday isn't precisely a model citizen. He's had help—investors, enforcers, inside information—that have gotten him where he is today."

"And the mafia threatened me?"

The glance he threw her was deadly serious. "Yes."

"Why? I don't know anything."

"Because you're his wife, Quinn. Because they think he cares if something happens to you. It's called leverage."

Quinn shivered and rubbed her arms. "He doesn't care. He cares about appearances, like if I try to divorce him, but he doesn't care if I get killed. He'd be the tragic widower then. He'd probably enjoy the sympathy."

"You aren't dying. You have me, and I'm not letting that happen."

She swung her gaze to his profile. He was handsome, like always, but there was more to him now than there had been when she'd known him as kids. There was a hardness. A darkness that said that while there might be scary things after her, he was even scarier.

"And I thought Hunter only hired you to keep me from running away," she murmured.

"I'm sure he did. But what he might not have realized was that he also hired the best protector he could find."

"I'm glad it's you. I don't know that I would trust anyone else."

They emerged from the garage. He flipped on the signal and sat waiting for traffic to clear. It was nearly two a.m., but Hong Kong was still alive with people.

"I won't let anything happen to you, Quinn."

She shivered, in a good way this time. "I know… What happens when Hunter comes home and I'm gone? Will he think I'm dead or that I ran away?"

Blade's hands flexed on the wheel for a second. "Honestly? I'm not sure he's coming home."

"I'm not sure I understand what you're saying."

"I'm saying that Hunter has more than one enemy who isn't pleased with him right about now."

"It's not in his nature to hide though. He'll try to spin it. That's what he does. No matter how bad it looks, he always comes out smelling like a rose."

Blade didn't look at her. "Not this time."

She wasn't sure why, but her heart skipped. "What exactly are you saying? That he's going to pay this time? That he won't get away with it?" He didn't say anything, and her frustration swelled. "Don't hide things from me, Blade. I have a right to know."

"Yeah, I guess you do… He's not coming back, Quinn. Not this time. He can't."

"Can't?"

He turned to meet her gaze head-on. "He can't because he's dead."

Chapter Twelve

BLADE HADN'T WANTED TO TELL HER ABOUT THAT JUST yet, but he wasn't going to lie to her either. Hunter Halliday was definitely dead. Ian Black's people had found him with a bullet through the heart. Dead as fuck. They didn't know if it was Shan or someone else who'd done it.

Still, Blade wasn't going to tell Quinn the details. He hadn't liked the man, and it was clear their marriage wasn't a happy one at all. But she must have cared for him once, and that was the part that Blade had to tiptoe around. There was no need to upset her any more than necessary.

She gaped at him as he drove. He wasn't sure if she was going to cry. Just when he was beginning to worry about her, she started to laugh. Shock coursed through him.

But she kept laughing until tears streamed down her face.

"Quinn?"

She waved a hand. "S-s-s-sorry." She giggled.

"It's okay," he said, because what else could he say?

"I-I d-don't know wh-why—" She bit her lip and shivered hard—then she sobbed.

The shock riding his system was quickly turning to alarm. Crying was a more normal reaction, sure, but still not a good one because he had no fucking idea what to do about it. He didn't have time to pull over and drag her into his arms to comfort her.

"Quinn. You gotta stop, baby. You gotta pull it together. Fall apart when we're safe."

She waved a hand, gulping. "I'm sorry. Really. I'm just…" She drew in a few deep breaths, pressed her hand to her belly. Didn't say anything for a long minute.

"I'm stunned but I'm also relieved," she finally began. "And that makes me a terrible person, doesn't it? I'm relieved the bastard is dead." She swiped beneath her eyes. "He was good to me for a while. He made me feel special, and I adored him. But he changed. So I can cry for the Hunter I once loved— the one that wasn't real—and I can also be relieved that the terrible person he *really* was is no longer in my life. Right?"

"You can feel however you want to feel. You'll get no judgment from me."

She sniffled and sucked in a breath. "God, I feel terrible and yet I'm also happy that I never have to deal with his moods ever again. That he'll never slap me or pinch me or drag me to our room for sex."

The idea that Hunter had done any of those things to her made him want to howl. "Did he do those things often?"

Blade was proud of how even he made his voice sound. How normal.

"Not as often as he used to—well, except for the sex. He hasn't done that in about six months." She paused for several moments as she stared out the window. He couldn't see her face so he didn't know what she was thinking. "But it's over now and I'm free."

Not as free as he would like her to be. They still had to deal with the threat to her life. And with the aftermath of Hunter's death.

He was a wealthy, powerful man. And while she'd said there'd been a prenup, that didn't mean she wasn't going to be involved in the resolution of Halliday's estate.

Which meant she was still at risk, especially if the triad hadn't gotten their money. They'd keep coming for it, and they weren't going to care who they had to threaten—or kill—to get it.

"Do you know what's in Hunter's will?" he asked her.

She shook her head. "No idea. I mean, I don't expect to get anything, of course. I imagine it all goes to Darrin."

"Are you on any bank accounts?"

"Yes. Hunter had a procedure once and he was worried about his ability to do business while in the hospital. He put me on the account so I could do his bidding. Before you ask, he didn't trust anybody who worked for him to execute things precisely as he wanted. In fact, he thought they might try to oust him. Anyway, that's neither here nor there. So yes, I'm on the account. But my signing authority is limited. Hunter had to approve anything over ten thousand dollars." Her eyes widened as the implications of Hunter's death hit her. "Oh my God, this means I have full control of the account now, doesn't it?"

He flexed his fingers on the wheel. "Technically? Yes. But it's probably not wise to do anything crazy. The estate will come after any money that isn't yours, and they'll come after it hard."

"I wouldn't steal anything," she said a touch indignantly. "I just thought maybe I could give the household staff some bonuses. Hunter never did. Lupe needs a new car—she's the housekeeper in Dallas and she's been with him for ten years now—and I'd like to give it to her. Things like that."

Of course she would. Quinn had always been sweet like that. And he wanted her to be able to do it, but now wasn't the time.

His brain churned with the things he knew about the situation. She could sign checks. She had access to Hunter's bank account. If the triad knew that, they wouldn't give up trying to collect the debt. They'd take everything they could get their hands on if they got to her. And then they'd make sure she disappeared for good.

He glanced in the rearview mirror, looking for anything out of the ordinary. It would have been prudent for the triad to secure Quinn before killing Hunter, but a man like Shan might have let his anger get the best of him. Shan probably wouldn't have thought that taking Quinn would be difficult. His people knew where to find her, after all.

Quinn hugged herself. "Where are we going?"

"We're getting the fuck out of Hong Kong."

"How? You aren't planning to drive out, are you? I don't think we'll get too far."

"No, we're not driving. I have friends who can get us out. We're going to meet them right now."

She looked suspicious. "What kind of friends?"

"Friends like me. Men who've done this sort of thing many times before."

She yawned suddenly, her jaw cracking. "Sorry."

"It's understandable. You had a long day."

She nodded. "I'm tired and overwhelmed—and I'm just going to let you do what you do. I don't even want to know right now. Is that okay?"

"More than okay," he told her. "Go to sleep, Quinn. I'll wake you when we get where we're going."

"I don't think I can sleep," she whispered. Too many thoughts racing through her head, no doubt.

"Just lean back and close your eyes. See what happens."

She did as he directed. Five minutes later, she was out.

––––––––

QUINN DIDN'T KNOW how long she dozed, but she snapped awake in a panic, a little scream on her lips. It took her a few moments to remember where she was and who she was with. And what had happened to put her here.

Blade was beside her, big and calm and comforting. The interior of the car glowed brightly, and she realized they were in a parking lot with huge floodlights shining down.

She sat up and blinked. "Where are we?"

"We're waiting for our contact to meet us."

"Contact?" She pushed her hair out of her face. She'd never gotten to shower, so her hair was wavy and full. "It sounds like we're in a spy movie. Did you make a chalk mark on the sidewalk?"

He grinned. "Nope. They'll find us without that." He turned to look out the front windshield, presumably searching for something, his fingers tapping on the steering wheel. "I've got friends who will help us. Just waiting for one of them to show up and get us to the airport."

"Why can't you drive us there? Abandon the car in long-term parking and forget about it."

"Do you really want to stroll through passport control?"

"I don't think we have a choice."

One corner of his mouth lifted. "Now that's where you're wrong. It's all in who you know."

A van pulled up and flashed the headlights three times. Blade flashed back. There was an answering flash and then he turned off the ignition and opened the door. "Come on, let's go."

"To that van?"

"Yep."

She grabbed her bag and opened the door, striding around the front of the car to meet him. The air was crisp at this hour, and Hong Kong was beautiful as the sun began to peek over the horizon and wash the water pink.

Blade put a hand against her back and propelled her softly but firmly toward the van. The door slid open at the last second and two men smiled at them.

"You made it, frogman."

"Was there any doubt?"

The man who hadn't spoken yet snorted. "There's always doubt with the new recruits. But you passed." He reached out a hand for Quinn.

She hesitated.

"It's okay," Blade said. "I work with these guys."

She took the man's hand and he helped her into the van. A moment later, Blade flopped beside her, dropping his backpack onto the floor next to her tote bag.

"Mrs. Halliday," the first man said, extending his hand. "I'm Jace."

She placed her hand in his. He was leanly muscled and surfer-boy handsome. He looked like he'd be tall when he stood up.

"Call me Quinn," she said.

"Quinn, then." He jerked his head at the other guy. "The one who helped you inside is Brett."

"Hey," Brett grunted as he settled a mean-looking rifle on his lap.

"And driving this bus is none other than our man Colton. We're gonna get you to the bird safe and sound."

Quinn turned to Blade. "Bird?"

"Plane," he said. "These guys are former military. Mostly. We speak a different language sometimes."

She looked at each of them in turn. They didn't have short hair or uniforms, but she could believe they'd served. They all had that determined look that she recognized from the past couple of days with Blade. It was a look that spoke of supreme confidence and utter certainty that they could handle any job put to them.

"Any sign of pursuit?" Jace asked.

"Nope," Blade replied. "We got out pretty quickly."

"And that's the plan right now. Get out fast before the authorities can shut down all traffic in or out. So hold tight, ladies and gentlemen. Colton is about to remind us why his family used to run moonshine during Prohibition."

Quinn grabbed the seat as the van shot forward

and then careened left before straightening again. The lights outside the van windows sped by. Eventually, after some twists and turns and what she suspected were near misses, they pulled to a stop.

"Gate's up ahead," Colton said. "Best hide them."

Jace pointed to the bench seat beneath their asses. "Y'all need to get inside there until we're through. I'll throw a blanket over it."

Quinn's lungs constricted as she looked down at the box she sat on. "It's small," she managed to squeeze out.

"It is. Sorry about that."

Blade gave her hand a quick press. "It'll be fine. I'll go on the bottom and you can lie on top of me."

He tugged her upright and Jace threw the lid off the bench. Blade quickly got inside, lying flat on his back. Quinn tried not to panic as she stumbled to the edge. Blade lay inside on his back, his eyes shining up at her.

"Come on, baby," he said. "You can do it. It won't last long."

Jace was waiting. "Soon as we're through, you can get out again. These bastards are lazy, promise. But we left with three and we don't need to return with five."

"And if they find us?" Quinn asked.

"They won't. Money will exchange hands before that point, if necessary. It'll be enough."

"Okay," she whispered. She stepped into the

coffin-like structure, feet between Blade's legs. He held up his arms, opened them.

"Come on, Quinn. You can do this."

She dropped down and stretched out over him. They touched everywhere, chest to hip to crotch. As the lid went down over her back, flames roared through her body at the contact with Blade. He put a hand behind her head, pressed her cheek to his chest. She felt his lips make contact with her hair. A shudder rolled through her. It was such a simple contact, and so profound at the same time.

"Don't make any noise," he whispered. "It'll be over soon."

Her heart felt like a squirrel on crack and her blood roared so loud in her ears that she wasn't sure if she'd even hear a noise if she made one. The tailpipe was louder here, the vibrations stronger. There was a hole at one end of the bench, and she focused on that. Stared at it and at the movement outside it. There wasn't much, but it was enough.

She was much too aware of Blade's body. How strong and big it was and how she responded to it. Her skin was on fire. Desire swam in her veins. In spite of her fear at the tight confines, liquid heat flowed through her on waves of flame, pooling between her legs.

The van lurched forward again, and the box vibrated around them. She must have made a sound because Blade's fingers moved in her hair.

"It's okay," he whispered.

She wouldn't have heard it except that his mouth was so close to her ear. His breath was hot against her, his body even hotter. And there was something else too… a growing hardness pressing into the apex of her thighs. Pressing against flesh that was already aching for want of him.

The van rumbled to a stop. Voices sounded outside the window. And then the engine shut down and Quinn turned her face into Blade's chest and tried to calm the hammering of her heart. She wasn't cut out for this stuff. She was a mouse compared to these men. She liked routine and quiet. God, she'd thought she was bored day after day with Hunter not letting her go anywhere, but right now she wished she was back in her bed with a good book. Or maybe with Blade.

The van doors opened. She could see light coming in through the hole. Two men with machine guns spoke rapidly. The man called Jace was closest to them.

"Hold up, hoss. Did you say you're looking for a runaway? We don't have any of those. We don't pick up hitchhikers."

Blade's grip on her tightened. The guard said something else in Chinese. Jace responded in kind. Then he said something in English that chilled her blood.

"Be my guest. We've got nothing to hide."

The guard clambered into the van and started banging around. Quinn squeezed her eyes shut and prayed. Something hammered on top of the bench and Blade tightened his arms around her when she would have made a noise.

"Dude," Jace said. Then he started speaking in Chinese. A few moments later, the man clambered out of the vehicle, the doors slammed, and the van was moving again. The lid popped up and Jace peered down at them.

"Told ya," he said with a grin. "Bastard wanted money."

"Yeah, I heard," Blade replied. "But the runaway he was talking about is Quinn. Somebody got an alert out pretty damned quick, don't you think?"

"It's a triad. They probably own half of Hong Kong."

Blade pushed her upright, and Jace helped her from the box. She sank down on a seat opposite, grateful to be breathing fresh air but also sad that she was no longer pressed up against Blade. No longer feeling the long, hard length of him pushing into her pubic bone.

He climbed out of the box and dropped it shut, then sat down on it again. "Any more checkpoints?"

"Nope, that's it. Almost there."

Within minutes, the van rocked to a stop and the doors popped open. A gleaming jet sat a few feet away, stairs pushed up to the open door. The jet was plain white, nondescript. The engines whined a little higher as the group jumped from the van and headed for the stairs. Jace went first, followed by Brett. Blade pushed her in front of him. Colton brought up the rear, but not before he spoke to someone waiting nearby and handed them the keys to the van.

Quinn stepped onto the jet and then stopped as she entered the main cabin. It wasn't at all what she expected. She was accustomed to traveling in Hunter's jet, which had been outfitted with as much luxury as he could get. But this one was a military command post, complete with computer banks and a conference table at one end. There were plush seats surrounding it and there was a hallway leading to the rear of the aircraft, but she couldn't see what was beyond it.

Blade put a hand against her back and propelled her forward. A man emerged from the hallway, smiling broadly as he saw them. He was tall, handsome, with black hair and dark eyes and a rough sort of masculinity that would have made her heart throb if not for Blade.

"Well, well," he said. "What did the cat drag in?"

"Ian," Blade said from behind her. "This is Mrs. Halliday. Which you know."

Ian came forward and held out a hand. "Indeed I do. Hello, Mrs. Halliday. How are you?"

She took his hand because it was expected, but she wasn't sure she wanted to. "Tired. Confused. Overwhelmed."

"Yes, I imagine so. Why don't you follow me? I have a place where you'll be more comfortable."

She hesitated, glancing at Blade over her shoulder.

"It's okay," he said. "I'll go with you."

Ian didn't look insulted by her hesitation. He simply waited.

"Thank you," she replied. "I'd appreciate that."

They went down the hallway and came out into a cabin that had lay-flat pods. "Sit wherever you like," Ian said. "Unfortunately, there's no time for beverages. We're departing immediately."

As if to punctuate that statement, the aircraft engines spooled up.

A woman's voice came over the speakers. "Ladies and gentlemen, we need you to take your seats and buckle up. We're cleared for departure and we'll start our taxi in approximately two minutes. I'll update you as soon as we're airborne."

Quinn sat down and buckled her seat belt. Blade sank into the pod beside her and did the same. Ian took one across the aisle.

Quinn leaned toward Blade, pitching her voice low. "Who is he?"

"Right now, he's the man who's getting you out of here. And he's my boss." Blade frowned. "Other than that... I have to be honest and say I don't really know."

"Well, that's comforting."

Blade snorted. Then he took her hand in his and held it. She liked the warm feelings spreading through her. He hadn't touched her like this when they were teenagers. She'd have given up potato chips for good to have had him hold her hand back then, but he'd never shown the slightest inclination.

"Yeah, sorry," he told her. "But he's one of the good guys. That much I'm pretty sure of."

"Pretty sure?" Quinn glanced at the man who scrolled through his phone, seemingly oblivious to their conversation.

"It's as good as I've got. But he's getting us out of here, so let's focus on that."

She was trying to. But she was also focusing on her hand in Blade's. "I like you holding my hand," she said softly.

His eyes were hot as they met hers. "I like it too."

She sucked in a breath. "When we were in that box in the van…"

"Yeah. Sorry about that."

"I'm not."

He lifted a hand to her cheek, brushed her skin lightly. Tenderly. "I've wanted to touch you like this since I first saw you again. But I couldn't." His brows drew low. "And I'm not sure it's such a good idea now."

"Why not?" Because she craved his touch. Just like this if it was all she could get. More if he'd give it to her. She'd been crazy for him back in high school. She still was. Of all the people she'd ever known, he was the only one who'd stood up for her when she most needed it. And now he was doing it again.

"Because I don't want to stop at just a touch. I

want things I shouldn't want, and touching you only makes it worse."

The plane was picking up speed now, charging the runway. Her pulse raced faster and faster. She took a deep breath. And then she laid her heart on the line.

"I want those things too, Adam. I always have."

Chapter Thirteen

Shit.

He was in so much trouble here. Quinn's green eyes gazed up at him with such hope and admiration. She wanted him, and God knew he wanted her. But guilt wouldn't let him enjoy this moment at all.

He'd ghosted her. They hadn't seen each other in eight years, but he could have stayed in touch. He just hadn't made the effort. Because even though she'd been his friend those last two years in high school, he'd failed to realize how much that friendship had meant to her. It meant something to him too, but after he joined the Navy and got busy, he'd let it slip.

Losing his phone hadn't helped because he'd never taken the time to search her out on social media and connect again. He'd meant to, but the more time that went by, the easier it was to put it off until he'd convinced himself that she wouldn't even want to hear from him after so much time. That she was living her life and having fun.

Reluctantly, he pulled his hand from her cheek. Her gaze clouded.

"I shouldn't have said those things," he told her. "Now isn't the time."

"When is?"

He glanced toward Ian. The man looked preoccupied with his phone, but Blade didn't believe it for a second. Ian Black wasn't the ultimate spy because he minded his own business, after all.

"When we're alone," he said.

She sighed and nodded and turned her face toward the front. But she didn't let go of his hand, and he didn't try to pull it away.

The plane lifted off the runway and climbed skyward. Relief flooded him, at least for the moment. He'd successfully gotten her out of Hong Kong—but her problems weren't over yet. The triad would be looking for her. There were others who might as well —Beijing, the US government, and Darrin Halliday. They'd all be interested in knowing where she was and what she was doing once Hunter Halliday's death was widely known.

After the plane reached ten thousand feet, a flight attendant appeared and asked if they wanted drinks. Blade ordered a bourbon. He could use a hit of alcohol right about now.

Quinn ordered a sparkling water. Ian also ordered bourbon, winking at Blade when their gazes met. The drinks came and Blade tossed his back. Ian did the same. Quinn sipped and flipped through a magazine she'd found. The flight attendant brought another bourbon. Blade sipped it, savoring the flavor this time.

An hour later, Quinn lay asleep in her pod and Blade glanced at Ian. The man jerked his head toward the war room they'd been in earlier. Blade unclipped his seat belt and stood. They made their way to the front. Jace, Brett, and Colton sat around the table, drinking and talking. There were a couple of other people at the computers, monitoring the red dots on the screen. Support staff.

The whole damned thing looked like HOT. Same kind of setup, same kind of team monitoring the screens.

"Fellas," Ian said. "Thanks for another mighty fine extraction."

Jace tipped his chin at Blade. "Your girl okay, man?"

His girl? Yeah, maybe she was. Maybe she always had been.

"She's fine."

"She was a little freaked at the checkpoint. Don't think she liked the close quarters with you, stud," Brett said with a grin.

Ian took a seat. Blade did the same. These were good guys, though they weren't quite what he was used to. They didn't have to adhere to any military regulations, though HOT was fairly flexible in that as well. But HOT was still active duty, and they still had rules to follow. Black's Bandits, as they were known, could do whatever the fuck they liked. And the only person they reported to was Ian Black. He couldn't bust them in rank and pay, but he could still eject them from his tribe and make it hard for them to find work elsewhere. So maybe they were a lot like HOT in that respect too.

"I'm pretty sure it was the threat of a Chinese prison that had her worried," Blade said.

"Yeah, probably so. She's a gorgeous lady. I wouldn't have minded cuddling up with her in that box for a bit myself."

Blade kept his cool. "You'll have to find your own girl. This one is mine." Because why deny it? She was his. What he planned to do with her was another matter altogether.

"So we need to talk about what happens next," Ian said.

He'd been thinking of nothing else. "Once the world knows Halliday is dead, they'll be looking for his widow."

Ian nodded. "Yep, they will. Mrs. Halliday is about to become very popular."

"So what's your plan to protect her? Or do you care about that?"

Ian arched an eyebrow. "Easy, sailor. We just got her out of Hong Kong, didn't we? What makes you think I don't care?"

"No offense, but I don't really know what your motivations are," Blade replied. "You wanted information about her husband's dealings with Chinese technology companies. I got you what I could, but that's over now. So maybe she's not useful anymore."

Ian leaned back, kicked his legs up on the table, and folded his hands behind his head. "I'm not offended. I know what you think of me, but I also know why I do what I do. Mrs. Halliday will be safe. We'll put out something vague about her not wishing to be bothered, suggest she's in seclusion while she mourns, and you'll be with her. Take her back to your place and keep her there until I tell you otherwise."

Blade frowned. He'd been liking the plan up to that point. "Don't you have a safe house where she can stay?"

"What, getting tired of spending time with your old friend? Nobody will think to look for her with you. Plus I'll put eyes on the place. We'll know if something is amiss. You have a security system, right? Cameras, alarms?"

"Yeah, I do. And for the record, I wasn't suggesting you stash her somewhere so I could back out of the mission." He'd fully intended to go with her, but he'd thought she'd be in a safe house. Not *his* house.

"Sounded like it to me, but okay," Ian murmured. "What kind of system you got?"

Blade frowned. "My security is good enough. Infrared, night vision, perimeter alarms."

"You set it up yourself?"

"With my team, yeah."

It was the nature of his business to be paranoid, after all. And, if he was willing to admit it, taking Quinn home with him wasn't actually a bad plan. He'd be more comfortable at his place, that's for sure. He knew the lay of the land, knew his system. He'd bought a small place in the country a few miles from work, because when he wasn't on duty, he liked to be where he could hunt and fish and relax on his own terms.

It was easier than renting, where he'd have to explain long absences to somebody and arrange for bills to be paid. At his own place, everything was on automatic withdrawal. He stopped the mail and he could be gone for months. Nobody would know. He even had a deal with a neighbor. Thirty bucks a week during the growing season and his lawn was mowed. The guy had a zero-turn mower and liked to ride it. He put on his tunes and went to town. It was an ideal arrangement.

"Then your place it is," Ian said. "If it gets too hot, we'll move her. But for now I think it's the best plan. You'll call your SEALs anyway, soon as you get there. The more eyes the better."

"For all I know, my team is gone."

Black made a face. "Yeah, could be, huh?"

It grated on Blade that he wasn't assigned to his SEALs at the moment. They could be on a mission somewhere without him, and that bugged him. They'd get a replacement for him, or they'd run it without him. They were trained to do so in case they lost a man. Always a possibility.

"You like pressing my buttons, don't you?"

"I like pressing everyone's buttons. It's what I do." Ian's eyes sparked like granite. Hard, assessing. "Anybody who can't handle the heat is a person I don't need on my team. What HOT does is important. What I do is important too. I know you don't like me —not many do—but I'm a patriot. I work for the good of this country, same as you."

"You've worked at cross-purposes to us before." The time he'd tried to sell their women to desert nomads, for instance. Or, and this one Blade hadn't been around for, the time Ian Black had kidnapped a HOT operator and basically threatened the free world with a lethal virus if he didn't get his way.

"And I will again if I have to. Whatever it takes to uphold the Constitution and protect our way of life."

Blade frowned at the man. But he got what the dude was saying, and there were other incidents to prove what he said was the truth. The time Ian had rescued the colonel from certain death, for instance. "I can respect that."

"I've got spies on the ground, Blade. We're watching out for her." He steepled his fingers. "I probably shouldn't tell you this, but you need to know she's got a price on her head now that her husband's dead. The triad wants her. Hell, Beijing might too, though I've had no confirmation of that."

No, he didn't like fucking hearing that at all. Everything had happened so fast that he hadn't gotten the real information he'd wanted about Halliday's operations. He had some video of Halliday with a triad boss. That was it. It wasn't the smoking gun they'd been looking for, and it wasn't enough to protect Quinn from the people who'd be trying to find her.

"I'm not surprised. Do you have any idea what's in Halliday's will?"

Ian shook his head. "No. He was notorious for changing it when he was pissed, so it's got everything to do with how he was getting along with his son at the time. Quinn could inherit a lot—or nothing at all."

That didn't surprise him in the least, though based on his observations of Hunter and his wife, Quinn was the one on the outs this time.

"She had signing authority on the bank account," Blade said, "But only up to ten thousand. With Halliday gone, she can sign anything. The triad probably knows that."

"Jesus," Ian swore. "That would explain why they want her so badly."

"Do we know if it was the triad who murdered Halliday?"

Ian frowned. "No, but they're the most likely culprits. There's also Beijing to consider. Halliday was a bit of a loose cannon with the triad breathing down his neck. And the deal to supply the terminals was already done. Maybe Beijing didn't need him anymore since that was wrapped up tight. They could have sent someone from the MSS to eliminate him."

Blade hadn't thought of that possibility. It was plausible though. The Ministry of State Security was the Chinese equivalent of the CIA or MI6. "Shit."

"Yeah, shit is right," Colton said. "Either a Hong Kong triad murdered an American billionaire or the Chinese government did. Not sure which is worse."

"Oh, I'd say the government is worse," Ian said. "That might trigger a response from President Campbell."

Blade thought of Garret "Iceman" Spencer, the Alpha Squad operator who was married to the president's daughter. Campbell was no lightweight, according to Ice. The man was tough, focused, and he took his position as the leader of the free world very seriously. If he had to send a message to Beijing, he would.

"Probably true," Blade said. "Campbell won't take it lying down if the government ordered the murder of an American citizen."

Ian motioned to the flight attendant. "Whiskey all around." Once the man returned with the drinks, Ian picked one up and fixed them all with a frown. "Better drink up, boys. The shit, as they say, is about to hit the fan."

———

THE PLANE LANDED on a private airfield in Maryland nearly twenty hours later. Quinn was tired in spite of the fact she'd slept on the plane. Her internal clock was totally fucked. Blade ushered her to an SUV and tucked her inside. He stood talking to Ian Black for a few minutes, and then he climbed inside and inserted a key into the ignition.

"Where are you taking me?" she asked as he pressed his foot to the gas and the SUV crawled forward.

"Home," he said, glancing at her.

"Hunter didn't have a house in DC. He was looking at one, but he hadn't finalized the purchase—"

"My home," he interrupted. "I'm taking you there for safekeeping."

Quinn couldn't think for a long moment. "Safe-keeping?"

"There will be people looking for you. They won't look for you there."

She supposed that was true. "Have you heard from Darrin yet?"

"No. We don't know what's in the will. And Hunter's death isn't public knowledge yet."

It was still hard to believe Hunter was gone. She'd despised him, but all she'd wanted was escape. Not for him to die. "It will be though, won't it?"

"Yes."

"What's going to happen?"

"Truthfully? I don't know. There'll be a lot of people interested in you."

Her belly ached. "I don't know what to say to any of them."

"Don't worry about it just yet. We're going to keep you hidden as long as possible."

"Forever?" she joked. "Because that would be almost long enough."

It was an hour later when they pulled up to a single-level brick ranch house. It was so different from anything she'd experienced with Hunter. And nothing like the semidetached house in England in which she'd grown up. But she knew it was a ranch based on all the HGTV she'd consumed in the past couple of years.

There was a garage, and Blade pulled into it after pressing a button in the SUV to lift the door. Once they were inside, he shut off the engine and took the key from the ignition.

"Home sweet home," he said. "It's a lot smaller than your place in Hong Kong. And there's no Li-Wu inside to anticipate your every need."

The heat of embarrassment danced across her skin. "I don't need that stuff."

"I know. Just warning you though."

She followed him from the vehicle, waited while he unlocked the door, and then stepped into a small kitchen with dark cabinets and a white stove and fridge. So different from the professional-grade appliances she'd had. And yet it was more inviting. Cozy. And very neat, as if he never really used it.

"I like it," she replied.

"You don't have to be nice."

"I'm not being nice. It reminds me of home in a way."

He tossed his bag down on the floor. "I've got a guest room. It's small but clean. The bath is in the hall. There's only one bath in this house, so we have to share it."

"It sounds delightful." What the heck was wrong with her? On the plane, she'd told him she wanted him. And now she couldn't tell him she wanted to sleep in his bed *with him* instead of in a room by herself? Really?

If she'd had a normal marriage, it would be too soon. But she hadn't and it wasn't. And she didn't feel guilty about that either. Hunter had repeatedly demonstrated his lack of respect for their marriage vows when he was alive anyway.

Blade flipped on lights as he moved through the house. Quinn followed, curious about the place where he lived. It was bigger than her parents' house had been, but not big at all. The entire thing would fit into the expansive great room in Hunter's Texas house.

When Blade finished, he turned and spread his hands, encompassing the combination living/dining room. "It's not huge, but it's mine."

"I had no idea you were a neat freak."

He dropped his hands and laughed. "I don't like clutter. It gets dusty. Besides, I move too much to have a lot of crap."

She walked toward the couch. It was big and tan and looked comfortable. "May I sit?"

"Sure. You need anything? Something to drink? Eat?"

"You asked me that on the way here. I'm fine. I still have my bottled water from the plane." She pulled it from her tote and set the bag down before sinking onto the couch. She wiggled her butt on the seat. "Oh my. It's like a big squishy hug, isn't it?"

Amusement curled the corners of his mouth. "I guess you could say that. I picked it because it's big enough for me."

"It does have a very deep seat. I could disappear in this thing."

"Well, try not to."

Something hit the window and Quinn jumped. But Blade didn't look at all worried. He strode over to the rear door and pulled it open. A big gray tabby cat sat there. It tilted its head back and meowed.

"Hey, buddy. You're out late," Blade said.

Quinn's heart squeezed. "Is that your cat?"

"Nope. Well, you gonna sit there or come in?" he asked the cat.

The cat walked inside. Swaggered inside, more like. Quinn watched Blade and the cat saunter toward the kitchen together.

"It's not your cat but you let it in?"

Blade grabbed a can of cat food from the pantry and proceeded to open it up while the cat did figure eights around his legs. He dumped the food in a bowl and set it down. The cat dived in.

"This knucklehead is nobody's cat. I thought he belonged to the neighbors down the road, but they said he shows up and they feed him, then he takes off again. He never stays. Doesn't stay here either. I feed him when he wants it, but otherwise he does what he wants."

"What's his name?"

"Don't know. I call him Buddy or Dude most of the time."

"I had a cat," she said softly, her heart squeezing even tighter than before. The pain was still fresh sometimes, but mostly she dealt with it. "Hunter gave him away."

Blade's head snapped up. "Wait a minute—you had a cat and your husband *gave* it away?"

She nodded. "He did."

"Motherfucker."

"Yes, I certainly thought so. I checked to make sure Tigger was okay—and he was. I send money for his care. Hunter didn't know that. I still have a little bit of money in my own account, and I set up a transfer to the people who adopted Tigger."

Blade stalked toward her. She didn't know what he was planning to do, but when he sank down on the couch and dragged her into his arms, she didn't protest. Why would she?

"Fucking hell, Quinn," he growled, his breath hot

against her hair. "I'm sorry you had to endure that man for so long."

She lay with her cheek against his chest and an arm over his midsection, spreading her hand over his hard abdomen. She could stay like this forever if he'd let her. "I made a bad choice," she said. "But I didn't know until it was too late."

He pushed her hair from her face, tucked it behind her ear. Tipped her chin up so he could see her eyes. "You okay?"

"I will be. I think I need a shower and maybe ten hours of sleep." She bit her lip, dropped her gaze from his. "I don't want to sleep alone, Adam."

"I told you what I want to do to you. It hasn't changed. But Quinn, I'm not sure it's a good idea. You're tired and emotionally exhausted, and that's the kind of bridge that once you cross it, you can't go back."

She tried not to let his words sting. But they did. "I know. And I don't expect you to do anything, but maybe if you'd hold me like this for a while, I wouldn't feel so lost."

He blew out a breath. "It's gonna kill me, but yeah, I can do that. If that's what you need."

Chapter Fourteen

BLADE CHECKED THE PERIMETER THROUGH THE cameras and armed the alarm system while Quinn disappeared into the shower. He heard the water turn on and he couldn't help but picture her stepping under the spray. Soaping her body, her hands gliding over her breasts, down the delta of her belly, between her legs.

"Stop it," he growled. No damned sense getting worked up when he'd just promised her he'd sleep with her and hold her all damn night.

Okay, not all night. Just until she fell asleep. He could do that. He could survive it. He'd survived far worse, hadn't he? Being a SEAL was no walk in the park. He'd gone on countless missions, and so far he'd walked away from each one. So a few minutes cuddled up with Quinn Evans Halliday would be torturous but survivable. He could handle it.

Except he didn't really have to. Quinn wanted

him. He wanted her. That kiss they'd shared in the market in Tai Po had been utterly explosive. He'd wanted his share of women, fucked his share of women, but he'd never felt quite that level of yearning before. He'd told himself it was their shared history causing it. And the forbidden element. She'd been another man's wife at the time. He respected that barrier, even when the husband was the kind of asshole Halliday had been.

But now she was a widow. No longer off-limits. He could spend the night deep inside her and nobody would care.

Except he had to be careful. Quinn wasn't someone he could treat like a hookup. She was more than that. She was his friend, and he'd already been a shitty friend once before. He couldn't do it again. If they had sex, it would get awkward. She'd get hurt in the end because he wasn't a forever kind of guy. Never had been.

And then there was his job. It wasn't the sort of job a guy who wanted picket fences and kids did, even though he had teammates who were successfully negotiating that minefield at the moment. He'd watched them with interest, but never longing. His emotional outlet, when the shit got rough, was fighting. He'd learned mixed martial arts in Hong Kong, and when the pressure got to be too much and he needed a release that wasn't sexual, he headed for the underground fight scene.

No, he definitely wasn't a forever kind of guy. But

Quinn was a forever kind of girl. And he wouldn't hurt her for anything.

It was only ten p.m., so he got his phone off the charger and dialed. It was answered almost immediately.

"Blade, what's up?" Alex "Camel" Kamarov asked. "Everything okay?"

"Yeah, man. I'm home."

"We heard you'd been reassigned. We've all been wondering what was going on. Can you talk about it?"

He thought about what Ian had said to him about calling his team. That sounded like tacit approval to him. "Some of it. But not on the phone."

"I can be there in twenty. We'll get the guys together—could take another couple of hours."

Blade laughed. "Not tonight, Camel. I've just spent the past twenty hours or so on a plane. I'm going to bed. But I'd like the team to get together as soon as possible. I'll tell you what I can, but the thing is, I'm pretty sure I'm going to need your help at some point in the near future. FYI."

"You know you don't even have to ask. We've got your back."

Yeah, he did know that. It was the greatest part about being a SEAL. About being HOT.

"How's Bailey?" he asked. "She still treating you right?"

Camel snorted. "Bailey is the fucking light of my

life, man. It's only been a couple of weeks since you last saw her."

"Yeah, I know. But she might have *seen* the light since then and stopped putting up with your ass."

"Hardly."

"What about Kayla and Ana? Neo still pretending he's not interested in her?"

Zack "Neo" Anderson was their teammate, and ever since Bailey's sister Kayla had arrived, Neo had seemed partial to the blonde and her baby. But he'd never actually asked her out.

"Man, I don't know what's up with Neo. He hasn't been around for a week. Kayla refuses to talk about him, or so Bailey says. I honestly don't care, so long as nobody's unhappy. They can figure it out for themselves—or not. Not my problem."

Blade heard the shower shut off. "I think it is your problem whether you want it to be or not. Kayla is Bailey's sister. You're gonna hear about this for a while."

"Jesus. Thanks, Blade. Why don't you disappear again for a while?"

Blade laughed. "I might. Right now though I've got my own problem to deal with."

"Seriously? What kind of problem?" Camel sounded entirely too interested.

Blade thought about playing it off, but the truth was they'd all know soon enough. "I had a best friend in high school. We lost touch and she, uh, married someone. But he's dead now and she's here with me. That's all I'm telling you for now. You'll find out more tomorrow."

"Fucking tease," Camel said laughingly. "Fine, tomorrow."

They talked a few more seconds, and then Blade hung up and sucked in a deep breath as he heard the bathroom door open. Quinn came down the hall, hair in a towel, another towel wrapped around her body. His dick immediately sat up and took notice.

"I, um, don't have anything to wear to bed. I didn't pack pajamas," she said.

"I'll give you one of my shirts." He went into the kitchen and opened the double doors where the washer and dryer were hidden away. He grabbed a clean navy-blue T-shirt that said Navy in yellow letters and took it back to her. It was an XL, which meant it would probably come down to her knees or thereabouts. Not as much coverage as he would like, but maybe it'd be enough.

"Thanks." She smiled at him tentatively, then spun on her heel and headed for the bathroom again. He watched her go, thinking that of all the things he'd ever thought would happen in his life, having Quinn in his house wearing a towel and making his dick hard simply by breathing wouldn't even have made the top ten.

He went into his bedroom and threw back the covers. He'd considered going into the guest room and getting into bed with her there, but that bed was only a full-sized while his was a king. He could hold her until she fell asleep and then put an acre of mattress between them so he could make it through the damned night without losing his mind.

Why had he agreed to hold her again?

Oh yeah, because she'd asked him to and he couldn't tell her no after everything she'd been through. The cat story had nearly killed him. Speaking of cats, Dude, aka Buddy, was sitting by his bowl in the kitchen and licking his paws. Blade strode over and looked down at him.

"You staying or going tonight?"

Dude looked up at him and shrugged. Okay, not really, but the look the cat gave him was definitely a shrug.

"All right then. I'm going to bed. If you're staying, that's fine. I'll let you out in the morning."

Jesus, he was losing it. He was having a conversation with a damned cat. A cat that wasn't answering. He went over and took out a bag of dry food, poured some in a different bowl, and set it down. He took out one of those travel litter boxes from the closet, peeled off the paper, and set the thing down in a corner. He kept a couple of them around because sometimes Dude didn't want to go back outside after he'd eaten. So far, there'd been no accidents.

He wouldn't even have known about the tempo-rary litter boxes if not for the neighbor. "Piss anywhere but there and you're never coming inside again," he said sternly.

Dude simply raked him with a disdainful glare.

Blade shook his head and went back to the bedroom. A few minutes later, Quinn came in. Her damp hair hung down her back, and her face was scrubbed free of the remnants of her makeup. His T-shirt hung to her knees, as he'd predicted. Thankfully.

She twisted her hands into the sides of it. He wondered if she knew or if it was an unconscious gesture. "Hey."

"Hey," he replied. Then he patted the bed. "Get in. I'm gonna shower too."

"Okay."

She looked nervous. He stopped in front of her and put a finger beneath her chin. "You don't have to do this, Quinn. You can change your mind about sleeping with me."

"No. I want to."

"It's just sleep though."

"I know."

"Then why are you nervous?"

The corners of her eyes crinkled. "You can tell?"

"Of course I can tell. You're practically vibrating with it."

She sighed. "You have no idea how often I thought of this when we were teens. How I wanted to be your girl. I wanted you to hold me close all night long. I'm sure I wanted other things too, but I was more vague on that than I should have been."

He frowned. "Meaning?"

"Meaning I didn't quite know what was supposed to happen. Of course I knew in the abstract, but I was shockingly ignorant too. Combination of factors." She waved a hand. "None of that matters right now. What matters is I feel safe with you and I'm so very glad Hunter hired you."

A sliver of guilt pricked him. Hunter had hired him, it was true, but there was so much more behind it that he didn't want to tell her just yet. And that's what made him feel like a jerk. He hadn't gone to Hong Kong to protect her at all. He'd gone there to spy on Halliday—and her since nobody had known if she was part of Hunter's conspiracy or not. She wasn't, however, and that was one of his greatest reliefs.

"I'm glad he did too."

She laid her palms against his chest. Curled her fingers into the fabric of his T-shirt. "If you hadn't been there, I'd probably be dead."

He didn't think there was any probably about it. If the triad had killed Halliday, they'd have come for Quinn and leaned on her for money. Then they'd have killed her too. And if it had been one of Halliday's other business partners? Well, there was no telling what would have happened to her. Getting her out of Hong Kong had been the best thing he could've done.

"Don't think about it. You're here, you're safe, and we'll make sure you stay that way."

"How long do you think I'll have to hide?"

He pulled in a breath. "Honestly? I don't know. But you're welcome here as long as you need it. And if the boss says to move you, I'll go too."

She smiled up at him.

He suddenly couldn't breathe as well as he should. "Damn, you're beautiful," he said. "I should have told you that years ago."

"Thank you. And it's okay. It's probably a good thing you didn't, actually. I already idolized you. If you'd told me that, I'd have been even more lovesick than I already was. I might have tied myself to that tree in front of your house and refused to leave when you told me you were joining the Navy. It could have been ugly."

He searched her sparkling gaze. It took him a good few seconds to realize she was teasing him. Sure, there was a hint of truth under the joke, but she wasn't being entirely serious.

"I'm sorry if I hurt you, Quinn. It was never my intention."

"I know." She shoved him away and crossed her arms. "Now go shower. I'm tired and I want to go to bed."

"Yes, ma'am. Be right back."

But when he got back, she was under the covers, her small body curled into the center of the mattress, sound asleep. He breathed a sigh of relief. Or maybe it was disappointment.

He grabbed one of the pillows and headed for the couch. He'd turn on the television, distract himself for a while. Maybe, when he was tired enough, he'd return. Or not.

Yeah, it was going to be a long night.

Chapter Fifteen

QUINN WOKE UP WHEN SOMETHING SOFT AND FURRY settled against her side. "Tigger," she breathed before she remembered where she was. She reached down and touched the cat who'd lain beside her. He started to purr. Tears pricked her eyes, but she swallowed them down.

It was dark in the room and since she was unfamiliar with her surroundings, it took a moment for everything to come into focus. She turned her head, searching for Blade, but she was alone. Disappointment flared inside.

"How are you, sweet kitty?" she asked, scratching the cat. He purred.

She didn't know what time it was or how long she'd been asleep. All she remembered was standing close to Blade, her palms on his chest, and then stepping back and telling him to shower. She'd climbed into bed to wait—and that was the end of that. She'd clearly missed his return, and she was certain he hadn't gotten into bed with her at all at that point.

The cat jumped down and Quinn lay there, wondering what to do. Go back to sleep or get up and search for Blade? What if he was in the other room, sleeping?

Then she'd leave him alone, wouldn't she?

She flipped the covers back and climbed out of bed. A quick stop in the bathroom to pee and swish around some mouthwash, just in case he was awake, and then she headed down the hallway and into the tiny living room.

Blade lay on the couch, the light from the television flickering over his face. And his bare chest. Lord have mercy. He was heavily muscled, with tattoos on his arms. His face was in profile to her as he looked at the TV. He had a scruff that she wanted to rub her hand over.

She took another step forward and he looked up, his dark gaze landing on her. "Everything okay, babe?"

His voice was gravelly, as if he'd been asleep and just woke up.

"Fine. The cat woke me."

"Oh man, I'm sorry. I should have put him out." He pushed to a sitting position and ran a hand through his hair. Muscles flexed and bunched. Her mouth watered. He wasn't like those guys at the gym who were too pumped, too focused on their upper body to the detriment of everything else. He was big and proportional and so seriously in shape that her insides twisted at the sheer beauty of him.

"No, don't worry. He got into bed with me and purred for a while. It was nice."

Blade looked surprised. "Huh, really? He's never gotten in bed with me. If he stays overnight and wants out, he comes in and yowls. Works every time."

He levered up off the couch and strode into the kitchen where the cat sat by the food bowl. She watched as he reached into the cabinet for another tin of food, muscles rippling across his back. Her heart swelled with emotion as he opened the can and dumped it in the bowl. It was silly, but she couldn't help it.

"Why do you take care of a cat that isn't yours?"

He looked up from washing his hands. "It's not a hard thing to do and it doesn't really cost me anything other than time and a few bucks for shots here and there." He shrugged. "Besides, it's the right thing to do, don't you think?"

She did. She hugged herself though she really wanted to go over and hug him. "It is. I love cats, but my parents wouldn't ever let me have one. Tigger was my first. I had him for five years."

"I'm really sorry, Quinn. If I could get him back for you, I would."

"I know. He's in a good home though. It wouldn't be fair to the family who adopted him if I asked for him back. But they know if anything changes to contact me. I'd have found another home for him if they had."

"Because Hunter wouldn't let you have him."

"No, he wouldn't have. He didn't like me to have anything that made me happy. No friends, no pets, no life outside of him and his ideas of the perfect wife."

Blade opened the fridge and grabbed a beer. "You want one?"

She hadn't had a beer in years. Hunter thought it was too coarse for a lady. Wine was acceptable, but not beer or liquor. "Yes, that would be lovely."

He popped the top on two beers and came over to hand one to her. They were standing in the middle of his living room. "You want to sit?"

"That would be lovely."

Geez, could she sound any more nervous, repeating herself like she didn't have a brain in her head? She went over to the couch and took a seat at one end. Blade sat down on the other. He reached out to clink beers with her. Then he upended the bottle and took a healthy swig.

She took a sip. The beer was creamy with a bite at the end. It tasted better than she'd expected after so many years of not drinking any. "So I guess I fell asleep."

He nodded. "Yep. I came back and you were out."

"Did you sleep at all?"

"After a while. I came out here to lie down. I didn't want to disturb you getting into bed."

"Don't lie, Blade."

He glanced at her. Then he nodded. "All right. I didn't want to get into bed with you because it was going to be sheer fucking torture."

Heat blossomed beneath her skin. "I'm not sure how to take that."

"Take it like I'm a man who's attracted to you, Quinn. That's definitely how it's meant."

She took another drink. Her heart was racing like she was that desperate high school girl again. And yet she wasn't. She'd done so much to improve herself. She was pretty now and she knew it.

"This is awkward, isn't it?" she asked.

He laughed. "Uh, yeah. Definitely."

She toyed with the bottle. "For a lot of reasons. I had a crush on you, but you thought of me as a little sister or something. Then we lost touch. And now my husband just died and I'm sitting here thinking about how you look without your shirt on."

"Yeah. You feeling okay about that, by the way? I don't mean about the way he died. Just that he's gone now."

"You think I should feel sorry he's gone?"

"I didn't say that. It's been a few hours and your thoughts could have changed. That's all."

She shook her head. "Nope. I would have preferred a divorce and never to see him again, but I'm not going to miss him however he left. I'm sorry for Darrin. I don't think they had the best relationship, but I think maybe it'll be a blow since his mom is gone too."

"She died skiing in France."

Quinn shouldn't be surprised he knew that, and yet she kinda was. "Yes. Hunter used that to elicit sympathy from me when we were dating. When we married, I found out how he really felt. He said she was a gold-digging cunt." She laughed bitterly. "It took him a few months to say those things about me, but he did sometimes."

"You make me wish I'd kicked his ass."

"Okay, well, enough about me," she said brightly, because this was starting to get to her. "Maybe we should talk about you for a change."

"What do you want to know?"

"Why aren't you married?"

He practically choked on the swallow of beer he'd just taken. "I haven't met anyone willing to put up with me and the life I lead."

"You wouldn't give up being a bodyguard?"

He pressed his lips together in a flat line. "I'm not a bodyguard, Quinn. I'm a private contractor who gets things done. The assignment varies."

"Okay. And that means you can't get married?"

"No, it doesn't. I have teammates—er, friends, who are married or getting married. It's a hard life though. Takes a special relationship to weather it."

"So there's hope for you."

"Yeah, there's hope."

"That's good." She sighed. "I can't imagine I'll ever get married again. Though I suppose it's possible. With the right person. And believe me, I'll make damned sure it *is* the right person if I ever say yes again."

The cat sauntered over and let out a big meow. Quinn jumped.

Blade laughed. "He wants out." He picked up his phone, tapped a few buttons, and then got up to open the door. The cat darted out. "User!" Blade called after him.

He thumbed the screen of his phone and then set it down. "Alarm system," he said at her look.

"Oh."

"Don't open any outside doors if you wake up before I do."

"I won't."

"My cameras are on the exterior. I'm not spying on anything you do in the house."

"I didn't think you were."

"It crossed your mind for a second."

"Okay, yes, it did."

"Did you know much about Hunter's business before you married him?"

"I read up on him after we met, so yes, I knew. I thought he was brilliant. But later I came to realize he really wasn't as smart as he wanted everyone to think. He had a business partner early on. Jasper Door. He was the one who designed the machines they used to build their business. Hunter pushed him out years ago. If not for Door, I don't think Hunter would have been as successful as he was. He had the connections, but Door had the technical skills."

"Door had a massive heart attack about ten years ago."

"Yes. And Hunter started taking credit for much of Door's work after his death. Even some of the articles I read said Hunter had been the visionary. But he wasn't. I learned that through simple observation." She set the beer bottle down, though she'd only finished half. "It's going to be a huge mess when everyone finds out he's dead. A lot of people didn't like him. And a lot thought the sun rose and set around him. He was very polarizing." She clasped her hands in her lap as she thought about everything that was still to come. "I'll have to go to his funeral and pretend to be the grieving widow. I'll have to listen to those people offer sympathy and wax on and on about him being a great man while I just want to scream inside."

"You won't be going to his funeral. It's too public. We can't take that risk, Quinn."

"You really think someone is going to want to kill me too?"

"I think it's possible. You have access to his money, at least for now. And there are a lot of people who'd like to get their hands on some of it. If he didn't pay his debt to the triad, they'll be first on the list of people looking for you. And we don't know who else he might have owed money to."

"People die owing money. It's not a crime." But she knew it was more than that. So much more.

And so did Blade. "Depends on who you owe the money to, doesn't it?"

Quinn wished she could hibernate through all this and then wake up and her life would be normal again. Just her and Blade and nothing else to get in the way. No danger, no propriety, nothing.

"So how long do you think I'll be in hiding?"

Blade frowned. Then he shook his head. "I don't know."

"Don't leave me. Please. You're the only one I trust."

He reached over and took her hand. Warmth flooded her. "I'm not leaving you, Quinn. I'm in this until the end."

———

BLADE WANTED nothing more than to protect her. To make Quinn's world safe again. But there were so many variables, so many possibilities, and the reality was they didn't know who'd killed Hunter Halliday or what they might do next. Maybe they wouldn't give a shit about Quinn. Maybe the triad had gotten their money and they were done. Or maybe the estate would be resolved immediately and Darrin Halliday would inherit, which meant the triad would go after him.

Or, if it had been Chinese intelligence agents who'd killed Hunter, they might not care what happened next at all.

Yeah, too many fucking variables to see a clear path. Which meant Quinn was safest when she stayed hidden.

Her gaze dropped to their hands. His did too. He didn't know why he'd reached out, but now that he had, he was having to deal with the electricity sizzling through him. The hot need pounding into his veins. It was crazy that he could be so affected by this woman. His brain told him that he knew her, that there'd never been a spark between them in high school, but his heart and his cock told a different story.

There was definitely a spark now. A glowing coal deep down inside that threatened to catch fire and burn all his inhibitions about her to the ground. He was on the verge of withdrawing his hand when she put her other hand over the top of his, encasing his fingers between her palms. Her touch was warm.

"Do you feel that?" she asked softly.

He was in the process of dragging his eyes from their hands to her face when he got stuck on her nipples. Nipples that made little points in the T-shirt he'd loaned her. Her breasts weren't small, but they were firm and round and her nipples were like the cherry on top of the sundae. He wanted to see them more than he wanted to draw his next breath.

"Blade?"

He jerked, forced his eyes to hers. "Uh, yeah."

"I lusted after you in high school, but it never felt like this. This is… intense."

"Yeah, it is." His cock was already swelling. Aching.

"You know what I think?"

She could think? Hell, he couldn't string two thoughts together at the moment. "What?"

"I think, maybe, we should give in to it. Just this once. Get it out of the way. Maybe it's nothing and we'll feel normal once we release this pressure."

"And if it ruins our friendship?"

She laughed softly. "Oh, Blade. Do we really even have that anymore? I mean, I care about you a lot, and I don't want to lose you again, but we're relying on an old relationship to call ourselves friends. I hope we *will* be real friends again. I sincerely do. But right now I can't think of anything but what it would feel like to have you inside me." Her gaze dropped. "God, I can't believe I just said that. I'm scared to death right this moment, but I also feel like I've been caged for far too long and now I'm free. I want to do what feels good and to hell with the consequences."

He was a little in shock at that speech. And a whole lot turned on. "I care about you too," he said. "It's important to me that I treat you right this time, Quinn."

His feelings were such a tangled jumble right now. He cared about her and he wanted to wrap her around his cock and drive her crazy too. He wanted to erase her bad experiences with Hunter Halliday, not that it was possible, but he wanted to. He wanted Quinn to be *happy*.

"Then kiss me and let's see what happens. Maybe nothing will. Maybe we'll both be like, eww, this is my bestie, I can't do this. Or maybe we'll be like holy hell, where have you been all my life. Besides, friends can have sex. It happens all the time."

He couldn't believe what he was hearing. First of all, there was no eww about this. Not from him. He'd tried to conjure up those little-sister feelings he'd once had, but they were forever changed. Quinn was not his sister and never had been. His cock knew it even if his head kept trying to throw ice water on the flame.

And second... "Wait a minute—are you suggesting we can be friends with benefits?"

"I'm saying it happens. People get lonely and needy and they may not have a romantic attachment, but they can have sex to relieve the loneliness and make themselves feel good. Having sex isn't a commitment."

He snorted a laugh. "Okay, who's the guy here? Because you sound a lot like you're trying to talk me into it. And, Jesus, I sound like the reluctant girl who thinks you won't respect me in the morning."

Her eyes sparked at that, but she didn't let go of his hand. She scooted closer to him, but not so close she was touching him anywhere but their hands. Shit, she was only wearing a T-shirt. He could have it up and over her head in a split second. And then he could be sucking those tits and filling his hands with them.

"You won't regret it, baby," she said, making her voice deeper before it cracked with a laugh.

"You're crazy, Quinn. But I fucking adore that about you. Always did. Seems I missed the shit out of you and I didn't even know it. So, yeah, I'm cautious because of that—and because you've been through a lot. I don't want to take advantage of you."

"Take advantage of me. I want you to."

His dick wanted him to as well. Badly. "When was the last time…?"

"The last time Hunter and I had sex? About six months ago. He preferred professionals."

Blade frowned. He couldn't imagine. The man had Quinn—classy, sweet, funny, beautiful Quinn—and he'd preferred to fuck whores? It didn't make a damned bit of sense.

"But the other night when he…"

Shit, why bring that up right now? *Dumbass.*

"When he said my lipstick wouldn't show up on his dick?"

"Yeah."

"That was the first bit of interest he'd shown in months. And it terrified me, I admit it. I was glad when the Chens arrived instead."

"So was I." Because if Hunter had dragged her away, he wouldn't have been able to let it happen. Something inside him clicked as he stared at her, like a key fitting to a lock and turning the tumblers. His feelings dropped into place, and he knew what he was going to do. What he had to do. Consequences be damned. Because Quinn deserved to be worshipped, not terrorized.

He tugged on her hands, pulling her toward him. "Come and sit on my lap, Quinn. I'm about to rock your world."

Chapter Sixteen

A SHUDDER ROLLED OVER QUINN. *OH DEAR HEAVEN.* She'd unleashed the beast and now butterflies swirled in her stomach at the look on his face. He looked intense. Hot. Focused.

But she wanted this. Wanted it more than her next breath.

Quinn straddled his lap, her legs shaking. She curled her fingers into his shoulders. His hands settled on her waist, holding her lightly but firmly. She sank a little deeper onto him, until her silk-clad crotch met the hard ridge of his erection.

She might have whimpered. He reached up and pushed her hair back over her shoulders. His broad hand curled around her neck, his eyes blazing hot as he looked up at her.

"You still sure about this?" he asked, his voice husky. "Last chance to stop."

She bit her lip as she nodded. "I'm sure."

He tugged her down to his mouth. Her eyes dropped closed. But he didn't kiss her. She could feel him a whisper away, but nothing happened. She opened her eyes questioningly.

"For the record," he whispered, "that was a lie. Anytime you want to say no, you can. I'll respect it, even if I'm balls deep inside you. This only works when we both want it. Understand?"

A shudder ran down her spine—whether at their proximity, his words, or the specific picture of what balls deep inside her meant, she didn't know. "Yes."

"Good."

He kissed her, a full frontal assault of her mouth that had her moaning softly as her body incinerated in the flames. She'd had sex with a couple of men besides Hunter, but she didn't ever recall this deep ache, this hard, hot need that raked its claws through her over and over.

She hurt, but in a good way. She had never known it was possible to feel like this. Sex had always been a need, a pleasurable release, but it had also been disappointing in its own way. Maybe she'd read too many romance novels, but she'd always expected something *more*.

Right now she felt like she was getting it. And it was amazing.

Blade had one hand curled around her neck and the other on her hip. His tongue sucked hers. Every sweet tug set up an answering throb in her sex. Her panties grew damp as her body sent all its resources to prepare for an invasion she desperately wanted.

Quinn speared her fingers into his hair, curled them against his scalp, kissed him with all the fire and passion she'd been holding in for so long. His hand moved from her hip to her thigh, slipping beneath the material of the shirt she wore. She shuddered with anticipation as she thought he intended to touch her where she craved him the most.

But he kept going, his fingers sliding up her torso, beneath her breast, around the curve of it, his thumb raking across her nipple. She stiffened and moaned into his mouth. He kissed her harder, deeper, demanding everything she had to give. And then he slipped both hands to the hem of her shirt and started to tug it upward.

He broke the kiss long enough to rip the shirt over her head, spreading his hands over her back and turning her, dropping her onto the couch, coming down on top of her, his legs between hers, spreading her wide enough to accommodate his hips. And all while continuing to kiss the daylights out of her.

"Jesus, Quinn," he said as he broke the kiss, pressing his hips into hers, his cock riding against the thin silk of her panties. "You're driving me crazy."

She lifted her arms, threaded them around his back, ran her palms down to his ass and then pressed herself up, grinding against all that hardness.

"Same here," she said. Or maybe she panted it.

He dropped his mouth to hers all too briefly

before sinking down to suck a nipple. There was no preamble, no warm-up. He just went for it—and Quinn thought she might come apart any second. Her back arched as she thrust her nipple into his mouth. He cupped both breasts in his hands—big, rough hands—and then sucked each one, flicking the sensitive tips until she thought she might go mad.

"Blade... please," she moaned as he drove her higher. She wasn't sure what she was asking for, but when he dropped lower, dragging his tongue along her torso before hooking his fingers into her panties, her breath choked into nothingness.

His gaze met hers over the scrap of fabric separating her sex from his view. "I want to lick you, Quinn. Do you want that?"

"God, yes."

He grinned. "Glad to hear it." And then he tugged her panties over her hips and down her legs, stripping them and dropping them onto the floor before using his shoulders to bump her legs open.

She was torn between embarrassment and anticipation. This was Blade—Adam—her teenage crush, lying beneath her legs and looking at her like he could eat her alive. It was her every naughty fantasy come true. She might not have had the knowledge when she was a teen, but she'd figured it out since—and he'd figured into her fantasies quite a lot in the early days.

"How do you want it? Lots of teasing before sneaking up on the main course or diving right in?"

"If you don't touch me immediately, I will expire," she declared.

He laughed. "That's my girl."

And then he touched his tongue to her clit, and stars began to coalesce behind her eyes. "Blade," she gasped. "Oh, wow, that's so good."

"That's right, baby," he answered. "I'll take care of you."

He spread her wide and licked her hard and fast, driving her body higher and tighter until everything exploded in a bright, hot shower of sparks that stole her breath and her voice for long moments.

Quinn fisted the cushions as she arched her hips up to his mouth, riding his tongue, taking her pleasure where she wanted it. He didn't stop, didn't tire, didn't let her down until she cried out and pushed him away because she couldn't take another moment of the intensity.

Quinn turned her face into the back of the couch, squeezed her eyes shut, and breathed deeply as the tremors shook her. She wanted to cry and laugh and shout for joy, but she did none of those things.

"Be right back," Blade said.

She nodded. Her body was cool where he left her lying without his heat, but he was soon back, ripping open a condom and rolling it onto his cock. She blinked at the sight of him hovering over her, one knee between her legs, the other foot on the floor, his sweatpants gone.

His body was a beautiful sight to behold. Hard,

muscled, and tattooed, he was like a bad-boy fantasy to her good-girl ways. She'd never smoked, hardly drank, and she'd only ever dated the preppy put-together boys once she'd lost enough weight and gotten enough self-esteem to date at all.

But Blade—oh, he was every girl's bad-boy fantasy come to life. The biker, the rough-and-tumble boxer, the hard-assed former Navy SEAL turned professional bodyguard. This was the man who fought for your honor instead of paying someone else to do it for him.

"You okay?" he asked, and her heart did a flip. Bad and sweet.

"Yes. Never better." She meant that too.

He was stroking his cock. It was big and beautiful, like him, and her only disappointment was that she hadn't gotten to touch it and play with it first.

"You still want this?"

She managed to roll her eyes. "Are you trying to back out? Because I'm not amused, mister. I need to feel your cock inside me."

He arched an eyebrow. "Dirty talk, Quinn?"

She felt the blush rolling over her. "Sure, why not?"

He lowered himself, captured her mouth with his. She sighed and stretched, kissing him lazily. And then she felt him, that big bold part of him poised to slide into her body, and she shivered with excitement. And, yeah, probably a little bit of fear. It had been a long time, and she wasn't sure how this was going to feel.

She needn't have worried. Blade slid inside her slowly, letting her stretch to accommodate him. He didn't shove his way in and he didn't jab her. He was a master at the long, smooth glide. When he was seated deep inside her, he stopped moving and just lay there, letting her body adjust.

Quinn wrapped her arms around him, slid her hands to his ass, and grabbed on. Even his butt was hard. It was such a turn-on after she'd been neglected for so long.

"You feel amazing," he told her. "It's everything I can do to take my time. I just want to pound into you until I blow. But we'll save that for another time."

She loved the feel of him inside her. The way it felt to lie beneath his big, powerful body and know he had her pleasure and her feelings foremost on his mind.

"Another time? Are you saying there will be?"

"After that orgasm you just had, what do you think? Willing to do it again? Or is it too eww for you?"

She couldn't help but laugh, even though what was going on between them was serious. "No eww here. Just a lot of mmmm."

"You taste mmmm," he said. "And you feel fucking fantastic."

He moved his hips, sliding partway out of her and then pushing back in a little harder. Quinn gasped, but in a good way. Her nails dug into his ass and her hips pressed upward into his.

"Stop talking, Blade. I want you to fuck me good and make me come again."

He withdrew all the way before slamming into her. "Honey, that's what I want too."

There was no more talking. There was only moving, bodies sliding together, hips rising and falling, bodies meeting again and again. Blade tried to be easy on her, she could tell, but she urged him to give her even more. He answered her challenge, rocking into her harder, pressing her to the limit. His eyes locked with hers as the tension between them spiraled tighter. She wanted to look away because it was too much, but she couldn't.

Her feelings threatened to spill free, to tell him in words what this meant to her. What *he* meant to her. Because there was no way this was anything less than an emotional connection. She couldn't have felt like this with anyone but him.

"Blade," she whispered, overwhelmed as he rocked into her.

"Yeah, baby. I feel it too. Now come for me."

"I'm going to."

"I know you are, gorgeous."

And she did, her body splintering into a million pieces as she cried out. He didn't stop moving though. He dragged it out, heightening the pleasure until she was limp with it. Then he followed her over the edge, groaning as he poured himself into her. It was the most intense, most beautiful sexual experience of her life. She only hoped he felt the same.

BLADE GOT up and went into the bathroom to dispose of the condom. He stood there for a long minute, staring at himself in the mirror, asking what the fuck he'd just done. Not because he regretted it.

Because he wanted more. Not just a little bit more. A lot more.

But why? Was he tangled up inside because of their history? Or had fucking her really felt that damned amazing? When she'd come around his cock, her body arching into his as her mouth fell open, her tits bouncing as he'd slammed into her, he thought he'd never seen anything more beautiful in his life.

And then his release hit and he'd been stunned by the intensity of it. He'd ground his hips into her, groaning, ejaculating so hard he felt like the top of his dick had blown off.

He glanced down at his cock. It was still hard. Still ready to go again. Jesus.

He scrubbed a hand through his hair and sauntered back to the living room. Quinn was on the couch, T-shirt pulled back over her head, fumbling with the panties he'd stripped off her.

She glanced up at him, her movements arrested as if she'd been caught stealing from the till or something.

"What are you doing?" he asked her.

She lifted her chin. "Getting dressed."

"Why?"

She looked adorably confused. "Um, we're finished?"

He stalked over and took the panties from her hand. Then he balled them up and threw them across the room. "No, we really aren't," he said, sinking down over top of her, pulling the T-shirt up and over her head as he did so.

She squeaked as he tugged her beneath him. "Blade," she gasped.

"Yeah, Quinn? You got a problem with this?"

"I, uh… oh my God," she moaned as he dropped his mouth to a nipple and sucked it between his lips. "No. No problem at all."

"Once isn't enough," he told her as he cupped her tits in his hands and pushed them together. "I thought I made that clear."

She licked her lips and he dipped his mouth to hers, sucking her tongue. When he let her go, she made a little panting noise.

"I thought you were just being nice," she said.

He frowned. "Nice?"

"You were horny and you hadn't gotten off yet, so you could have just been saying it—"

He put his hand over her mouth. Gently, of course. Her eyes widened, but not in a way that said she was scared. "I don't *just* say anything, Quinn. I said it wasn't enough, and it wasn't. Now if you tell me you're done, I'll respect that. But if you tell me you're just as hot for me as you were the first time, then I'm going to eat your sweet pussy again before I turn you over and fuck you from behind. I won't let you finish that way though. I want you facing me so I can see your eyes when I take you over the edge. I want to see you come. You good with that?"

Her mouth had dropped open just a little bit during his speech. She snapped it closed now. He could see the pulse in her neck, throbbing quickly, and he could see the effect on her body as a flush pinkened her creamy skin.

"I am *so* good with that," she said in that proper British accent of hers.

"Tell me to eat your pussy, Quinn." Because he wanted to fluster her even more. He liked it when she was pushed out of her comfort zone. Because once she got there, she let go and soared.

The blush deepened. "I don't think I can say that…"

"Why not? You told me to fuck you earlier. Now tell me to eat you out. Tell me to lick your pussy and I will."

"You won't do it if I don't?"

He almost laughed, but he didn't. She was looking for a reason to say it. If she needed that, then he'd give it to her. "That's right, baby. No licking until you ask for it."

He could see the concentration on her face. "Okay. Then I guess I must ask you to lick me. Um, lick my pussy, I mean. Please?"

Blade grinned. "Oh baby, you have so got yourself a deal."

He dropped down her body and made good on his word, licking her into a frenzy so hot she fisted both hands in his hair and rode his face while she came. Then he turned her over and fucked her from behind. When she was on the edge, ready to explode a second time, he withdrew and turned her over so he could watch her face while she fell apart.

It was, without doubt, an addictive experience he wasn't going to tire of anytime soon.

Chapter Seventeen

QUINN WOKE BLUSHING. WHAT ELSE COULD SHE DO? When she turned her head and saw the man in bed beside her, his dark lashes fanning over his cheeks, his naked chest bared to her gaze, the blush was inevitable. Especially when she thought of what she and Blade had done together. The way he'd thrust his body into hers, hitting pleasure points she hadn't realized existed. She'd come hard, repeatedly, in spite of her belief it wasn't possible.

It *was* possible. Especially when you had a hot man with a magic tongue between your legs. Hunter had *never* done that to her. She'd had so little experience before her husband, mostly because she'd been uncertain of herself even after she'd lost weight, that she hadn't realized precisely how much a man could enjoy licking a woman into orgasm.

The couple of men she'd slept with before Hunter hadn't had quite the same effect as Blade did. He was, quite simply, a sex god. For which she was profoundly thankful. She'd learned things, namely that sex really could be as amazing as it was in the novels she read.

She pushed the covers back, slowly, intent on getting up and sneaking to the bathroom. Blade's eyes popped open as he flipped toward her. A big arm dropped over her torso, anchoring her to the bed.

"Quinn," he breathed.

"Hi," she said, the blush deepening, burning from somewhere deep inside and spreading over her entire body.

He pulled her closer, nestled his nose against her neck. "Where you going, baby?"

"Pee," she said.

His grip loosened. "Okay. But if you want an orgasm before breakfast, you better get back here quick."

Her body liquefied, little tingles of excitement zipping through her from head to toe. "Who's making breakfast?"

"If you come first, I am. If you don't, then I guess it's you."

She placed her palm against his cheek. It was a bold move for her, but she liked the way his stubbled cheek turned into her palm, scraping it.

"So it's a contest," she said. "Who comes first wins."

He grinned. "Yeah, something like that."

I love you.

Quinn stiffened as the words sprang to mind.

What the hell? She swallowed her tongue before she could do something stupid—like say them. She had no idea if she loved him. How could she? She hadn't seen this man in eight years—and he hadn't even been a man then. He'd been a boy. You didn't necessarily love someone you'd had a crush on.

But her heart beat hard and insisted she did know. She'd *always* known. It wasn't just a crush. Which meant…

No. It wasn't true. It couldn't be true. They'd had sex once—okay, a few times in one night—but that didn't make it love. Crushing on someone in high school didn't make it love. It just didn't.

"I'll be right back." She jumped out of bed and went into the bathroom to take care of business. But of course once she was there she couldn't miss the opportunity to freshen up. By the time she returned, Blade's eyes were closed again and he was sprawled across the bed. She almost tugged on her clothes and headed for the kitchen to make coffee, but he lifted his lids and gazed at her, his eyes hot.

"Ready?" he asked, his voice gravelly.

She hesitated. "You sure you don't want to go back to sleep?"

He flipped the covers back and patted the mattress beside him. "Honey, I'd rather be balls deep inside you any day. Get back here and let me make you feel good."

Quinn's belly flipped, but she forced herself to walk back to the bed. And then she hesitated on the edge, but Blade had no such qualms. He dragged her down and rolled her beneath him. Then he tongued her nipples, one after the other, before dropping down to spread her wide with his fingers. Her heart skipped a beat as she gazed at him poised between her legs, his expression sensual and hot.

"You want my tongue?" he asked.

Her pussy ached in anticipation. "Of course I do —but what about you? Isn't it your turn?"

He dipped down to touch his tongue to her clit. "Soon, baby. But first you have to come."

"Blade," she gasped. "Oh God."

"Yeah, baby," he said before he buried his tongue in her body, licking, sucking, and manipulating her into a screaming orgasm that shook her down to her soul. "God, you taste good," he said before climbing up her body and thrusting his tongue into her mouth. She opened to him, excited, her body craving more. They kissed hard, tongues gliding, mouths pulling and sucking. His cock nudged at her entrance and he tore his mouth away, groaning.

"Condom," he said. "Got to get it."

She tightened her legs around him. "I-I told you I hadn't had sex in six months. And I'm on the pill— because Hunter didn't want any more kids, ever. He'd have made me get rid of it if I'd gotten pregnant."

He stared down at her, looking angry. Maybe she shouldn't have invoked her dead husband at a time like this.

But then he spoke. "I always wrap it up. I haven't

been bareback in years. And I get tested regularly for the job."

Her stomach bottomed out as the import of what he was saying rushed in. "Then fuck me bare. If you trust me. I understand if you don't," she finished in a rush.

"I trust you," he said on a growl. And then he plunged into her, his naked cock thrusting to the hilt.

Quinn moaned at the feel of him inside her with nothing between them. He was hot and hard and silky smooth. His eyes were closed, his jaw clenched tight. But then he opened them again, staring down at her.

"Holy fuck, you feel good. So wet, Quinn. So tight and velvety." He pulled out and then thrust home, deep. "Goddamn."

Quinn gripped his ass, held him to her. "Fuck me hard," she gasped. "Please."

He stilled. "Dirty talk, baby? Really? You blushed so hard last night."

She looked up at him, at this man who was buried deep inside her, his cock throbbing in the most intimate places in her body. Love rushed through her, hot and swift. "I know. But you're teaching me there's nothing to be ashamed of. Fuck me until I come again. I know you can. I know I have so much more left to give."

He reached down and hooked his arms behind her knees, spread her wide until every movement of his body caused her to shudder with pleasure. She was vulnerable, open, but she wasn't scared. He started to move, pumping slowly, grinding his hips into her.

"Is that good?"

Her eyes closed. "Yessss…"

He moved faster, harder, thrusting his body deep into hers. There was nothing between them. Nothing but skin and emotion. At some point he let her legs go, wrapped his arms around her, and pumped into her as she spiraled higher. As if he knew what she needed. What she craved.

Quinn reached for the peak, straining to find it— and then she came, gasping his name, her body exploding as his cock ground against her clit, dragging out the pleasure as she pulsed around him.

"Quinn—fuck," he groaned as he stiffened and shot a stream of hot semen into her body. He kissed her when his body finally stopped jerking. "That was fucking amazing."

"Yes." She licked her lips. "But one of these days I want you come like that when I'm sucking you, okay?"

He kissed her again. "You want to suck me off, Quinn? You sure?"

Her heart hitched. She knew he was thinking of Hunter and what he'd said to her. "I'm sure. Is that okay with you?"

She said it like a challenge. He laughed, still deep inside her. Still hard. "Honey, it's definitely okay with me. You want to suck me off, I'm fine with it. But if you change your mind, I understand. You don't have to do it."

She was slightly offended. "As many times as you've licked me, I think I owe you."

He kissed her yet again, her taste still vaguely on his lips. She didn't mind it. "You don't owe me anything, Quinn. If you don't want to, I'm not upset. If you do, then I'm ecstatic. Believe me."

"I want you as happy as I am."

He smiled down at her. "I'm pretty happy right now. You're hot, wet, and tight. And I just came inside you. Doesn't get much better than that."

"How many times do you think you can come before the real world intrudes?" she teased.

He thrust inside her, his cock still hard. She moaned softly. Was that her G-spot? She didn't know, but fucking hell, it felt amazing. Like a shower of sparks every time he moved.

"I don't know," he growled. "But I intend to find out."

IT WAS NEARLY ELEVEN in the morning when he finally got out of bed and showered. Blade didn't want to wash Quinn off him, but he needed the water to wake up. He stood under the spray and let the sharp needles of hot water pound into him.

Jesus, he'd messed up. Or maybe he hadn't. But he'd fucked Quinn, his best friend from high school, until his dick was sore and he couldn't possibly go another round without some rest.

Except, hell, it had felt *amazing*. Like it was more than fucking but less than what he imagined love might be. He'd watched his teammates who were in love, and none of them had a single doubt about how they felt.

Blade, however, didn't know what this was. It was an amazing physical connection. No doubt. But wouldn't something as profound as love come with incontrovertible proof that's what it was?

Of course it would. His teammates had been hit with lightning or some such bullshit and they just *knew*. He didn't know. All he knew was he cared for Quinn and he couldn't wait to fuck her again.

Which wasn't going to be all that long since they were in the same house with nothing much to do except wait for orders. He'd barely dressed when he was imagining stripping Quinn naked and eating her pussy while she curled her fingers into his hair and screamed. He'd always loved eating pussy, but he'd never obsessed about it. Until now. All he could think of was spreading Quinn's legs and licking her pretty pink folds until she begged him to stop. It was fucking intoxicating.

"Shit," he muttered as he got dressed and tried not to let his hardening cock determine how he spent the day. If he fucked her again, they'd both be sore.

Instead, he went into the kitchen and started to fix breakfast. The deal had been whoever came first won.

He'd always intended her to come first. He set about cracking eggs and putting bread in the toaster. When the food was ready, he carried it on a tray to the bedroom.

Quinn lay on her stomach, her back exposed as the covers had drifted down. Blade made a noise that might have been a whimper as he stared at the curve of her back. He could run his fingers down that curve, between her buttocks, and into her wet pussy. Then he could follow it with his dick, thrusting until they both came.

Except, dammit, he'd made breakfast and she needed to eat. He went forward and sank onto the bed beside her. Her red hair was a gleaming mess on the pillows, her skin creamy and pale. She made a noise and turned over, her breasts popping free of the covers.

Oh fuck, those pretty nipples. So pink, so responsive, so beautiful. Blade itched to take her breasts in his hands, to press them together and lick her nipples while she moaned. Hell, he wanted to fuck those breasts they were so pretty, but he'd spring that on her another time. Maybe in the shower when he could come all over her chest and she could wash it off right away.

Jesus, Quinn made him horny. The fantasies he had when he thought about her were intense. Exciting. Dirty.

"Quinn," he said, clearing his throat, determined

not to enact any of his hot imaginings while trying to bring her breakfast.

Her eyes fluttered open. It took her a moment to focus on him. When she did, her smile was so pretty it made his heart clench. "Blade," she breathed.

He wondered that she'd switched to calling him Blade so easily. She'd known him as Adam, and she occasionally called him that, but mostly she'd switched to Blade as if she'd called him that his whole life.

"I brought you breakfast."

She pushed herself up on an elbow. "Did you?"

"Fair's fair. You came first."

She snorted softly. "You planned it that way."

He set the tray on the bed beside her. "Damn right I did. A gentleman always comes last."

He picked up the fork and pushed it through the eggs.

"I want to make you come," she said, and his insides clenched.

"You do, Quinn. So hard I can't think for a long time after."

"No, I want you to come first. I want to make you crazy."

"You do make me crazy. But eat what I cooked for you, and I'll let you make me come first the next time."

She frowned as if she were disappointed. But then her stomach growled and she pressed a hand to her belly. He held up the fork with eggs. Her frown grew. And then she ate the eggs and he grinned at her.

"Fine. I'll eat," she said. "But your turn is coming."

He couldn't wait.

Chapter Eighteen

AFTER BREAKFAST, QUINN SHOWERED. THINKING OF Blade and all they'd done together made her so sensitive she considered turning the stream onto her clit and letting herself come. It wouldn't have been the first time she'd used the shower to climax, but it seemed like too much of a waste to do it with him so close. He could make her come so easily. A finger in the right place, a tongue—a cock.

"Stop," she said softly. "Too much of that and you won't be able to walk."

Her legs were already shaky, and her sex was slightly sore. Apparently you really could have too much sex. She frowned. Too bad, because if it weren't for that, she'd be trying to get Blade naked again.

His body was a wonder to her. The muscles so hard and smooth, his skin so silky and beautiful with its decorative ink. His cock made her belly drop with longing. It was long, thick, and he knew how to use it to drive her to heights she'd never experienced with a man.

Quinn turned the hot water down and let cool water stream over her body. It was necessary in order to tamp down the flame licking higher inside her.

She finished showering, got dressed in a T-shirt and jeans, and blow-dried her hair until it was still damp but not soaking wet. Then she emerged from the bathroom and went to find Blade. He was on the phone when she entered the living room.

"Yeah, we'll be there in a few minutes. Just waiting on Quinn... and she's done," he said as he turned and made eye contact with her. He smiled, and her heart did a ridiculous throb thing that actually hurt. She put her hand on her chest and rubbed.

"What was that about?" she asked when he ended the call and slipped the phone into his pocket.

He put his hands on his hips and frowned at her for a moment. She started to get worried when he didn't speak. Then he blew out a breath and said something that made her stomach roll.

"I haven't told you the truth, Quinn."

Oh boy. "You're married, right?" Because that was the worst thing she could think of.

"Nah, not married. But I'm not quite who I said I was. I didn't leave the military... I'm still a SEAL."

"Okaaay... So what does that mean?"

"I'm not a bodyguard. Never have been. I was, uh, *tasked* with the job of protecting you because we had a connection and because I speak Chinese fluently."

She was trying to process what he was saying. "But why? Why would anyone send you to be a bodyguard for me?"

"Because you're Quinn Halliday. Because your husband was a rich man with military contracts and suspected allegiances to the Chinese that might allow them to spy on American military operations."

Quinn blinked. Suspected allegiances? Hunter had been superpatriotic, or so she'd always thought. He'd often denigrated her for her accent, telling her that America was the greatest nation on earth and Britain was puny and weak. She'd ceased reminding him that she was actually an American as well as a British citizen because it only made him angry. He'd told her to talk like an American if she was so damned American. She'd only once pointed out that Americans came from many countries and some still spoke with accents. That had earned her a swift backhand across the mouth.

"Are you telling me that Hunter was colluding with the Chinese to allow them to spy through his processors?"

Blade's brows lifted as if he was surprised she'd figured it out. Then he nodded. "That's exactly what I'm saying. I was there looking for proof of his crimes."

Her heart thumped and her eyes stung. *Stupid Hunter.* "And did you find it?"

"No. Unfortunately. The situation escalated far too quickly. It went beyond what any of us suspected."

So Hunter had been a traitor to his nation. Of course he had. Anything in pursuit of the almighty dollar. Something else occurred to her then. "And what about me? Was I a suspect too?"

The corners of his mouth tightened for a brief moment. "Yes." She tried not to feel wounded. "But it was clear to me from the beginning that you weren't involved with Hunter's schemes."

She supposed that was something. "I'm glad to hear it… So who were those people in the van? The man on the plane who you said was the boss?"

"He's the boss, all right. Just not *my* boss. Or not my usual boss."

Blade came over and took her hand, folding it in his. She was slightly torn over letting him. In one respect, she loved when he touched her and this was no exception. In another, he'd obviously been keeping secrets from her. Not terrible secrets, but she still couldn't help feeling a bit betrayed anyway. Especially that she'd been a suspect in the first place.

"You're about to meet my teammates, Quinn. I trust them with my life—and with yours—and I know they can help keep you safe."

"Why are you telling me these things now?"

He looked down at her hand clasped in his, then back up at her. Their eyes met. Held. Her heartbeat quickened.

"I probably shouldn't. Nobody's gonna be happy about it. But you're my girl, Quinn. That's why."

"What's that mean, I'm your girl?"

He frowned as if he were thinking about it. "It means I've got your back. I'm not abandoning you this time. We're friends. For real. I'll fight for you if I have to. I won't let anyone tear you down again."

"I appreciate that," she whispered, her throat suddenly tight.

"Are you pissed at me?"

"A little. But I understand why you didn't tell me before now. And I don't know that it would have made a difference anyway. You came back into my life, and I'm thankful for it however it happened."

He tugged her into his embrace. "Yeah, me too."

He pushed her hair over her shoulder, caressed her cheek. She tilted her head back to stare up at him. To gaze into those eyes that she wanted to lose herself in. Her heart hurt looking at him. Because she wanted *everything* with him. He was what she'd been waiting for her whole life. But once more, she was stuck in a place where she couldn't tell him that. Because what if it wasn't what he wanted? What if she lost him by doing so?

It was just like being back in high school and crushing hard on him, except this time they'd actually had sex. But that didn't mean he was hers.

"I don't know where this is going," he said, "but I like where we've been so far."

Her pulse careened out of control. "Color me surprised that a man likes sex." She grinned.

"I do like sex," he said, the hint of an answering grin on his lips. "But I really like sex with *you*, Quinn."

"Bet you say that to all the ladies."

He let his palms slip down her sides to her hips, dragged her against him. He was hard and her belly churned with need. "No, I really don't. Sex is sex. It feels good and I like it a lot. But sex with you… There's something slightly addictive about it."

She pushed her hips into him and his breath hitched. "Only slightly addictive? I'm insulted."

"Okay, it's more than slightly addictive. I told the guys we'd be there in a few minutes, but right now all I want to do is strip you naked and bend you over the back of the couch."

"I want that too… but I think I won't be able to walk if you do." She hated to say it, because she really did want him buried inside her, but she had to be realistic.

He snorted. "It's okay. My dick wants to fuck you, but there'll be repercussions if I do."

She blinked. "Really?"

He bent down and pressed a quick kiss to her mouth. "Yeah. Men get sore too, baby. Best give it a rest for a few hours."

He stepped back and tugged her toward the kitchen. "Get your purse. We're headed over to my team leader's house. Everyone will be there, including the women."

Quinn's nerves spiked. She was going to meet his friends? Oh holy shit. And women? They could be the worst sometimes.

"You okay?" he asked, and she knew her nerves must be showing.

"Uh, sure. Just a little nervous."

He put an arm around her and pulled her into his side. "I watched you work the room that first night when Hunter insisted you go to that business dinner, and then the night of the party at your place. You're amazing, Quinn. You know how to talk to people, even though it's something you work at. You'll be fine."

She loved that he knew she had to work at it. That it wasn't natural. He'd known her when she could barely say boo to a ghost, so he knew how far she'd come. Yet another reason she loved being around him. He knew who she really was.

"I will be. I know. But these are your friends, not Hunter's business associates. I didn't care what they thought about me. I care what your friends think."

"They'll like you because I do. Promise."

Like. It wasn't what she wanted, but it was a start. "Okay. I hope you're right."

"I'm right. Now come on, let's get going. I want you to meet everyone. And I want to get a plan in place for taking down whoever killed Hunter. I won't believe you're safe until we've got the bastard."

IT WAS HALF an hour to Dane "Viking" Erikson's place. When they arrived, the cars belonging to Blade's teammates sat in the driveway and on both sides of the street. A sense of relief flooded him. He didn't doubt Ian Black's ability to get the job done, but there was just something about having his friends involved that made it even better.

He parked and then took Quinn's hand when she joined him at the front of the vehicle. He didn't care if his buddies ribbed him over it. Quinn was special to him, and he didn't mind admitting it.

They went up the sidewalk. He didn't have to ring the bell. The door opened and Ryan "Dirty Harry" Callahan stood there, looking as big and menacing as he could. Then he broke out in a grin.

"Dude, wow. I want a special assignment if it gets me a girl that looks like this one."

"Mind your manners, Dirty," Blade growled. "Quinn is a lady."

Dirty performed a mock bow. "Of course. Pleased to meet you, Lady Quinn."

He was surprised when Quinn laughed. "Not literally a lady," she said in her proper English accent. "Just Quinn will do."

Dirty looked smitten. Blade was more annoyed than he'd thought possible.

"Quinn." Dirty took her free hand and kissed it. Blade tried not to lunge for his throat. "Pleased to meet you."

Blade slapped at Dirty's hand. "Let her go, asshole."

Dirty laughed, but he dropped Quinn's hand. "You got it, Blade. Looks like you've been initiated into the club."

"Initiated? What the fuck are you talking about?"

"The PW Club, dude," Dirty said as they stepped into the foyer and he closed the door behind them. "You're gonna fit right in with Viking, Cage, Cowboy, Cash, and Camel."

Quinn shot him a puzzled look, no doubt at the litany of odd names. He shook off the annoyance he felt with his teammate and the Pussy Whipped Club, a name they'd come up with as teammate after teammate seemed to fall under the spell of a woman, and explained. "Nicknames. Like Blade. It's easier that way." He jerked his head at Dirty, who was definitely on his shit list at this point. "This one is Dirty Harry, though we just call him Dirty for short."

"And what is the PW Club?" Quinn asked politely, shifting into social mode.

Blade squeezed her hand and led her into the house. "Nothing, baby. It's Dirty being juvenile."

She didn't ask for an explanation, and he didn't offer. Instead, he walked her into the big open-concept kitchen and living area that Viking shared with his DEA agent wife, Ivy. The team was gathered around the giant island, laughing and talking. They all looked up when he walked in with Quinn. He had an urge to gather her to him, but he didn't do it.

"Quinn, this is my team."

"Hi," she said with a little smile and a wave that he knew cost her a lot of introverted energy.

"Hey there," Viking said. "Welcome, Mrs. Halliday."

"Thank you."

"You can call her Quinn," Blade said. Viking shot him a look that said volumes. He pressed on anyway. "You may know her as Mrs. Halliday from the files, but Quinn and I went to high school togethcr. Wc were best friends."

"That's right," Quinn added. "Please do call me Quinn. I prefer it. I wasn't happily married to Hunter Halliday, and while I'm not happy he was killed, I'm not sorry he's out of my life."

There was a bit of a stunned silence for a long moment. Blade had told Viking on the phone that Halliday was dead, so it wasn't news to the group, but it was the first time any of them had heard how Quinn felt about it. After an awkward moment, Miranda Lockwood McCormick sashayed forward, her golden-blond perfection as stunning as always, and held out her hand.

"I'm Miranda. I'm married to that one over there," she said, pointing at Cowboy. "He's an ass, but he's gorgeous and he's mine."

"Hey," Cowboy said, sounding slightly offended. "I'm not an ass."

Miranda laughed. "Yes, you definitely are. But I love you anyway."

And just like that, the ice was broken. The other wives and girlfriends came forward to welcome Quinn while Blade's teammates laughed and added their own encouragement. By the time all the introductions were made, Quinn had settled into what Blade thought of as her hostess mode. She might not be the hostess, but she acted like one, expressing interest in other people, asking questions, being concerned about their comfort.

He stayed by her side, but she didn't actually need him. She'd transformed herself into what was required. He knew it would cost her later, because at heart she was an introvert, but he was proud of her.

"So, what's the story?" Remy "Cage" Marchand finally asked when they'd exhausted the chitchat.

Blade pulled out a barstool for Quinn so she could sit at the massive island.

"Thank you," she murmured.

He bent to kiss her cheek. "You're welcome, baby," he said, uncaring that his teammates were studying him closely. He kept a hand on her hip as he stood behind her and met Cage's gaze evenly. "The story is that Hunter Halliday is dead, which you already know. He was murdered in Hong Kong two nights ago, though the media still hasn't picked it up yet. Mendez tasked me to Ian Black, who sent me to infiltrate Halliday's household and find out who he was working with on the military deal." He'd explained the basics of that deal to Viking earlier, and he knew his team leader had informed everyone else.

"I didn't get that information. All I know is that Halliday owed money to a triad and the boss came to collect. His name is Shan—but whether or not he's the one who ordered the hit, I don't know."

"So we don't know who killed Halliday or why. Or precisely who is after Quinn."

"Nope, we don't know either of those things." There was a bounty on her head, but they didn't know who had issued it. Yet. "Quinn has access to Halliday's money, at least until the news of his death goes public and the estate gets involved. Someone looking for what they're owed might come after her to get it."

"I take it there were no transfers before Halliday's death?"

"None that Black's people could see. Which means the triad didn't get what they were looking for. Now either they've written that money off and they're using Halliday's death as an example of what happens when you don't pay up, or they didn't pull the trigger and they still want what's owed."

The doorbell rang just then, and every SEAL in the room shifted into high alert. So did Viking's DEA agent wife Ivy and CIA operative Miranda.

"Expecting anyone?" Viking asked softly.

"Nope," Ivy said. "Could be a kid selling stuff for school."

"Yeah, could be. Except school's out right now, so that's not the most likely explanation."

"No, probably not," she replied. "Unless you

ordered more of those BBQ supplies you're always looking at online."

Viking frowned. "I didn't. But you love when I smoke ribs."

"I do indeed. Order all you like."

"All righty, then," Viking said. "Guess I'll go answer it."

They were all quiet as Viking headed toward the front door. Blade exchanged glances with his teammates. Most likely it was nothing, but they were trained to think of worst-case scenarios. Made them seem paranoid to an outsider, but it was the job to always consider what might happen.

"Oh for fuck's sake," Viking said, his voice drifting back to them. "What do you want?"

The answer didn't reach them, but the door shutting did. Viking came striding back into the room. And Ian Black walked in behind him.

"Hello, kids," Black said cheerfully. "What a lovely gathering."

"Speak of the devil," Cage murmured.

Cowboy shifted his stance and looked annoyed. Out of all of them, probably Cage and Cowboy were the two with the most reason to dislike Ian Black. He hadn't done them wrong, but he'd definitely played a part when their women were in danger.

"I have to assume there's a reason you're here," Viking said. "Care to enlighten us?"

"What, no offer of a beverage?"

"Would you like a drink?" Ivy asked, smiling sweetly.

"No thanks," Ian said. "But I appreciate your asking."

"For fuck's sake," Cash "Money" McQuaid grumbled. His wife, Ella, squeezed his arm and said something in his ear. It didn't stop the grumbling, but Cash didn't say anything else that was audible to the rest of them.

"How are you today, Mrs. Halliday?" Ian asked.

"I'm fine, thanks. How about you?"

"Peachy." He let his gaze slide over the group of them. "I knew you'd all get involved. Just remember this isn't officially your op, okay? You don't want to cause any grief for your soon-to-be General Mendez."

No, they definitely didn't.

"Is this a social call or what?" Cage finally growled out.

Ian folded his arms over his chest. He was a tall man, well-muscled, with the kind of suaveness that spoke more of board rooms than combat. And yet he was a warrior down to his core. Blade had seen it in action more than once, and he'd heard tales from Alpha Squad too. Ian Black was no pushover.

"Not a social call. Halliday wasn't killed on Shan's orders. I've got a source in the triad, and he's reporting that Shan is pissed and losing his shit right about now. Halliday owed him around thirty million, give or take a few bucks for the vig—that's interest if you don't know."

Quinn gasped.

Ian zeroed in on her. "Yes, Mrs. Halliday, your husband was deep in debt to Chinese mobsters. And they aren't the only ones. There might not be a Halliday Tech Solutions left after this is all over, I'm sorry to say."

Quinn folded her hands in her lap and straightened her spine. Blade could feel the strength rolling through her as she dug down deep.

"I don't care for me, but there are people who depend on Hunter for their jobs. I care about what's going to happen to them. And Hunter's son. He would have inherited the business someday."

"Not today," Ian said. "Hunter changed his will about a month ago. He gave a controlling interest to you. You're in charge of HTS, Mrs. Halliday."

Blade felt her body go stiff. "That can't be right. Hunter didn't think very highly of my intelligence, so he wouldn't leave me a controlling interest in his company."

"He would if he were angry with his son. And if he didn't actually expect to die but only wanted to use it as a club to control Darrin."

Quinn was trembling. "Yes, he would do that," she said quietly. "That is very much how he operated."

"Well, then. Congratulations, Mrs. Halliday, because you are now the majority shareholder in HTS, however long it lasts."

"You just said the company was going broke," Blade grumbled. "This can't be a good thing for Quinn."

"Probably not, no. But it's hers to deal with for the moment. And the news is about to hit the wires."

"Well, hell," someone said.

"I don't want it," Quinn replied, sounding the slightest bit desperate. "I'll sign it all over to Darrin. He can deal with it."

"You can't. Your husband thought of everything, as petty tyrants usually do. No transfers of shares for one year, and nothing without board approval."

"Can he do that?"

"Maybe not, but it'd take time to challenge it in court. HTS is a privately owned company. They don't have to play by the same rules as publicly traded companies do."

"Okay," Blade said. "So Quinn is the majority stakeholder in HTS. Her step-son is presumably the second-biggest stakeholder. Shan didn't order Halliday's death, which means someone else did—and Shan still wants his thirty million. Plus Halliday was in debt to countless other people we still don't know about, and the company might go belly up. Any more good news today?"

Ian tilted his head slightly and smiled. "We're no closer to getting evidence about any backdoor coding in those computers."

"Awesome," Blade said. "Just awesome."

"Texas," Quinn said, and Blade walked around to

see her face. She was nibbling her lip, her delicate brows drawn down in a frown as she concentrated on something.

"Texas?" Blade asked.

She lifted her gaze to his. "The Texas house. That was our main residence. Halliday Tech Solutions has offices in many locations, but Dallas is the headquarters. Hunter had a setup kind of like in Hong Kong, but he had cameras and sound. He also recorded all his phone calls. Insurance, he told me once. If he kept those recordings, they're on the hard drive in his control room."

Ian Black pushed his way to Blade's side, standing in front of Quinn and gazing down at her with barely suppressed excitement. "He recorded his calls? You're sure?"

"Oh yes. He recorded them sometimes in other houses, but the recordings all went to Texas. He was rather obsessive about it."

"Can you give me a floor plan of the house?" Ian asked.

Quinn frowned. "I could, but it won't do you any good. You need me to get in. Hunter's security there is tight, and they aren't letting you in."

"They don't have to let us in," Blade said. "Breaking in and neutralizing the opposition is kind of what we do."

"Yes, but why? If we fly down there, I can walk right in with a few of you at my side. I'll dismiss the security staff. Then I'll show you where the room is and you can get what you need."

"It's not a bad idea," Ian said.

Blade didn't like it. "It exposes her. We don't know who might be waiting for her to return."

"That's true, but she'll be walking in with a SEAL team at her side."

"As much as I'd like to do that," Viking cut in, "I don't think we can. We're still, uh…" He looked at Quinn, who didn't know about the secret organization they were assigned to. Blade could see the moment Viking's fuck-it meter pegged. He'd decided that Quinn was one of them now. "We're still HOT, and HOT isn't involved in this one."

Ian turned with a smile on his face. "Then you'll just have to join Black's Bandits, won't you?" He pulled out his phone. "Lemme just call Johnny and get that done."

"Dude, seriously, you think Mendez is going to pen-stroke us onto your books for a mission?"

Ian's face turned deadly serious and cool. "Yeah, froggie, I do."

Chapter Nineteen

THEY TOOK IAN BLACK'S PRIVATE PLANE TO TEXAS. Hunter had a plane too, but so far as Quinn knew, it was still in Hong Kong. Before they'd left the DC area, Ian had suggested she needed to go shopping. She'd looked down at her leggings and sneakers and realized he was right. Mrs. Halliday was elegant and poised, and she needed that poise if she was to walk into the Texas estate with a SEAL team and tell the security staff to stand down.

So a trip to the private airfield where the plane waited also encompassed a side trip to an expensive and exclusive boutique. Quinn had half expected her credit cards to be declined, but the charges sailed through and she soon had an expensive designer outfit complete with shoes and handbag.

She'd also stopped for makeup, though she decided to skip the jewelry. She had the diamond earrings and necklace she always wore, both modest, and she'd tucked her wedding ring into her purse before she'd escaped with Blade. She'd done it because it was expensive and it was hers—and she was practical enough to think she might need to sell it. She slipped it on, shivering a little at the feel of it on her finger. Her stomach roiled, but she could handle that.

She drew in a deep breath and mentally prepared herself for strolling into the Texas house. She hadn't expected to inherit a controlling interest in HTS. And she still wasn't sure she actually believed it. Just because Ian Black thought he knew what was in Hunter's will didn't mean he really did.

But Hunter had been a manipulative bastard, and controlling his son by threatening him with the loss of the company would have been just his style. So who knew if it was real or not, but it was certainly possible.

When the plane landed in Texas, a black stretch Hummer limo waited on the tarmac. Plenty of room for her and the nine men accompanying her. Yes, nine. Ian had made his phone call while the extremely large and menacing men in that kitchen watched him with barely disguised hostility.

And when he was done, he'd put the phone on speaker. A man's deep, gravelly voice had come on the line and informed the team they were off the books for the time being. She didn't know what that meant, but apparently it was good news for Ian because he looked smug.

She'd studied Blade, waiting for some enlightenment, but he'd merely shrugged and put his arm around her. After a few arrangements and the side trip, they'd met at the plane and boarded. Ian had been there to see them off, but he hadn't accompanied them.

Now Blade escorted her down the steps of the plane and onto the tarmac. She cursed the Louboutins she'd purchased for their narrow design and for making her feet ache. Beautiful shoes, but why the man couldn't make them a tad bit wider she did not know.

The men waited at the bottom of the steps for her, fanned out like an honor guard for the queen. They'd changed into suits for the occasion, and they all had the headsets like her prior bodyguards had worn. She knew they were armed as well because there was no way this group of badass men wasn't packing a lot of heat.

She walked on Blade's arm to the Hummer and climbed inside. He got in beside her. The men piled inside as well, taking up all the room. No one opened the minibar or acted at all like this was a fun time.

Just as the vehicle started to move, her phone began to ring. It shocked her because the only people who ever called were her parents or Hunter. She stared at the number she did not recognize, her heart hammering as a fine sheen of sweat broke out on her skin. She lifted her gaze to Blade's.

"I don't know who it is."

He took the phone and tapped the screen. "This is Mrs. Halliday's assistant. What can I do for you?"

She blinked at him, watching him frown. "No, Mrs. Halliday is not giving interviews. Thank you."

He stabbed at the screen and gave the phone back to her. It rang again. She stared at it, then lifted her gaze to Blade's. "What now?"

He reached over and tapped the button to send it to voice mail. "That's all you can do, Quinn. I'm afraid the media has the story."

"Well, we knew it would happen."

He took her hand and squeezed. "Yeah, we did."

"They won't stop now," she said.

"No, they probably won't."

"Time to buck up and play the grieving widow, I suppose."

"Yeah, probably so."

She looked at the men sitting on the seats lining the sides of the Hummer. They were grim and serious. But they made her feel safe. If she hadn't met them in Viking's kitchen, if she hadn't met their women… Well, maybe she'd feel differently. As it was, she was glad they were here.

"Thank you all for coming," she said even though it felt kind of silly to say it. They were here for something important, not for her. But it didn't matter, because she knew they would protect her anyway.

They all glanced at Blade and then back at her as if they were joined at the hip. It would have been comical if the situation wasn't so serious. "You're one of us now," Viking said. "We'll always be here for you."

She was overwhelmed with gratitude. These men had only just met her and they made her feel like she belonged. Like they were a tribe. She'd never had that with Hunter, and she knew now that she should have.

Blade lifted her hand to his mouth and kissed it. "You got this, baby. I'm behind you all the way."

She sucked in a breath. "All right then, gentlemen. Let's go in there and get those recordings. And pray they're what you need."

———

HUNTER HALLIDAY'S Texas estate was magnificent, of course. Over ten thousand square feet with a long circular driveway and automatic gates that opened once the Hummer rolled up and the guard came to the window. Blade had let it down and waited for the man to arrive. His expression changed when he saw Quinn.

"Mrs. Halliday. Welcome home."

"Thank you, Chris."

The gates opened and the Hummer passed inside. When they reached the front of the house, a man waited. The guard would have called ahead to let the household staff know Quinn was here, of course.

Blade opened the door and stepped out, then turned to help Quinn. Her hand pressed into his, small and hot and trembling. He squeezed to let her know it was going to be okay. Her gaze met his and her expression hardened as if she was telling herself to be strong.

"Mrs. Halliday," the man at the door said.

"Hello, Miguel. How are you?"

"I'm well, Mrs. Halliday. I have seen the news. I'm sorry for your loss."

Quinn dropped her gaze as if trying to maintain her calm. "Thank you, Miguel. It's a shock for us all."

They'd listened to the news on the way over. The reports were that Hunter Halliday had died of a massive heart attack. Ian Black's work, no doubt. It was far better than the world hearing that an American billionaire had been murdered in Hong Kong. The president would know the truth, as would the heads of US intelligence agencies. But there were some things you did not let be publicly known if at all possible. For the good of international relations, it was better that way.

"I've brought my own security," Quinn said. "With the uncertainty caused by Hunter's death, I feel it's best to protect myself until things are settled."

Miguel's dark eyes gleamed. Then he bowed his head in acknowledgment. "Of course, Mrs. Halliday."

The SEALs piled from the Hummer. They weren't wearing their typical tactical gear, but they still looked menacing. Dark suits, earpieces, weapons beneath jackets. Neo carried a backpack with a computer. Dirty had a duffel with equipment they might need for busting into Hunter's office.

And they were all, every one of them, capable of taking down any security forces that Hunter might have without firing a shot. It just remained to be seen whether or not they would need to.

Miguel's eyes widened at the sight of them all. But he wisely refrained from trying to prevent them from entering the house behind Quinn. Her heels tapped relentlessly against the marble of the soaring entry-way. There was a grand curving staircase on either side of the room, and the ceilings were at least twenty feet tall.

Miguel came in behind them and stopped.

Quinn turned to face him. "I'm sending my staff to Hunter's office to secure his files. You can tell your men to stand down."

The man seemed to think about it for a moment. His shoulders tensed, his eyes darted over them—and then he shrugged. "Mr. Halliday is dead. You're the boss now." He took his phone from his pocket and made a call. "Mrs. Halliday is on her way up. Give her what she needs."

"Thank you," Quinn replied when he ended the call. "Send your men to the perimeter. I expect we'll be inundated with news crews before long. I don't want to talk to them."

"Yes, ma'am," Miguel replied before turning and striding away, his phone already to his ear again.

Quinn's eyes met Blade's. She still looked so serious, but then a grin broke out on her pretty face and she winked. Blade winked back.

"Good job," he said softly.

"Thank you." She pointed at the stairs. "Hunter's office is up there. I'll show you where it is." She started for the stairs, her shoes tapping out that determined beat again, and a hot, possessive feeling flooded him. Quinn was confident even when she was scared. She was determined and sexy, and he wanted her so much it physically hurt.

But it was more than that. Viking had said she was one of them now, and Blade knew what that meant. It meant his teammate saw something in his face when Quinn was around. Something that said she was his and he intended to take care of her.

Was it love? Maybe it was. He'd never been in love before, but he knew this thing with her was different. The logical side of his brain tried to tell him it was too soon. The emotional side was saying *what the fuck, dude? You've known this chick for years, and you loved her as a friend long before now. So why not?*

Yeah, why not? At least he could let this thing play out and see where it went. Was it inconvenient? Yeah, it damned sure was. Quinn was a recent widow, and her life was going to be a mess for a while until everything with her husband's estate was sorted out. The timing couldn't be worse.

And yet he couldn't help how he felt. He'd be there for her through the whole thing. And if, when it was over, she still wanted to be with him, then they'd take it from there and see what happened. Maybe she could handle this life he led. Or maybe she couldn't. The only way to find out was to try.

They reached the top of the stairs. Viking and Blade moved to put Quinn behind them as they headed in the direction she told them to go.

"It's here," she said. The sounds of a soccer game on television came through the walls. "There's a sitting room and then Hunter's office. Inside there, he has a hardened room with his documents."

Blade and Viking exchanged a look. Blade knocked on the door. It opened a second later. A big man stood there. Another was on the couch. The game was on and the remnants of a fast-food meal lay on the coffee table.

"Hello, Hugh," Quinn said. "I think Miguel told you I was coming up?"

Hugh stepped back and opened the door wide. "Yes, ma'am. We were just watching the game and waiting for you."

"Excellent. Thank you so much for all you've done for Hunter and me these past couple of years. I am certain he was pleased with you."

Hugh frowned a little but nodded. "Thank you, ma'am. I'm sorry for your loss."

Blade got the feeling that none of Hunter's employees liked him very much. But they seemed to like Quinn.

"Thank you," Quinn said, reaching out and giving his arm a squeeze. Then she turned to Blade and his SEALs. "The office is in there. Please secure my husband's files for safekeeping."

"Yes, ma'am," Viking said, jerking his head at the SEALs. They opened the office door and went inside. Blade, Money, and Camel stayed with Quinn. They weren't needed inside, but they did need to stick with Quinn and protect her. Just in case these boys decided to do something stupid. Blade didn't think they would, but you never knew.

Viking's voice came over their earpieces. "It's a fingerprint scanner on this damned vault. We'll need to cut our way in with a torch. That's going to take some time."

"Copy that," Blade said. "Mrs. Halliday, it's going to be a while," he said to Quinn.

Quinn seemed to consider that statement for a second. "Very well. Gentlemen," she said to Hugh and the other man, "would you please join Miguel? The media is about to descend on us, and I'd like you to keep them out. I'm offering you all double pay for handling the situation with subtlety and class. No incidents, please."

"Yes, ma'am," the two said in unison before exiting the room. Nobody said anything while the footsteps echoed away from them. Then Blade turned to Quinn and grinned.

"Way to go, honey."

"I don't think they liked Hunter very much. He paid them extremely well and he demanded loyalty, but he wasn't very nice about it. They stayed because of the money, not because they liked him."

"His mistake," Blade said.

"Indeed."

Inside the office, a light flared as the torch went into action. Quinn's head snapped up, her eyes widening.

"Steel door," Blade told her. "Only way in is to torch it."

She nodded. "How long?"

"About five minutes, give or take. Depends on the steel."

She folded her arms over her chest and started to pace. "I just want it over."

Blade went and put his hands on her shoulders, forced her to look at him. Her green eyes were so pretty, so filled with anxiety. He wanted to kiss her, but now wasn't the time.

"We're professionals, Quinn. It'll be over quicker than you think. Then we'll be on the plane home again."

"Home? Do I even have a home anymore?" She looked around the room they were standing in. "This isn't my home. Never was. I hate it."

He tugged her into his embrace, put his chin on her hair and held her close. "Right now your home is with me. If you want it to be."

Her fingers curled into his suit jacket. "I do want that."

"Then you have a home, don't you?"

Chapter Twenty

IN THE END, IT TOOK THE SEALS PRECISELY TWELVE minutes to bust into Hunter's vault, locate his server, and download everything. Then they unhooked it and stuffed it into one of the transport bags they'd brought with them. She only knew that because Blade told her so.

While they'd broken into the vault, Blade and Money had escorted her to her bedroom so she could grab some more clothing. There was very little she wanted, but she took some jeans and button-down shirts, a couple of pairs of slacks, and two dresses with some heels. She had clothes in every house that Hunter owned, but nothing of real import. The things she'd had in her own apartment before she'd married him had ended up being sold or given away.

There was jewelry in the safe in her bedroom, but she didn't want it. It was gaudy stuff that Hunter had given her to show off her trophy-wife status, nothing important or meaningful. Once she'd stuffed things in a suitcase, Money took it from her and they escorted her down the stairs and into the marble foyer. The rest of the SEALs came pounding down the stairs and met them.

"Ready to rock 'n' roll?" Viking asked.

"Ready," Blade said.

They headed for the exit and stepped out, surrounding her as they hustled her toward the Hummer. Once they were all in, the vehicle headed down the drive. Miguel and his men were on the perimeter as news vans began to line the street outside the estate.

"Oh holy shit," Quinn breathed. She didn't want to deal with any of this.

Blade put a hand on her knee. "It's okay. We'll get you out of here."

"Let me talk to Miguel, please."

Someone communicated to the driver and the Hummer rolled to a stop. Blade powered the window down and called out to Miguel. He turned and sauntered over to the side of the vehicle.

"Thank you, Miguel," Quinn said. She felt it was important to win over Hunter's people, just in case. And she intended to do right by them so long as she could. The will might prove otherwise, but for now she had access to money. "I intend to fulfill my promise to pay you and your men double for dealing with this. But I think it's best if I leave and go somewhere they won't find me. I'll be in touch."

"Yes, ma'am. If you need anything, you only have to ask. My men and I are here to serve you now."

Quinn smiled though her heart skipped with the excitement of it all. "Thank you so much."

Miguel stepped back, the window rolled up, and the Hummer eased down the drive and out the gates. Reporters surrounded the vehicle, shouting questions, but the driver navigated through them handily and without anyone getting hurt. Soon they were picking up speed and heading back to the airport.

Quinn turned to stare out the window at the traffic. This was only one small victory today. The battle wasn't over yet. She still had to deal with the fallout from Hunter's death—there were people depending on her, a company on the brink of disaster, and possible treasonous evidence on the files the SEALs had taken from Hunter's vault.

But for now she was sitting next to the man she loved, his thigh was pressed against hers, and he'd told her she had a home with him. It wasn't a declaration of love—but it was something.

He put an arm around her and she leaned her head against him, secure in the warmth of his body and the protection of his teammates. Her phone buzzed incessantly in her purse, but she didn't take it out to look at it.

They reached the airport in record time. The engines were already running, and the instant they were on board and strapped in, the plane blazed into a takeoff roll. Within moments, they were in the air.

As soon as the buzzer sounded for the ten-thousand-foot threshold, the SEALs were up and making for the control room they'd passed through earlier. Quinn went with them.

Neo took the hard drive they'd used to copy Hunter's audio and plugged it into one of the terminals. The rest of them sat at the conference table, buckled their seat belts, and waited. Blade brought up another screen, and Ian Black's face appeared.

"Well, that was fast, froggies. Did you get the goods?"

"We got Halliday's server. Loading the audio now."

"Excellent. It'll take time to listen to it all, but good job, guys. Guess Johnny really does hire the best."

Viking snorted. "Was there any doubt?"

Ian laughed. "Nope, none at all. But you know I have to annoy the shit out of you before I can compliment you."

"You're a laugh a minute, Black," Cage said. "I don't know why the colonel puts up with you."

Ian shook his head. "Yeah, you damned well do. Because I'm the best there is—and I have loose morals when loose morals are required. Not something you boys do well."

Quinn had no idea what they were talking about, but she liked Ian. He was acerbic and aloof in many ways, but she sensed there was a heart in there. Some of the prickliest people in her experience were some of the most damaged. They put up those walls to keep people out, not because they disliked people—though it was part of it, perhaps—but because they'd been hurt before and they didn't intend to be hurt again.

"No, probably not," Viking said. "But I guess it's good somebody can."

Ian gave him a mock salute. "Bring the plane straight home, children. No excursions. Daddy's waiting."

Viking laughed. "Over and out… daddy."

Ian's laugh was even louder right before the call screen closed.

"Why does he call you froggies?" Quinn asked.

Blade snorted. "Frogmen is another name for SEALs. Because we're combat swimmers. Ian thinks he's funny."

Quinn smiled. "I think he's funny too. He doesn't seem to care what anybody thinks. And every one of you big bad men cringes when you have to talk to him. If that's not funny, I don't know what is."

Blade blinked at her. Then he grinned. "Well, fuck. Got me there."

"He's an asshole," Cage interjected. "But I guess he's a good asshole, all things considered."

Nobody disagreed.

They settled in for the trip. There was nothing else to do now that they'd sent the files to Ian. Some of the SEALs slept. Some watched videos or talked. But Blade took Quinn to a pair of seats as far from the others as he could get.

They held hands and the second they were seated, he tugged her toward him and kissed her. Quinn melted into him, her palm on his cheek, a little moan in her throat as his tongue stroked hers.

Then he broke the kiss, cupping her cheeks in his hands, and gazed into her eyes. "I've been wanting to do that for hours now."

"Me too. There are a few more things I'd like to do as well."

"I think there's a bed on this plane."

She wasn't sure if he was serious or not, but her eyes widened as she searched his. "Let's find it then."

He laughed. "I'd love to, but the guys would probably notice. Then they'd tease me, which means they'd embarrass you because you're an introvert."

"Some things are worth the hassle."

He kissed her again. "So's waiting until we've got hours to spend in bed together."

She put a hand on his arm, slid it up the fabric of his suit jacket. "I like this suit on you. It's very sexy."

"I'll let you take if off me if you like."

"I would definitely like."

His gaze turned serious. "You doing okay, Quinn? That was a lot of stress back there."

"I'm fine. Really. I just kept picturing Hunter and what a jerk he could be when angry, and I knew if I wasn't a jerk, I'd get a good response. Because while Hunter was no doubt mostly charming with Miguel and his guys, there would have been times when he was a dick."

"I didn't want you to come with us, but it was a good thing you were there. It would have been harder to get inside, and there could have been casualties. Not a good thing for any of us when the op involves Americans."

She leaned back on the seat and gazed at him. "So this is the kind of thing you do all the time, hmm?"

He frowned slightly. "It's one of them. Oftentimes the reception is far more... hostile. This was a picnic compared to most of our missions."

"What do you think will happen if Ian finds what he wants?"

Blade drew in a breath. "Honestly? I don't know. There's no doubt that HTS will lose the contract, and that's going to hurt the company financially. Beyond that, it's hard to say."

Quinn chewed her lip. "A lot of people are going to be hurt by this."

"I know. But there's not much you can do about that, honey. Hunter created this situation when he contracted with the Chinese to put those chips into his systems. That's nobody's fault but his."

"I don't know how to be in charge of a company," she said, voicing the fear she'd had since Ian Black had so casually dropped the bomb that she was inheriting the controlling interest. Not that she didn't hope he was wrong. She definitely did. But what if he wasn't?

"You have a board of directors. Take their advice.

That's all you have to do. Maybe they'll be able to save the company. You never know."

"And if there's no evidence on those recordings?"

Blade drew in a long, slow breath. "Then I guess the military is fucked when those new mainframes arrive. But we really, *really* don't want that to happen."

"Can't somebody test the equipment first? Find out where the vulnerabilities are?"

"I'm sure the Chinese have thought of that. The first components won't show a vulnerability. It'll be the later stuff that's got the holes into the system."

Quinn was thinking. Hard. "Can't I cancel the contract on my end? Just put a stop to the manufacturing?"

"Maybe. But I doubt it's an easy process. You still need the board's approval, and that's not likely to happen."

Quinn laid her head back on the seat. "Then I guess I'd better hope that Ian finds what he needs."

Blade looked at her with a slightly puzzled expression. "You have absolutely no doubt that he's right? What if your husband was just an asshole instead of a traitor?"

Her stomach twisted. But she didn't waver. "Oh no," she said softly. "I'm pretty sure he was both."

———

THE PLANE LANDED in DC around midnight. The SEALs descended onto the tarmac. Blade wrapped his arm in Quinn's and led her down the stairs. She was still dressed to kill in a bandage dress and sky-high heels, her diamond wedding ring winking like a fucking beacon. When they reached the bottom, the guys milled around, waiting for their ride back to the rendezvous point.

Neo and Dirty tried not to stare at Quinn, but they couldn't quite help themselves. Their gazes raked over her body and the formfitting dress that showed all her curves. Blade tightened his hold on her arm, tucking her against his side possessively. She didn't seem to mind. She pressed into him, smiled up at him, and his heart thumped.

"You need us tonight?" Cage asked, pushing his way to the front of the SEALs.

"Maybe a couple of you to make sure the perimeter wasn't breached. After that, no."

Cage nodded. "Sending Neo and Dirty. That okay with you?"

Of course it was those two single motherfuckers. Blade had thought that Neo was interested in Kayla Jones, but maybe he was wrong. Wouldn't be the first time.

"Yep, fine with me."

The vehicles arrived and they split up. Fifteen minutes later, they were at the rendezvous point, piling into their own vehicles and preparing to drive to their respective homes. Debriefing would happen tomorrow.

Blade opened the truck door for Quinn and then

hopped in the other side. Neo and Dirty were behind them, firing up Neo's Mustang. He gave them the signal and they started toward his house.

All was quiet when they arrived. Blade checked the cameras and intrusion-alert system on his phone. All was fine. Still, he entered the house first, Neo behind him while Dirty watched Quinn. The house was untouched.

He went back to retrieve Quinn. Dirty was eyeing her while pretending he wasn't. Blade shot him a hard look that said *don't touch.*

Dirty shrugged.

"You need anything else?" Neo asked.

"No, I think we got it."

"Call if anything changes," Dirty said. "Black's guys are five minutes away. We're headed home, but we can be back in ten to fifteen if you need us."

"Roger that."

The two of them faded into the night and Blade shut the door. Quinn had disappeared. He set the alarms, set up the cameras, and turned off lights as he trailed after her. She wasn't in the shower. He went inside the bathroom, brushed his teeth—she'd been there moments before because her toothbrush was still wet—and then headed for the bedroom.

Quinn was near the window, bandage dress and heels still in place. Her ass was magnificent in the tight fabric. His dick started to swell as he walked up behind her and put his hands on her hips. He dropped his mouth to her neck, nudging her lush red hair aside.

"What are you thinking about, baby?"

"Life," she said.

He licked a trail along her neck as she tilted her throat away. "Life doesn't always make sense, Quinn."

"You're telling me?" She moaned softly. "Three nights ago, I was Quinn Halliday, frigid wife of Hunter Halliday. Now? Gracious, now I'm ready to do anything to get your cock inside me."

His gut clenched. "You don't have to do anything, Quinn. All you have to do is say yes."

"Yes. So much yes."

He turned her in his arms. Their eyes met, searching, and then he crushed his mouth down on hers. There wasn't much he could say, still too much he didn't know.

"Quinn," he breathed into her mouth, her tongue hot and wet against his.

"Blade… Oh how I want you. It hurts to want you this much."

"What do you want, baby? Tell me."

He could feel the blush rolling over her delicate skin. Her entire body heated by several degrees. "You know what I want. You. Your mouth. Your cock. In me, on me. All of you."

"You've got that. All of it."

He pulled her into him but she hesitated. He met her gaze.

"This is crazy, right?" she asked. "It can't last. You

want me now, but what about next week? Next month?" She shook her head. "I don't think I should believe this thing between us."

He put his hands on her thighs, pushed the bandage dress up, over her sweet hips. "Quinn, I don't care what you believe. The truth is that I've never felt this way before. Yeah, I know you. We were friends first. But now? Now all I want is to fuck you so good you can't think of anyone else."

Her breath hitched. "You already do that."

He snorted. "I didn't have much competition. But, honey, you see those men tonight? Those men sniffing around you? Neo and Dirty would sell their souls for the chance to taste you. I could see it on their faces. And the last fucking thing I want is for *you* to see it. Or, worse, respond to it."

She couldn't help but laugh. "Adam, seriously?" Her palms cupped his cheeks. Her body stepped into his. "Don't you have any clue how I feel about you? Any clue at all? You're my savior, my hero. The man I adored in high school. The man who makes me horny now." She trailed a hand down his chest, his abdomen, down to his groin, cupping his burgeoning dick. "*This* is what I want," she whispered, squeezing. "You. Fuck me, Adam Garrison. Please."

Fucking hell, he needed no more incentive than that. He stripped the bandage dress from her body, turned her away from him, and put her hands on the dresser. She wore tiny panties and a matching bra that he snapped open with one hand. Her tits spilled into his palms and he tweaked her nipples as she gasped.

"What are you doing to me?" she asked a touch breathlessly.

He dropped his mouth to her shoulder. "The same goddamned thing you're doing to me."

He dragged her panties to the side and swept a finger into her hot pussy. She was wet for him. So damned wet. He pushed his way into her while rolling her clit between his thumb and forefinger.

"Oh," she gasped, her head dropping, her hips thrusting backward. Impaling herself on him.

"Quinn. You're so beautiful."

"I don't want this to end," she said. "I never want it to end."

He lost control then, fucking her hard, thrusting into her body while she pushed back against him. He wrapped a hand in her long red hair and twisted, dragging her back toward him.

"Yes," she moaned. "Yes."

He fucked her harder, shoving her into the dresser while tugging her backward at the same time. "Quinn. Jesus."

"I'm coming," she moaned.

And then she stiffened around him, crying out. He thrust harder, faster, until his own orgasm burst from him in a hot rush. He laid his head against her shoulder, panting, waiting for his wits to return. Emotion coursed through him, making his gut clench and his eyes sting.

"Blade," she whispered.

He could feel his semen, hot and fluid, dripping from her body. He withdrew, turned her in his arms, and swept an arm beneath her legs, lifting her. She gasped, but then she put her arms around his neck as he carried her to the bed. He laid her down on it after dragging the covers back, then climbed in beside her. She turned into him, sighing.

"You make me happy," she murmured against his skin. "So happy."

He held her tight. His heart was full, his head full too. Full and confused. *Love*, his heart whispered. *This is love.*

You don't really know that, his head said.

"You make me happy too," he told her. "Go to sleep, Quinn."

She yawned against his neck. "Yes." A minute later, she was out.

Chapter Twenty-One

QUINN WOKE UP GASPING FOR AIR. IT RUSHED DOWN her throat and into her lungs, and she dragged in more of it as she sat wide-eyed in Blade's bed and thanked God she could actually breathe.

"Quinn? What's wrong, baby?" Blade sat up beside her and put a hand on her back.

"I was dreaming." Her eyes stung with tears. "And I couldn't breathe. I literally could not draw in air—then I woke up gasping."

He rubbed circles on her back. "Do you remember the dream?"

"Hunter was in it. And you. But no, I don't remember what happened. Not really. He was shouting at me at one point. That's about all I can remember. I just wanted you to save me."

He pulled her into his embrace as he scooted back against the headboard. "I'll always save you, Quinn. That's my job."

She put an arm over his abdomen, turned her cheek into his chest. He smelled like forest and spice and maybe a hint of leather. It wasn't cologne. It was his natural smell along with deodorant and soap. It was a scent she found comforting.

"I'd like to get to a place where I don't need saving," she said against his skin. "A place where life is just life and it goes on day to day without any drama."

He chuckled. "Well, yeah, of course. Though you should know that life with me isn't going to be drama free."

Life with him. She liked the sound of that. "Are you a drama queen, Blade?" she teased.

"Hardly. I have a dramatic profession though. I need you to understand that if we're going to try to make this work."

Her heart was still racing from the dream and being unable to breathe, but now it raced for another reason. "Are you talking about the future?"

"Does that bother you?"

"No, not at all."

He pressed a kiss to the top of her head. "It's like this, Quinn. We have history, and we have now —and we might have tomorrow too. If we both want it and we work at it. Is that something you want to do?"

Quinn frowned. It didn't sound much like a confession of love, but then again he was a guy, and guys in real life weren't as romantic as the guys in the romance novels she'd read. Though maybe this wasn't romance at all. Maybe it was just hooking up and having a good time.

But did she really want to push for that conversation, or was she just going to be happy to move at his pace? And maybe it wasn't a bad pace considering she was the recently widowed wife of a rich man and people would be paying attention to what she did. Shacking up with her bodyguard right after her husband died was probably going to make some tongues wag.

"I want to be with you. But I suspect my life is about to get very complicated in the next few weeks—so I guess the question really is, how are *you* going to handle that?"

"I'll handle it," he said. "You'd be surprised what some of the guys on my team are handling. What did you think of Ella?"

Quinn blinked. "Ella? Tiny, gorgeous woman with your teammate Money, right? They're married, I think."

"They're married. Ella is a princess. Actually, she's a queen in exile. Her country doesn't have a monarchy anymore, but she's still the queen. So Money married a literal damn queen—and there are people who bow to her and everything. It's kinda crazy."

"Wow."

"Yeah, wow. You know who Gina Domenico is, I presume?"

"Of course! She's a huge star. Love her music."

"She's married to a guy who used to be on a different team than mine."

"Seriously?"

"Seriously. So you see, I can handle your life. I've got friends to call if I need advice for dealing with an important woman."

Quinn couldn't stop herself from snorting. "I'm not important."

"Yeah, you really are, babe. Like it or not, you're important—and probably a lot more wealthy than I'll ever be. So think about that too. I live in a small house. I travel for work a lot. I do dangerous things. If you don't want that kind of drama, being with me isn't going to work."

She didn't get a chance to reply because his phone suddenly pinged with an alert and scared the crap out of her. But what he did next scared her even more. Blade shot out of the bed in a second, dragging on the jeans and T-shirt he'd left lying nearby and reaching for his weapons. His expression was utterly hard and businesslike.

"Get in the closet, Quinn. Don't come out until I tell you it's safe."

She clutched the covers to her body. "What's happening?"

"Closet. Now. Put on some clothes. Get your shoes on. Don't come out until I tell you." He bent down and kissed her swiftly on the mouth. "It'll be okay. Just do what I tell you."

"Okay."

He ran from the room, guns drawn. Quinn bolted from the bed and grabbed her clothes, dragging them on quickly. She'd just started on her shoes when gunfire rang out. Her heart climbed into her throat as the firing continued. Her first instinct was to find Blade and make sure he was okay.

But she did what he'd told her to do and got into the closet instead, hunkering down against the wall to wait. It was all she could do.

That, and pray.

――――――

THE MOTHERFUCKERS HAD FOUND HER. Blade headed for the cache of weapons he kept in the hall closet and dragged out the duffel, reaching inside for loaded magazines and the AR-15 he kept ready to go.

He had his phone in one hand and hit the speed dial for his team leader. Viking answered on the second ring. "Blade? What's going on?"

The man sounded remarkably awake for someone who'd probably been dead asleep a second ago, but then again all the SEALs had that ability.

A weapon discharged outside the house, saving him an explanation. Viking swore. "Goddammit, we'll be there as soon as possible. Where the fuck are Black's people?"

Blade would like to know that too. "No clue. Call that motherfucker, would you, and tell him I'm going to rip his head off and shit down his throat the next time I see him if somebody doesn't get their ass over here and sweep these fuckers up."

"Copy that. Any idea what you're dealing with?"

"No. My perimeter alarm went off. Someone's breached the garage. Now they're firing, probably at the door. They're coming for Quinn. I'll hold them off as long as I can, but I'm gonna need some backup."

"On the way. Hold tight."

"Roger that."

The phone went dead and Blade waited for the enemy's next move. He didn't have to wait long. The door to the garage burst open. Blade took aim, preparing to spray that end of the room with fire the second somebody materialized. But nobody did.

Instead, something sailed into the room and landed on the floor with a thud. Blade didn't need to wonder what it was. He launched himself toward the open bathroom. It was the closest room to him and the tub was iron. Quinn would be safe in the bedroom, but he had to get behind cover quickly and pray he was able to come out again firing before they could get to her.

Blade's legs pumped him toward the opening. Another moment and he was tumbling into the tub, arms and legs banging into the sides, breath leaving his body as he hit hard.

But he had no time to take inventory of his aches and pains before the living room exploded in a concussion of sound and flame.

QUINN SCREAMED as the house rocked beneath her. Burning wood and gunpowder—or some kind of explosive residue—permeated the air. One of the shelves above her fell, clothes on hangers dropping onto her head and surrounding her in a cocoon of fabric.

Just like in the dream, she suddenly couldn't breathe. She kicked and pushed and got the clothes off her, then she shoved the door open. Parts of the bedroom wall were missing and fire raged through the holes in what used to be the living room and kitchen.

Fear welled up in her soul. Fear for Blade. "Blade," she screamed, stumbling from the closet, her ears ringing from the concussion of sound that had rolled through the house a few seconds ago. "Blade!"

She started toward the door. It swung inward, and she flung herself toward him, so happy he was alive. But it wasn't Blade at all, and she stopped, frozen, as fear flooded her.

A man in a gas mask stood there with a weapon pointed at her chest. She turned to run—where, she didn't know—but he reached out and grabbed the back of her shirt, jerking her toward him.

"Not so fast, Mrs. Halliday," he growled. A moment later he bound her wrists with a hard plastic zip tie. Another man emerged, also holding a gun and wearing a gas mask.

"He's dead," the man said. "Buried beneath the

rubble. That blast was overkill, dude. All we needed was to stun the motherfucker, not blow the house up. What if you'd killed her too?"

"Yeah, well, I didn't. Did you put a bullet in him to make sure he's dead?"

"I sprayed the area where he last was, yeah. But I'm not gonna dig through that shit just to find him. If he's there, he's hit. Believe me. And we need to get the fuck out of here before his friends arrive. Mr. Shan won't accept failure. We might as well put bullets in our own brains if we don't deliver the goods. Because he'll do it for us if we return empty-handed."

Quinn started to scream as the man's words sank in. They'd killed Blade? Oh God no. Please, no.

"Shut that bitch up," the man who'd been speaking said.

The first man spun her around and slapped her hard across the face. "Keep screaming, bitch, and you'll wish you hadn't. Shan wants you alive but he didn't specify whether or not you needed all your parts. I'd be happy to cut your tongue out for you."

Quinn clamped down on her tongue, gulping back her tears. She didn't care if they killed her, not if Blade was gone, but she also wasn't ready to give up just yet. What if he wasn't dead? What if they'd missed him and he was alive beneath the rubble? He'd said he would always protect her. So she was going to believe it for as long as she could. She was going to believe until he saved her. Or until Shan killed her.

One of the men dropped a dark cloth over her

head, enveloping her in blackness. Then he picked her up and threw her over his shoulder like she was a sack of potatoes. She thought about fighting, but again, she had to stay alive as long as she could and give Blade a chance to find her.

Because he would. He had to. He'd promised.

Chapter Twenty-Two

A COUGH WRACKED BLADE'S BODY. SOMETHING HEAVY pressed down on him. He stilled and tried to remember what had happened and where he was. It didn't take long for his wits to return. He'd been in bed with Quinn when he'd gotten an alert on his phone. He'd gone to fight, but someone had thrown an explosive device—and he'd dived into the iron tub in the bathroom.

He was still in it. He was breathing in plaster and burning wood and sulfur, and the remnants of the bathroom and the roof pressed on his shoulders and back. He had enough room to maneuver just a little bit, but he wasn't going to be able to push his way out of here on his own. Because he had no idea how unstable the material above him was. Dear God, he hoped Quinn was safe. She should have been okay in the closet, which was the farthest point in the house—

but whoever had come for her was going to have no trouble finding her now.

Which had certainly been their plan in using an explosive device. Neutralize him and grab her. But fuck, what a risky maneuver. And a very unprofessional one. Whoever it was, they were more hired mercenary than trained operator. Overkill was never acceptable for a pro.

Blade could smell fire. He didn't think it was coming for him though. The water pipes had burst and soaked the wood around him. Trickles of water dripped onto his back as it made its way through the labyrinth of wood. He had to hope there was enough water to hold the fire at bay—and the choking smoke —until someone could get to him.

He fished his phone from the pocket he'd tucked it in, thankful it was still there and praying like hell it not only worked but that he could get enough of a signal to make a call. The screen lit up as he pulled it out. He couldn't see it too well because he couldn't bring it up to his face, but he managed to thumb what he needed and call the last person he'd talked to.

"On the way," Viking said. "ETA in eight."

"Need to make it quicker," Blade rasped, praying his teammate could hear him. "Explosion. I'm buried in the bathtub. No idea where Quinn is, but she was in the closet in my bedroom. She should be safe—but they'll probably grab her."

"Fucking hell. Hang on, man. We'll be there in four."

"Go after her. Send someone else to help me."

"We'll assess when we get there. Hang on."

The rubble above him shifted. He barely managed to hold on to the phone. "Viking, you copy?"

There was no answer, and he knew the call must have dropped. He held the phone tightly but didn't try to call again. There was no point. All he could do now was pray his teammates found Quinn before it was too late.

"Garrison! You in here?" a voice called.

Blade strained to hear the sound again, to identify the voice.

"Blade!"

It was Jace Kaiser's voice. One of Ian's men. Blade mustered up all his strength to shout, "Here! I'm here!"

"It came from over there!" Brett Wheeler this time.

There was scrambling overhead, and then the pressure started to lift as they cleared away boards and fragments of wall. A current of fresh air reached down to him, and he breathed it in gratefully. He could still smell fire and sulfur, but the breeze must be coming from the opposite direction and blowing some of it away.

The sound of fire trucks and police sirens sounded in the distance, growing closer. The boards lifted, dust rained down on his head—and then there was an opening above him.

"He's here," Jace said. "You alive, Blade?"

"Yeah," he managed. The digging continued and then his shoulders were free. Another couple of minutes and they'd uncovered over half the tub. Blade pushed himself upright on shaky feet and sucked in a deep lungful of air. "Quinn," he croaked out.

Jace and Brett exchanged looks, and Blade's belly hardened into a knot. Please, whatever it was, just let her be alive.

"They've got her," Jace said.

Blade's entire body was shaking. And not from fear. "I thought Ian said he'd have eyes on my house. He fucking told me that on the plane from Hong Kong. So where were you guys when those assholes arrived?"

Brett frowned. "Five minutes away at the local motel. We were in the car as soon as those guys tripped the perimeter."

It should have been enough response time, and yet it hadn't been. Jesus.

Firetrucks and police cruisers turned into the driveway and sped toward the house. Dealing with the responders would take a good few minutes, but thankfully the SEALs arrived right as the questioning started. Viking took over talking to the firemen and cops while a paramedic checked Blade out and made sure he wasn't injured.

He wasn't, though he was going to have some bruises from how hard he'd landed in the tub. A black car pulled up and a man climbed from the back. Blade saw red. He jerked away from the paramedic and stalked toward Ian Black, who stood there staring at the house, a hard frown on his face.

Black didn't seem to notice him approaching, but Blade realized it was a ruse when the man suddenly focused his laser gaze on him. "I wouldn't," Ian said coldly, and Blade halted, fists clenching at his sides.

"I grew up fighting on the streets of Hong Kong," Blade said mildly. "Pretty sure I can take you down with a minimum of fuss."

"Maybe so," Ian said in Mandarin. "Or maybe not. You ever wonder how I can speak Chinese? The truth of the matter is that you have *no* fucking idea about my background or what I'm capable of. Besides, hitting me isn't going to get her back any quicker, is it?"

"Who took her?"

"Shan hired a couple of mercenaries. Obviously not from me, or they'd have done a better job."

"You were supposed to have eyes on the place. That's what you said."

"And I did have eyes. I also have ears to the ground. The intel on Shan only just arrived. Do you want to hear it, or do you plan to stay butthurt?"

Blade tried not to growl. He didn't quite succeed. "One of these days, I *will* kick your ass. But first I want Quinn back."

Money and Camel drifted over to stand behind him. He could feel them scowling even if he couldn't look at them just yet.

Ian sighed dramatically. "Boys, boys, boys. Will

you never learn?" He flicked a hand as if dismissing flies. "No time for the macho posturing, children. You still belong to me, and we have a mission to prepare for."

He turned and folded himself back into the car, closing the door and powering down the window. He raked them with a glare reminiscent of something Mendez would do. "Kaiser and Wheeler will escort you to my office. I suggest you make it quick if you want to rescue Mrs. Halliday before Shan gets his money and decides to dispose of her."

———

QUINN SAT in the car they'd thrust her into and tried to stay calm. She couldn't see anything because the sack—or whatever it was—was still on her head. Her wrists were bound tightly. No matter how she twisted and turned her arms, the bindings stayed tight. There was no give at all as the hard plastic cut into her skin. She didn't think she'd cut herself because she felt no sting, but it wasn't far off if she kept struggling.

The men talked, but not about anything that mattered. The only thing she'd gleaned from them was that Shan was the one who wanted her, which meant he still wanted his money and expected her to provide it. She didn't know where they were taking her, but she expected they'd soon end up at an airport and she'd be on her way back to Hong Kong before very long.

When the vehicle slowed and finally came to a stop, she assumed they were at an airfield. But when one of the men yanked the door open, the odors of fish and water assailed her instead of jet fuel.

A hand came down on her shoulder and propelled her forward. She stumbled once or twice, but then her foot hit the hollow metal of a gangplank. The man propelled her harder and then jerked her to a stop right as her foot came down on air.

Two broad hands spanned her waist and then he dropped her onto her feet on what she could only assume was the deck of a boat. Then he was driving her forward again. Finally he let her go and she fell to her knees with the sound of a television in the background and the clinking of ice against crystal.

The sack was unceremoniously ripped from her head. She craned her neck to look up at the man standing over her and her heart skipped a couple of beats. She'd seen him before, when he'd come to Hunter's party several nights ago. Hunter had seemed agitated and the two of them disappeared into his office.

It was sometime that night, after the man had left, when Hunter left home and never returned.

"Ah, Mrs. Halliday. How lovely to see you again," he said with the hint of a smile. As if they were standing in an opulent ballroom surrounded by polite society. "We have not been formally introduced, but my name is Mr. Shan. I did business with your husband."

Quinn wanted to scream at him. Then she wanted to spit in his face and tell him to go to hell. But those were the actions of a crazy person—and she was anything but crazy.

"I remember you. You came to the party."

"Yes, I did indeed."

Her heart raced and her stomach twisted. "My husband was murdered, Mr. Shan. I don't know anything about his business."

Shan's smile widened. He shot a look at the man over her shoulder. "Mrs. Halliday is uncomfortable. Please help her—gently—to a chair."

The man seized her elbow and lifted her. Then he moved her toward an overstuffed chair in the yacht's gleaming interior and plopped her down on it.

"Restraints."

A knife appeared and the plastic gave way. Quinn rubbed her hands over the red indents in her skin. They stung now that the blood was returning, but she hadn't been cut.

"Would you like a drink, Mrs. Halliday?"

"Who killed Hunter?" she asked and then bit her tongue. She hadn't meant to say it, but the words popped out anyway.

Shan tilted his head to the side and then shrugged. "It was not me, I assure you. He owed me fifty million dollars. It would be stupid to kill him before I got paid."

Fifty million? Ian had said thirty—but she wasn't

telling Shan that. She wasn't about to admit she knew a damned thing about it.

"I don't have fifty million dollars," she forced out. "I don't even know if I'm in the will. My husband and I weren't happy together, Mr. Shan. He didn't trust me."

"Your husband is dead, Mrs. Halliday. And you have access to his accounts. You will transfer my money or you will join your husband in heavenly slumber."

Quinn's mouth went dry. Her throat closed up. "I can't just access a computer and transfer the money. I don't have his password. The most I can do is go to the bank and initiate the transfer in person."

Shan's eyes glinted like glass. "Perhaps you could remember your password if I have Mason here give you some incentive…"

"Mr. Shan, quite honestly, I have all the incentive I need. I'm not brave and I don't have any intention of fighting you about this. But I don't have the ability to log on to my husband's account. He did not share that information with me. If you can hack into them, well, you could transfer your own money and you wouldn't need me at all. But I'm as helpless as you to get into them remotely."

Shan seemed to consider it. Then he strolled over and stroked a finger down her cheek before pinching her chin between his fingers and wrenching her head backward to meet his angry gaze. "You would do well to recall the password, Mrs. Halliday."

"I-I don't know it. B-but I know where he kept it. And I know who to call to get it for me." She didn't know anything of the sort, but she hoped that Blade's team had gotten that information when they'd taken Hunter's server.

"A phone call, hmm? Do you think I'm stupid, Mrs. Halliday?"

"No. Absolutely not. But that's the best I can do."

"Knife, Mr. Mason," Shan said coolly.

Quinn's stomach rolled as Mason handed Shan his knife. It was a big hunting knife with a serrated edge. Her vision blackened, but she forced the darkness away. Though maybe fainting was a good plan, really. Shan grabbed her hand and wrenched it forward, laying her fingers on the arm of the chair. Then he poised the knife over her thumb and pressed down until blood began to trickle.

"You can still type without a thumb. Perhaps you will not miss it at all."

Quinn started to hyperventilate. "Please. Please. I don't know the information you want. I don't *know*."

Shan pressed a little harder, and pain blossomed. Quinn squeezed her eyes closed, wishing this nightmare could be over. If he was going to chop off her thumb, she just wanted him to do it. Tears streamed down her cheeks and a sob welled in her throat. The knife pressed harder and she moaned.

Shan swore and the pain lessened. She dropped her chin to her chest and started to cry. Her thumb was still there, though blood ran down her skin and pooled on the white arm of the chair.

"You will make this phone call," Shan said. "But if you are lying to me, Mrs. Halliday, I will take far more than a thumb."

Chapter Twenty-Three

BLADE AND HIS SEAL TEAM LEFT BEHIND THE RUBBLE of his house and followed Brett and Jace to a black building with black windows located on an unremarkable street in an unremarkable town in Maryland. It was in the corridor where other agencies were found, but it wasn't actually a part of any of the ones that Blade would have guessed.

In fact, he hadn't known that Ian Black even had a headquarters. The dude just seemed to appear out of nowhere when you least wanted him. He also seemed to be in all the hot spots of the world, often with an established basecamp and a network of informants that rivaled the bigger organizations for scope and depth.

They passed through security and followed Black's men into an underground parking garage.

"What the hell is this shit?" Cage muttered as they stepped out of Viking's SUV.

"You got me," Viking returned.

"Think Mendez knows about this?" Camel asked as he and the others who'd ridden over separately joined the group.

"Has to," Cowboy said. "But now I gotta wonder if Miranda does."

"That's what you get for marrying a CIA spook," Money said. "You never know what's going on in that pretty head of hers."

Jace and Brett walked over, looking uptight and serious.

"This way," Jace said, heading toward one of several exits. It turned out to be a freight elevator. They all piled in, and Jace stabbed the number five button. The elevator cranked its way upward. The doors opened on the opposite side of the elevator when they reached the fifth floor. But they weren't anywhere spectacular. It was a hallway with no obvious security.

But it had to be there. They all knew it too. Jace and Brett stepped out and the SEALs followed. When they reached a door at the opposite end of the room, the men stopped and turned back to them.

"Wait here," Jace said. He placed his hand against the wall, in no obvious location that any of them could see—and the door slid open like something in a sci-fi movie. Jace and Brett stepped through and the door shut again. The SEALs all looked at each other.

"Well, fucking hell," Money said.

"Black," Blade shouted, because he'd had just

about enough of this bullshit. "We don't have time for this! Quinn's in danger, and it's your fucking fault, so open the goddamned door and let us in so we can get to work, you motherfucker!"

His teammates blinked at him. A couple of jaws dropped. But, goddammit, he was pissed. He didn't have time for games or hand-holding or dancing around in circles while patting his head just so they could get inside Black's inner sanctum.

"Hold your horses," a voice boomed over speakers they couldn't see. "We're working on clearing you assholes to enter. Just a few more minutes while we get the paperwork in order, okay, pussycats?"

Blade went over and kicked the door that Jace and Brett had gone through. It was metal and his fucking foot stung. "No, it's not okay. Open the goddamned door!"

"Dude, back off," Viking said, clamping a hand over his shoulder and pulling him from the door. "We've got procedures at home too, right? We don't just let anyone in."

"We aren't just anyone," Blade growled. "The motherfucker knows us. He's worked with us before. This is bullshit meant to intimidate us."

"I do know you, assholes," Ian said over the speaker. "That's why this is going fast. Let my people finish and you'll be in."

Blade closed his eyes and counted. "I'm going to kill him," he said to no one in particular. "If Quinn is dead, Black is next. I don't care what the fuck happens to me, but he's going down."

There was a chime overhead. "Put your hand on the wall, dickface," Ian said. "Tile beside the door. All of you can enter."

Blade pressed his palm to the tile. The door slid open the same as it had for Jace and Brett. The SEALs strode through the door—and into a command center as high tech as any back at HOT.

There were banks of computers in the center of the room and giant screens lining the walls. On some of the screens were dots representing assets… just like at HOT. Blade stared. His teammates stared. They glanced at each other and then turned to look at the screens again.

There were about fifteen men and women, all in civvies, working on computers and watching the screens. Ian Black stood in the center of it all, arms folded over his chest, watching the SEALs. Blade hadn't realized it earlier, because he'd been blinded by rage and indifference, but the man wore a tuxedo. His shirt was crisp and white, the bow tie perfectly straight, the jacket unmistakably cut from expensive fabric.

"Where is she?" Blade asked, pushing past the disorientation and focusing on the most important part of this trip.

Ian turned to a man sitting to his right and said something. Shan's face popped up on one of the screens. "Zhi Wu Shan isn't just an enforcer, boys.

He's the Dragon Master for the Jade Tiger triad." Another photo appeared on the screen, this time of Shan standing on the deck of a very large yacht. "Mr. Shan recently arrived in Washington Harbor and is currently staying on the *Red Dragon*, the yacht he bought from a Saudi prince about a year ago."

"He's here?" Blade asked.

"He is here," Ian said. "Arrived a few hours after we did."

"He knew where we were taking her. How the fuck did he know that?"

Ian's expression was dark. "I have spies and agents in many dangerous places. Some of them aren't as loyal as they should be." He shrugged. "This pains me, but it's also the nature of what we do here at Black Defense International. Not everyone can handle the deep black kind of ops we do."

"So you're saying you have a mole."

Ian shrugged. "Maybe. Or maybe Shan has spies and agents everywhere too. It's a different game over here on the private side, gentlemen." He turned to look at the screen where a montage of Shan was playing. "Nevertheless, he's here, he's on the *Red Dragon*, and he has Mrs. Halliday."

Blade was ready to choke someone. "Then we need to go and get her. Why the fuck are we standing around looking at pictures?"

Ian turned back. "We're going, Blade. But Shan is no idiot. He'll be expecting company, and he'll be prepared for it."

Blade didn't see the problem. Neither did his team, because Cage and Viking were beginning to grumble.

"We're SEALs, Black," Viking said. "Commandeering ships is pretty much a guaranteed skill set."

"I'm aware. But——"

"Sir," one of the technicians at the nearest computer said, and Black's gaze snapped over to him. "Adam Garrison is getting a phone call. Should I let it through?"

Blade had forgotten about his phone. Hell, they all had their phones—and that shouldn't have been allowed inside a facility like this. But Black apparently had a way to take over the signals and intercept the calls. It was fucking genius, whatever it was.

"Let it through."

Blade's phone rang as he jerked it from his pocket. He didn't recognize the number, but it was a DC area code. "Garrison."

"Oh God, Blade. You're alive. Thank God you're alive." It was Quinn's voice, choking out words, and his heart squeezed hard. Jesus, she sounded scared.

"Quinn, are you okay?"

"I——" He knew she was trying to get a hold on her emotions. She must have believed he was dead. Not that he could blame her. He didn't know if she'd seen the rubble of the house or she'd been unconscious, but the fact he hadn't been there with her would have made her think the worst.

"Yes, mostly," she said, her voice wavering only a

little as she worked hard to be calm. "I n-need Hunter's bank log-in, Blade. I need to get into the account and transfer money."

Helpless anger welled inside him. Of course Shan wanted money.

"I'll get it, baby." But he didn't know if he could. What if that information wasn't in Hunter's files? He didn't need to tell Ian or his teammates what was being said. They were watching a transcription of the call on one of the screens overhead. It was instantaneous, which would have been impressive if Blade weren't worried about Quinn.

"I don't have a lot of time. Mr. Shan says——"

"*Nǐ hǎo*, Mr. Blade," Shan said. "You have an hour. I assume you know where to find me, yes?"

Shan spoke in Chinese, so Blade did too. A running translation, delayed by only a couple of seconds, began to play on the screen. "I have an idea where you are. You want me to bring the log-in personally?"

"Indeed I do. You will come alone. You will bring the log-in. You will call this number when you arrive. Someone will escort you into my presence. We will test the log-in together. Once it's done, both of you may go."

"And what assurances do I have that you'll let us go once you have what you want?"

Shan laughed. "None whatsoever. But I am not in the habit of wantonly murdering people who pose no threat to me. When I have my money, I have no more use for either of you."

"What makes you so sure I won't log into the account and take all the money for myself?" Because it had to be said.

Shan laughed again. "You certainly may, Mr. Blade. But three things will happen if you do. Number one, you will never see Mrs. Halliday again. And considering that you are her lover and apparently her childhood friend, I imagine that will be quite upsetting for you. Number two, I will hunt you down like the dog that you are. And then I will take great pleasure in killing you as creatively and slowly as I can imagine. And number three, if you do not arrive with the log-in in one hour, there will be an explosion at a local daycare tomorrow morning. It will be quite large and very messy. Many children will perish. So you see, Mr. Blade, if you care for this woman at all—for American babies at all—you will not fail to arrive with the ability to transfer my money. Goodbye."

"Holy fuck, that bastard is evil," someone said.

"He is definitely that," Ian replied.

Blade was trying to keep his cool. "What the fuck are we doing now? Do we even have Halliday's account log-in?"

"We do, actually," Ian said. "He kept everything on that server of his. We're not done with the recordings yet, but we've gotten tax returns, bank accounts, real estate holdings. It's all there—and Halliday was most definitely not clean. He didn't lie to Shan though. He doesn't have the kind of liquid cash that Shan wants in any of his accounts. He was in debt up to his eyeballs and awaiting payment on a few projects, most notably the mainframes for the military."

"So what the hell are we supposed to transfer into that madman's account? Fucking air and promises?"

"We'll come up with something," Ian said. "It would have been easier if he'd asked you to transfer the money without going to his location, but he doesn't trust anyone. He wants to do it himself."

"What about the daycare? Do you believe him on that one?"

"Unfortunately, I do. It's Jade Tiger's MO. Make threats and blow up soft targets if they don't get what they want."

"How the fuck are we going to find out which daycare?" Camel burst out. "There are hundreds of them in the metro area."

Camel's fiancée Bailey had the cutest little niece that lived with the two of them. Hurting babies was a sensitive area for any of the guys, but Camel was probably more sensitive than most after what he'd gone through with Bailey and little Ana.

"We're going to give him something he doesn't want," Ian said. "That's how we find it."

"That doesn't make any damned sense," Blade snapped.

"A little faith, kids," Ian said. "Now stop chattering like an old ladies' knitting circle and get ready to go. We've got a lot of shit to do and only about twenty minutes to get it done."

————

BLADE WAS ALIVE. Oh thank God, he was alive. She could have faith for a while longer. He would come for her. He'd promised he would and she believed him.

Quinn sat in the same chair that Shan's henchman had put her in earlier, her stomach twisting with fear, her heart pounding, her brain racing. She wasn't accustomed to this kind of stuff at all. She'd been bullied as a kid, sure. She'd been an introvert, and then when she'd lost weight and started fitness modeling, she'd gotten a lot of attention. Then Hunter entered her life with his own brand of intimidation.

But it wasn't anything like Shan's. She'd never feared that Hunter would kill her. Berate her, tear her down, slap her. But she'd never considered that he might actually kill her.

This man would murder her in a heartbeat. Especially if Blade didn't give him what he wanted. She had no idea what they'd discussed since he'd been speaking Chinese the entire time, but she knew he wanted money.

She didn't know if Ian's people had gotten the information she needed from Hunter's files. She didn't even know if it mattered. When she'd called Blade, she'd been grasping at straws. She hadn't known if he was alive, but she'd wanted desperately to know.

And then she'd wanted him to help her. She still didn't know if he could, because Shan was clearly still waiting for something, though he hadn't told her what. He was sipping whiskey and laughing at a Chinese show on his television. She couldn't see the TV, so she didn't know what it was.

He glanced down at his watch and over at her, then went back to his show. He didn't talk to her, didn't tell her anything, though the fact he hadn't killed her yet was a good sign. Or so she thought.

She let her gaze wander over the interior of the yacht. It was big, with a large living area and a dining room with a table that seated ten people. On the deck outside, she could see men moving around sometimes. They were armed with what she assumed were assault rifles. She couldn't see them clearly because of the reflections inside, but she saw silhouettes when they got close to the windows.

Definitely armed.

She didn't know how much time had passed—she wasn't wearing a watch and didn't have a phone—when Shan's phone rang.

He lifted it to his ear. "*Nǐ hǎo*, Mr. Blade."

She waited, her heart speeding up, as Shan spoke in Chinese. Then he dropped the phone and stood.

"Well, Mrs. Halliday, it seems as if your white knight has arrived. And he came alone, as instructed. Perhaps this night is looking up."

Arrived? Blade was here? She twisted her head around to look at the entrance. Within moments, there was a small commotion on the deck, and then the sliding doors opened and Blade stood there.

She couldn't stop herself from jumping up, but she didn't run to him because Shan had pulled out a pistol and leveled it at her.

"Good evening, Mr. Blade. I assume you've brought what I want?"

Blade's gaze raked over her and then he looked at Shan. "I have."

"Then please, enter and be seated at the table." He jerked the pistol toward the table and Blade strolled inside. He looked so good to her eyes. He was still wearing the clothes he'd yanked on when he'd left her in the bedroom. There were tears in the T-shirt, a rip in the jeans. She didn't know why, other than maybe he'd torn them when he'd had to dig himself out of the rubble. Clearly the man who hadn't taken the time to make sure he found and shot Blade had made a mistake.

Thank God.

Blade went over and pulled out a chair. Sat down.

"Mrs. Halliday," Shan said. "Join him."

Quinn moved on shaky legs. When she tried to pull out a chair beside Blade's, Shan interrupted. "Across from him, if you please."

Quinn obeyed. She sat down and stared at Blade, trying to tell him with her eyes what she hadn't had the guts to say before. *I love you.*

She thought about saying it now, but Shan's presence would make it ugly. She didn't want the first time she said it to be with him standing over them holding a weapon.

Though, dammit, she might have to. They might not make it out of here alive, and she wasn't dying without saying those words.

Shan called out something in Chinese. A moment later, a man in a suit entered. He was carrying a laptop computer. He sat down at the table and flipped it open, then quickly tapped out a few things.

"You may give my assistant the log-in. He will perform the transfer."

"How do I know you won't take everything in the account?" Blade asked.

"Once more, you do not. You're in no position to bargain, Mr. Blade. The log-in please."

Blade took a piece of paper from his pocket and pushed it toward the man with the computer. The man opened it up, then started typing again. Quinn's stomach twisted as she stared at Blade. She had no idea if he was bluffing or if it was real. But why would he come here at all if he didn't have some kind of plan?

The man at the computer looked up at Shan and said something. Shan walked around the table and stood behind him, staring at the screen. A small smile played at the corners of his mouth. Quinn had to think that was a good thing.

Blade was watching her, his gaze intent on her.

She stretched her foot out until she touched his. He didn't smile or wink or move a muscle. She understood it, but she wasn't capable of it herself. She had to touch him. Had to reassure herself that he was real and that she wasn't actually dreaming he was here instead.

Shan reached down and pressed a button on the computer. Quinn held her breath. If the transfer went through, maybe they'd walk out of here alive.

And if it didn't, at least she'd die with the man she loved by her side.

Chapter Twenty-Four

THIS WHOLE OPERATION WAS PROBABLY THE BIGGEST gamble of his life. Blade sat across from Quinn, staring at her beautiful face, knowing without a single doubt in his head that he was in love with her and wishing like hell he'd told her before now. Before this whole thing went to shit and Shan shot them before the team could storm the yacht.

"Your hand's bleeding," he said to her.

"I cut it," she said, dropping her eyes, and his gut twisted. He didn't believe her.

He shot a look at Shan, who was intently staring at the computer. If she was hurt, it was Shan's doing. He'd pay for that if Blade had anything to say about it.

"It's not too bad now," she continued. "The blood is drying."

Blade wanted to smash Shan's face in.

"This is taking too much time," Shan burst out.

Then he looked up at Blade. "What kind of con are you pulling, Mr. Blade?"

"None whatsoever. You got into the account didn't you? How can it be a con?"

He didn't dare to look at his watch because that would clue Shan in, but time was running out. His team had inserted into the water upstream from the harbor and they were making their way here using underwater propulsion devices to cut down on the time. They'd plant explosives on the bottom of the yacht and then scale the hull to cut down Shan's men before commandeering the bridge. The entire operation had to happen quickly and quietly, or the game was up.

Especially since Shan was armed and standing too far away for Blade to stop him before he could get off a shot. He'd been calculating the distance between them, but Shan wasn't stupid. He'd put Blade and Quinn across from each other and his man at the far end of the table. Blade would have to cross five feet at lightning speed—and do it from a sitting position. Not possible.

Quinn pressed her foot against his. He stared at her, willing her to understand him. Then he cut his eyes down toward the table. Again and again. Trying to tell her that when the action started she needed to dive under the protection of the table.

It wouldn't be much protection for very long, but it would give her a few crucial seconds. And seconds counted in this game. Very much.

Shan pulled the Glock from his side and pointed it at Blade. "If this transfer doesn't happen in the next sixty seconds, you are a dead man." He glanced at Quinn. "But I'll keep Mrs. Halliday for a while yet. She looks like she can warm my bed. If I can't get my money, I'll take it out of her body. First I'll fuck her until I'm tired of her. Then I'll put her into the trade. Redheads can fetch quite a price, you know."

Blade thanked God the man was speaking in Chinese. He didn't want Quinn to hear what Shan was saying. Didn't want her thinking of this man defiling her. It was bad enough that Blade had to think of it.

"It'll happen," he said, though it wouldn't because the entire interface was a fake. But what had to happen, and fucking soon, was that his team needed to arrive.

"Set a timer," Shan said to his man. "And here we go. Countdown time."

Blade sat very still, thinking hard. There was no way he was going down without a fight. No way he wasn't launching an attack of his own if his teammates didn't arrive in the next few seconds.

"Thirty seconds," Shan said. "Oh my."

"Maybe you have a slow connection," Blade said coolly. "You ever think of that?"

Shan snorted. "Twenty seconds."

"You really want to mess up this white interior? It'll take a lot of bleach to get the blood out."

"Ten seconds."

And that was the point of no return. Blade started to move—to do what, he didn't know—but Shan dropped the weapon before Blade's muscles twitched to life.

"And there it goes. Finally. But you aren't out of the woods yet, Mr. Blade. Now we must check my balance."

Blade's heart thumped. Adrenaline coursed through his veins, making it harder than hell to sit still and wait. He didn't know what Ian's people had done, but someone must have been doing some fancy computer work on the other end to make that bar complete its task. Still, there was no money, so Shan's account wouldn't have increased at all. Which meant death was imminent in a few more seconds.

There was a flash of something outside, nothing that made the slightest bit of noise, nothing that anyone would have seen if they weren't looking. But Blade was looking, and that flash gave him hope.

Shan's man was typing away on the computer, calling up Shan's accounts—or the Jade Tiger accounts—and time was winding down. The last grains of sand were falling in the hourglass.

"Where the fuck is it?" Shan's face turned red as the truth dawned on him. The Glock came up again, pointing, the finger stretched alongside the trigger beginning to curl into a hook. It wouldn't take much to fire—

The weapon fell from Shan's hand and skittered over the table as a shot burst through the window.

Blade launched himself at the gun, yelling at Quinn, "Under the table, Quinn. Now!"

She dropped, disappearing from view as men in tactical wet suits burst into the room, guns drawn. Shan reached the gun first and snatched it from before Blade's outstretched hand. Then he took aim, his eyes murderous, uncaring that he was outgunned.

Blade used his hands to flip himself over and then propel his entire body up and back, scissoring Shan's arm and twisting until the man dropped the gun. Blade would have broken Shan's arm, but Shan understood how to counter the move. He was free of the hold rather quickly, but Blade pursued. He kicked the gun toward the nearest SEAL and held up a hand to stop him from advancing on Shan. The man at the computer had been subdued and bound. But Shan had taken up a fighting stance in the middle of the room.

"He's mine," Blade said to his teammates.

"There's no time for this shit," Viking said.

"Won't take long," Blade replied.

Shan spit on the floor of his beautiful yacht. "That's what you think. Do not forget the bomb at the daycare. Do all you fancy fighting men wish to have the blood of children on your hands?"

"See?" Blade said. "This motherfucker needs an ass kicking."

"Fine," Viking sighed. "Just make it quick. We've got shit to do. And *don't* kill him, understand?"

Blade wasn't promising anything. He and Shan

circled each other, looking for weakness, looking for the moment to strike. Finally Shan launched himself with a jab to the head. Blade countered with an elbow to the face that sent Shan stumbling back. But Shan didn't go down. He grinned instead. Then he came hurtling back with a knee strike that caught Blade near the kidney.

Blade grunted and stepped back, then launched a round body kick. It was a risky move because Shan could grab his leg and twist, but Blade was fast and the blow landed against Shan's jaw and sent him flying. Blood dripped from his mouth, but still he smiled.

"You're much better than I thought you'd be," he said.

Blade didn't answer. He dived for Shan's legs and dropped him by sweeping them from underneath the man. Shan landed with an *ooof* against the hard floor. Blade jabbed at his head, landing punches designed to take the man out.

Shan countered with an elbow to Blade's jaw followed by an attempt to twist him off balance. But Blade was heavier than Shan and couldn't be shifted so easily.

"Fuck this shit," Blade muttered, rocking back into a straight arm bar that stretched Shan's arm hard and tight and threatened to snap it. It wasn't a move Shan could get out of and the man lay there, face twisted in pain, chest rising and falling with exertion.

Shan sucked in air. "You still lose," he spat out.

"All those children. And if you do not kill me, I will never cease to come for you."

"Enough," Viking said, sensing that Blade was reaching the end of his tether. Viking jerked his head at Dirty and Neo, and they came over and dragged Shan up, snapping steel ties onto his wrists and shoving him into the nearest chair.

Blade got up, blood trickling from a cut on his lip, head ringing from the blows Shan had landed. He sought out Quinn, who stood behind Camel, leaning around him to peer at the action.

Blade went to her, and she stepped out from Camel's protection, going into his arms as he opened them wide. She wrapped her arms around him and squeezed him tight. Blade put the unbloodied side of his face against her hair and breathed her in.

"I love you," he said softly, relief washing through him that she was alive.

She tilted her head back, eyes wide with shock. "You do?"

"Of course I do. Is it so hard to believe?"

She dropped her eyes and stared at his chest, fingers coming up to toy with one of the rips in his shirt. "A little. Maybe." But then her gaze met his again, her eyes shining. "I love you too. I think I always have."

Someone cleared his throat. Blade looked up, saw his teammates watching with varying expressions. Some were incredulous. Some smug—the bastards with women of their own, of course. They got it.

Not that his conversation with Quinn had traveled to everyone's ears, but it was pretty clear there was something significant going on.

Viking was standing close. He looked apologetic. "Okay, we've still got shit to take care of here. Can I get your attention for a little bit, Blade?"

He didn't stop holding Quinn. "Roger that."

Shan's eyes widened and his head snapped up as the yacht started to move. He hadn't expected that. Good. Blade took pleasure in telling the triad master what was about to happen.

"That's right, Mr. Shan. We're moving into open water. In a couple of hours, we'll be south of the District, out in the middle of the beautiful Potomac. There's an explosive device on the bottom of your boat. We're going to restrain you and your men and leave you all alone. And then, if we don't get the location of that daycare, the boat will explode. If you think you stand a chance of surviving the explosion and perhaps being rescued by the Coast Guard, I promise you that's not the case. You're going to be confined right over the spot where the device is planted. When it goes up, you go with it."

"But the daycare will still be gone," Shan said.

"Yeah, but you won't get to enjoy it, will you? If you tell us where to find that device, and we do, and nothing else explodes, then you get to live. You get to keep running the Jade Tiger triad and living the life of a rich, albeit sick and twisted, man."

Shan was furious. "I am not a stupid man, Mr.

Blade. I'll disclose the location. But remember, when I am free, I will hunt you down at some point in the future. You and Mrs. Halliday. So never stop looking for me, because I will be there one day."

"No, I don't think you will," Blade replied.

A phone rang just then. Viking's phone. He took it out and walked over to Shan. "It's for you."

Shan looked wary. "You have not answered. How do you know?"

"I know." Viking pressed the button to accept the call and put the phone on speaker so they could all hear.

"Hello, Shan," Ian Black said in English even though he spoke Chinese fluently. "I trust you are well?"

"Not at all. Who is this?"

"My name is Ian Black. I'm sure you've heard of me."

Shan's expression hardened. "I have."

"I have a message for you from Beijing."

"I do not believe you."

"You should. And you will, because I'm returning you to China as soon as this is settled. You will have a personal meeting at the Ministry of State Security, where you will be made to understand what the limits of your personal power entail. You're no match for the government, Mr. Shan. And that's what they wish you to know. Harm any of the men in front of you now, harm Mrs. Halliday—well, you will be worse than dead. And you know as well as I do that worse than dead *is* such a thing."

Shan's expression was still hard, but his skin had visibly paled. And no wonder. The MSS was the CIA equivalent, though with less checks on their power. "All I want is my money."

"I'm afraid that's impossible," Ian said. "You made a bad decision when you loaned money to Hunter Halliday. His legitimate debts will take everything there is before the criminal ones get a dime. Your debt was with him and he's dead. Time to write it off and move on."

"It's a lot of money, Mr. Black. Would you walk away from it?"

"I would if the alternative was life in a Chinese labor camp. Consider life as a free man payment in full."

Shan swore. His face was red again, but he finally shook his head as if clearing it. "Very well, I see the wisdom in your proposition."

"I thought you might. Now, once we've confirmed the location of the bomb you've placed, you'll be flown to Beijing where you get to have your meeting."

"Be sure never to cross my path, Mr. Black. I won't take it kindly if you show up in my territory."

"Noted. And that warning is mutual, Shan. I won't be so kind the next time."

The call ended and Viking pocketed the phone. "All right, gentlemen, let's get this tub to the rendezvous point. There's still a lot of work to be done before this shit is finished. Money, give this man some medical attention. Camel, you take care of Blade."

"Quinn needs attention," Blade said. "Tend to her first."

"Sit your asses down, both of you," Camel said, jerking his head to the table. They did as they were told. Camel took out a first aid kit and cleaned Quinn's wound. It started to bleed again and he sprinkled on a clotting agent before binding it up tight.

"What happened, baby?" Blade asked.

"Shan didn't believe me when I said I didn't know the log-in to Hunter's account. He, um, threatened to cut off my thumb."

Blade's gut turned to ice. He started up out of the chair, intending to go and finish the job, but Camel shoved him backward. "Sit the fuck down. It's over."

Blade growled. "He needs killing."

"I know he does, but it's not your job to do it." He shook his head. "Man, that was some kick-ass fighting. Personally, I wanted you to break his damned neck, but it's too late for that. Not to mention you were ordered not to kill him. You forget that?"

No, he hadn't forgotten. But it was more than that. He hadn't wanted to kill a man in front of Quinn. She didn't need that kind of memory in her head. How would it have affected her? Affected them? She knew what he did, but that didn't mean she needed to see it in action. She was a gentle soul. He wasn't.

"No, I didn't forget." Blade turned to Quinn. "But if I'd known for sure he did that to you, I'd have ripped his fucking head off—after making sure someone got you out of the room first."

She smiled as she reached up to caress his jaw. "I know you would, Adam. You've always been my hero protector, my knight."

"And I always will be, Quinn. Count on it."

"I believe you."

He kissed her to seal the deal.

Chapter Twenty-Five

QUINN SAT NEXT TO BLADE AND GRIPPED HIS HAND with her good one. The hand that Shan had cut was still throbbing, but it was starting to lessen since Camel had given her some painkillers from the first aid kit he had on his wetsuit. She'd been amazed at all the stuff the SEALs had carried, considering they were in wetsuits, which presumably meant they'd been in the water. But the wetsuits weren't ordinary ones, that's for sure. More like combat wetsuits or something.

She'd ask Blade about it later, but for now she was just thankful the SEALs were there. Thankful Blade was there and they were together. She'd thought—oh God, when Shan had been pointing his gun at Blade, she'd thought she was going to lose him. She'd thought Shan would kill him right in front of her eyes, and she didn't think she could take that. She'd thought, if Shan shot Blade, that she would launch herself at him and scratch his eyes out, consequences be damned.

But then Blade's team arrived and everything was well. Except for that fight between Blade and Shan, of course. She'd wanted to scream when his team let him fight, but she also knew he had to. And she knew he was damned good. She'd seen evidence of that when they'd been teenagers, though none of the bullies he'd fought for her had had any skills whatsoever. Shan did.

The yacht docked and Blade rose, pulling her up with him. They walked out onto the deck hand in hand. She was surprised to realize they hadn't docked at all. She'd only thought they had. There was a sleek black boat bobbing alongside the yacht. It was smaller than the yacht, but not by a lot.

The SEALs transferred Shan and his men to the other boat. Blade helped Quinn onto the rear deck, and then they watched as a new crew jumped onto the yacht and took over.

"Where are they taking it?" Quinn asked Blade.

"Probably somewhere that Ian can bug the thing from stem to stern with listening devices and cameras. Shan won't ever get any work done on that yacht again that isn't automatically transmitted to Ian's headquarters."

"You think Shan will keep it after this?"

"If not, he'll very likely sell it to someone else that Ian won't mind keeping tabs on."

"That sounds very Big Brother."

"And that's Ian Black in a nutshell."

Quinn shivered as they stood on the rear deck of the black boat and watched the yacht sail away. It wasn't cold out, but after everything that had happened, she was feeling a touch overwhelmed.

Blade put an arm around her and pulled her in close. "What happened when they took you, Quinn?"

It was the first time he'd asked her a question about tonight, but then they'd been surrounded by too many people on the yacht. Right now they were the only ones on the deck.

"Not much. They threatened me and put a sack over my head, then brought me to Shan. He thought I had the log-in and was being stubborn about giving it to him. He tried to cut my thumb off, but when I didn't cave, he must have realized I didn't have it. I told him I could get it though. That's how I called you."

"I'm glad you did."

"It was all I could think of." She frowned as she watched the yacht growing smaller. "So is there really no money in Hunter's accounts? Or was that a ruse?"

"There's some money, but not enough to cover his debts. He had personal debt and company debt, and they're all still tangled up. It'll take a while to sort it out, probably."

Quinn blew out a breath. "I don't mind being poor again. I really don't. Being rich didn't make me happy, but when I was on my own and working for everything I had, I was a lot happier. With myself and my life."

"It's gonna be a rough few weeks—or months. You still have a lot to deal with, and I have a job to do that'll take me away from time to time."

"You don't have a house either."

He snorted. "No, I sure don't."

"I'm sorry about that. It's my fault."

"No, it's Ian Black's fault if it's anyone's. If his people had responded faster, it might not have happened."

She thought about that for a moment. "True… but then I'd still owe Shan money and he'd still be coming for me. Maybe this way was best."

"Maybe so, but I won't be forgiving Ian anytime soon for letting you get captured. Scared the hell out of me when I didn't know where you were."

"I knew you'd come for me." Another thought occurred to her and her heart began to race. "Oh my God, Blade—what about the cat?"

"Shit." Then he shook his head. "He didn't come in tonight, so he was probably at the neighbor's. I'll call as soon as I can and ask if they've seen him."

"I hope he's okay."

"I'm sure he is. Dude is a smart little guy."

She believed him. He turned her until she faced him, then dipped his head and kissed her. It was like an explosion when their lips met. Heat, need, and electricity sizzled between them as they devoured each other.

He broke away long before she was ready for the kiss to end. "I can't keep kissing you. Not right now. I want too much, and this isn't the place."

"Hey," Camel said, peeking his head out the sliding doors. "We're ready to roll, so get your sappy, lovesick asses in here before somebody floors this puppy and you tumble off the back."

"Fuck you, Camel," Blade said good-humoredly. "You're one to talk. You don't take a piss without Bailey's permission these days."

Camel grinned. "I love that woman like crazy. You won't catch me denying shit."

They went inside and sat down on one of the seats against the wall. The motors revved and the boat shot forward like a high-performance speedboat. Blade wrapped his arm around her as she snuggled into his side.

"I can't wait to be alone with you," he murmured in her ear.

She couldn't wait either.

———

"HELLUVA MISSION, LADIES," Ian Black said as he walked into the room where the SEALs were waiting. They'd handed over Shan and his men and then been sent to change and shower before returning to the briefing room.

Quinn had been taken away too. Blade had protested, but Ian had asked him what he wanted her to do—hang out and wait around for him when she'd been through a rough time or be taken to one of BDI's hotel suites where he could join her as soon as they were done here?

He'd opted for the hotel, kissing her before she left and telling her he'd see her soon. She'd gazed up at him with trusting eyes and told him she'd wait up. He didn't think she'd be able to once he'd seen the weariness in her eyes, but he appreciated the thought.

Blade was tired too—and cranky as hell. At least he'd gotten confirmation that Buddy, aka Dude, was okay. He'd had a message from the neighbor, worried about his house and him and telling him to call at any time. So he had. Once he'd reassured them he was okay, he'd asked about the cat and gotten the information that he'd scratched on their door about an hour ago.

Now Blade just wanted to go to bed with Quinn and not come out for a few days. And the only way he was getting there was if they got this over with.

"Who killed Halliday, and is Quinn really safe now?" he demanded before Ian had drawn his next breath.

Ian arched a black brow. "Way to cut to the chase, kid. First, yes, she's safe. Shan won't cross the MSS, not if he wants to retain his little empire in Hong Kong. In the end, thirty million—he told Quinn fifty, by the way, so it's a good thing we padded the fake balance in the account—is a drop in the bucket for him. It was always about how it looked if he didn't force Hunter to pay up rather than the money itself. He didn't want to lose control of the triad, or lose territory to a rival triad, just because he couldn't force one asshole American to pay back what he owed. So it was mostly for show, though of course a man like that doesn't want to lose a penny either. Dragons hoard things, right? Well Dragon Master Shan's thing is gold, and he's missing some thanks to Hunter Halliday. He won't be happy about that, but he'd be even less happy in a labor camp."

"I'm sorry," Viking broke in, "but how the fuck do you have a contact in the MSS in the first place? Aren't they the ones we're worried are planning to exploit a backdoor in Halliday's microchips?"

Ian's dark gaze slewed to Viking. "I have many contacts that would surprise you. I'm a rogue and a mercenary, remember? I work for the highest bidder, not for God and country and apple pie. As for Halliday's chips, yeah, that's what we're worried about. But the deal isn't happening now, so it doesn't matter."

"You have proof of the coding?" Blade asked.

"Not yet, but we will. Halliday's recordings revealed some interesting information though. He was definitely working with Beijing, and he was being paid well for it. Of course, the man was also a shitty businessman and he made some bad investments in real estate instead of putting the money back into the company. He wanted to expand operations, but the properties he bought were shit properties. They would never work for new plants. Zoning was a problem, though he was trying to grease the skids with bribes. That's where a lot of the money went—land and bribes to officials."

He took a breath and let his gaze slide over them all. Blade didn't care for Ian Black very much, but he was learning to respect him. The man had principles. He walked a dangerous tightrope, but he'd never yet been on the wrong side of the important things. And he'd helped save Colonel Mendez when it mattered most of all.

"As for who killed him… a lot of people had motive, but it seems it was one of his employees who got there first. Richard Jenkins, HTS's new Hong Kong operations manager, hanged himself yesterday. He left a note."

Blade remembered the guy. Jenkins had watched Hunter Halliday a lot at the party, and not with the happiest of expressions. But that didn't mean he'd murdered his boss, even if he did blame the man for his marriage breaking up.

"And you believe that?" Blade asked. "What if it's a setup?"

"I do believe it." Ian sighed and shook his head. "It's more than the marriage ending. Halliday was fucking Jenkins's daughter back in Texas, a pretty girl who just turned twenty. He got her pregnant and then lost his shit when she told him. Forced her to have an abortion—stuck her on a plane and sent her overseas and had someone take her to a clinic where she didn't speak the language and didn't know what was going on. She told her mother—Jenkins's ex-wife—about it at some point. The mother told Jenkins, and not in a happy way. She blamed him for letting it happen, for working for such a guy. Anyway, according to the extremely detailed letter he mailed to his ex, he called Halliday and asked for an emergency meeting at the office at some point after Halliday had already left the party. Jenkins met him in the garage before he could go up. He confronted Halliday about what he'd done. Halliday laughed and Jenkins shot him. He'd bought an illegal weapon off the street about two weeks ago in preparation."

"Wow," Viking said.

"That's some shit," Dirty added. "Why'd he kill himself?"

"Insurance money. His policy pays out for suicide, and his daughter is the beneficiary."

"That's fucked up," Cage said. "She'd probably rather have her father than money."

Ian shrugged. "Sometimes people make a decision in the heat of the moment that they wouldn't otherwise make. He'd been planning to make Halliday pay for what he'd done, and he knew he couldn't get away."

Blade asked, "How is it your people didn't figure it out right away? Jenkins wasn't a professional, and they were following Halliday—who went to his office, right? Your people should have been able to make the guy."

"They followed Halliday from the party. He went

to meet with a rival triad enforcer, for God only knows what, but probably something to counteract Shan's demands. When he returned to the office, they peeled off. We had spies in his workforce, and access to the camera system. There was no reason to sit outside and wait. So Jenkins shot him in the garage, loaded him in the car, and dumped him near the docks. We were working on ballistics when we got the information that Jenkins had confessed. We'd have found him, but it was going to take some time to trace that weapon through the maze."

"The official story is he died of a heart attack. So what now?"

"There will be a correction," Ian said. "It won't reference the girl or her mother. But too many people have had access to the letter Jenkins sent for it to stay secret now, though it's possible it will all come out at some point."

Blade ground his teeth together. "So I'll have to prepare Quinn."

"Not a bad idea, buddy." Ian let his gaze wander over them all. "I'm releasing you back to HOT, effective tomorrow. Except you, Blade. You'll stay on as Quinn Halliday's protective detail until Shan is back in China and I get confirmation from my contact that he's gonna mind his own business."

"So she could still be in danger. Great."

"I don't think so, but I intend to make sure. I'll shoot the fucker myself if he makes one more threat, believe me." Ian turned toward the door. "You're dismissed for now, friends. Give the colonel a big wet kiss for me."

Ian walked out and Money started to laugh.

"What's so damned amusing?" Dirty asked him.

"I like that guy," he said. "I can't help it, but I do. Fucker's funny."

"Good thing," Blade replied. "I expect we'll be seeing a lot more of him in the months to come."

———

QUINN TRIED to wait up for Blade, but her eyes just wouldn't stay open. She'd showered and put on a T-shirt she found in the dresser, then sat in bed with the television going. The hotel she'd been taken to was nice, not too far from the building where Blade had gone to meet with his teammates and Ian Black. She hadn't wanted to be separated from him, but Ian had told her it wouldn't be for long.

One of his people had brought her here, made sure she was settled in the spacious suite, and said he'd be outside until Blade arrived. She'd peeked out the peephole from time to time, and the guy was still there. Leaning against the wall, scrolling through his phone.

She didn't remember falling asleep, but she woke up with a jolt, her ears straining to hear any noise. The television was still going. She started to mute it but didn't. Instead, she climbed from the bed, quickly unplugged the lamp, and picked it up before tiptoeing over to the door leading to the living area of the suite. She'd left the door open partway and she stood behind it, heart pounding, ready to smash someone in the face if they tried to attack her. No way was she getting caught again.

The door started to swing open and she lifted the lamp, gathering her will to act. She wasn't weak. She would never be weak again.

"Quinn?"

She cried out, her heart pounding as she jumped out of the way of the door. Blade swung it open and stopped in his tracks, staring at her.

"Redecorating?" he asked, nodding at the lamp in her hands.

She dropped the lamp and launched herself at him. He caught her against him, squeezing her tight, dropping his face to her neck and breathing her in.

"Blade! I heard something and I didn't realize it was you. After everything that happened——" She couldn't continue.

His hands roamed her back, squeezed her ass, pulled her against the erection straining in his pants. "I understand, baby. Thanks for not attacking, by the way. That would have been a pretty good headache."

She laughed softly. "Right. You'd have seen it coming and countered before I knew what happened. I've watched you in action, don't forget."

And he was magnificent, whether he was kicking high school asses or fighting for far darker reasons. She didn't like it when he was fighting at all. But after? Oh God, after… It made her hot to remember how lethally precise he was with his strikes. Like a blade.

"Mmm, want to watch me in action now? Because I'm thinking I need to be inside you, making you come."

"Oh yes, please. *Please.*"

They didn't make it to the bed. He ripped her T-shirt off and she shoved her panties down, then went for the belt on his pants while he dragged his own shirt up and off. His pants fell down his thighs, but before she could push them off he was lifting her, turning her, pushing her against the wall. Quinn wrapped her legs around his waist—and then she felt him at her entrance. Hard, insistent, hot.

He pushed inside her until they both groaned with the rightness of it.

"I love you," he said, his breath hot against her neck as he pressed his forehead to the wall behind her. Big hands held her steady.

"I love you. I always have."

"I've always loved you too, baby. But not like this. I wish I'd known. I wish I hadn't been so blind."

She gripped his face in both hands and dragged his head up until he was looking at her, his gaze spearing deep into hers.

"Listen to me, Adam Garrison. There's not a moment of my life I regret with you. Not a single one. You taught me to be strong when I was scared of my own shadow. I wasn't ready for you to love me like this back then. I wouldn't have known what to do with it."

"You give me too much credit, Quinn. You were always strong. You were crying when those bullies made fun of you, but you didn't run and you didn't beg. You took it. Those were mad tears, not pitiful ones. I may have showed you that, but I didn't create it."

She couldn't love this man more if she tried. It just wasn't possible. He was everything to her. Tears knotted in her throat.

"Listen to me," he said seriously. "I'm going to do everything in my power to give you the happiest life you can have. You're my girl, Quinn. You'll always be my girl. I'm going to love you with everything I have until the day I take my last breath. You're the sweetest, kindest person I know, and nobody deserves to be cherished more than you do. You feel me?"

"I feel you," she choked out as the first tear spilled. Because she couldn't help it. Because no one had ever put her happiness as their top priority. It was overwhelming.

"Don't cry, baby," he said. "It only gets better from here."

He kissed her then, their mouths fusing as their bodies started to move—taking pleasure, giving pleasure, driving them to the brink of madness before they crashed together in a shower of sparks.

Quinn would have thought his legs were spent, but Blade carried her to the bed and laid her down on it. Then he joined her, spooning her from behind, wrapping her in his embrace, his lips feathering along her shoulder.

"I didn't know I needed you until I saw you again," he said, his words vibrating against her skin. "I've spent so much of my life doing my own thing that I didn't think anything was missing. I was wrong."

"I've always known something was missing. I didn't know it was you until you came back into my life."

He squeezed her. "We're going to get through this together. You have to do what you have to do to settle Hunter's estate and protect your reputation, but when it's all over, we're going to live together. We're getting a kitten too. As many kittens as you want. And Buddy, because he's alive and well."

Oh, thank heaven for that. She sniffled. "Do you even like kittens?"

"How could anybody not like kittens? They're adorable."

She snickered. "Careful who you let hear you say that. Big, strong, tough Navy SEAL like you calling kittens adorable? Might be bad for your image."

"Don't care."

She turned in his embrace, sudden worry under-pinning her happiness. "Do you know who killed Hunter yet? Are we really safe?"

He kissed her nose. "We're safe. And yes, I know who killed him."

He didn't say anything else, and she searched his gaze in the dim light of the television. "Well?"

"It's not pretty, Quinn. But I'll tell you what I know."

When he finished, Quinn's mouth hung open. She snapped it closed as fury washed over her. "That poor girl. What a monstrous thing to do to her. And now she's lost her father as well."

"But you aren't surprised at what Hunter did."

"No, I'm really not. He was a horrible human being."

"Yeah, he was." He dragged in a breath. "I know I said we were going to live together, but I probably should have asked you. Do you want that?"

"Of course I want it! Why wouldn't I?"

"I don't know, but it occurred to me that maybe I was being a bit hypocritical considering how Hunter treated you."

"There's a difference, Blade. You might tell me we're doing something, but if I said no, you'd respect it. You wouldn't try to control me."

"No, I wouldn't."

"We're moving in together and getting a kitten and keeping Buddy in the style to which he's become accustomed," she said.

"And when you're ready, we're getting married."

She blinked. And then she smiled. "Yes, we definitely are. What about kids?"

"If you want them. But I think we've got a lot of practicing to do first."

"Practicing?"

He rolled them over and wedged her thighs open. His hard cock pressed inside her slick heat. "Yeah. I'm not sure I've got the right rhythm yet. I need to practice. You mind?"

She wrapped her legs around him with a little moan. "Practice makes perfect. I think you'd better try very, very hard to find the right rhythm."

"Oh, I'm gonna try hard all right. So. Very. Hard."

Quinn loved how hard he tried. She loved it so much that she woke him up a few hours later to try again.

Chapter Twenty-Six

45 DAYS LATER...

"MAN, it's nice to finally have you back with us, even if it's only for a party," Dirty said, clapping Blade on the shoulder and squeezing. "Sucks without you. Hope you come back to HOT soon."

Blade snorted. Dirty was about three whiskeys in and feeling no pain. The gang was at Money and Ella's new place, hanging out on the expansive back porch and patio with its views of the Chesapeake Bay, eating crabs and shrimp and drinking beer.

"I appreciate that," Blade said, squeezing Dirty's hand where it rested on his shoulder. "I miss y'all too."

And he did, though being tasked to guard Quinn for the past month and a half hadn't been a hardship at all. He'd traveled with her as she worked to clear up the messes in Halliday's business. His personal fortune, what he had left, had been held in trust so the business issues hadn't affected it. That was also why the money hadn't been liquid when Halliday needed it. He couldn't raid the trust.

Darrin Halliday inherited the bulk of the estate in the end, but Quinn had gotten a surprising amount of money from her late husband. She'd sat in the attorney's office with Darrin and listened as the terms of the will were read. Blade had been there, standing just inside the door as directed. When the attorney named the sum Quinn inherited, she'd actually gasped.

Fifteen million dollars might not be much for the wife of a billionaire, but Blade knew it was more than Quinn had ever expected to get. She didn't get the houses or cars, though she got her jewelry and a controlling share of Halliday Tech—which hadn't been worth much of anything until Darrin Halliday went to work.

The kid was a genius, and he'd slowly started to shed liabilities and restructure the company. He didn't resent Quinn, and she trusted him. It was a good relationship. The military contract had been canceled, and that hadn't been a good thing for the company, but Darrin had managed to find the silver lining in that as well. If he met his goals, Quinn could very well be an extremely wealthy woman in a couple of years.

Blade sought her out in the crowd, spotted her with Ella and Bailey. They were standing near the pool, drinks in hand, chatting like they were old friends. He loved that for her. Quinn had always been a loner, and being married to Halliday had isolated her from people even more. He knew it was hard for her to reach out as herself, but he thought she was doing it. Sure, she'd relied on her hostess persona at first, but she was really starting to bond with his team-mates' wives and girlfriends.

"How's the house coming along?" Dirty asked, drawing his attention. Dirty sank onto a chair and waited, bloodshot eyes firmly fixed on Blade's face. He'd never really seen Dirty get drunk, so he wondered what might be causing his friend to be so free with the whiskey today.

"The workers just finished the framing. Roof is next." He took a swig of his beer. "It'll be a few months yet, but Quinn and I are enjoying the RV."

They'd bought a big forty-footer and put it on the property so they could still live there while waiting for the house to go up. After talking about it, he and Quinn had decided to build a house similar to what had been there before. Nothing too huge, nothing too expensive. The property was nice, but it wasn't where they thought they'd want their forever home. So they'd rebuild something appropriate to the area, live in it until they decided to move, and then sell.

Kittens were on hold for the moment, but Buddy had claimed a spot in the RV whenever he wanted it. For some reason, that cat loved Quinn. He let her hold him and everything. Gave Blade superior looks too as Quinn scratched his chin and cooed to him. Like *Look at me, man. I'm the shit.*

Yeah, the cat *was* the shit where Quinn was concerned. And he was officially Buddy now. No more Dude. Quinn had said it was confusing and they had to decide. So Blade let her do it. Buddy it was.

The other guys drifted over with drinks in hand and took up seats around Blade and Dirty.

"We're glad you're here today. Look forward to you rejoining us someday soon," Viking said, raising his beer. The other guys did the same.

They all drank and then Blade cleared his throat. "I can't wait to get back to HOT. Though working for Ian Black is kinda cushy, you know? I could get used to it."

Cage snorted. "No you couldn't."

"Nah, probably not," Blade admitted. "Though he seems to do some pretty dirty missions out there in the world."

"He does, doesn't he?" It was Viking who said it though the question was mostly rhetorical so nobody answered. "And speak of the fucking devil."

They all turned to follow Viking's gaze. The man himself strode across the grass from the front of the house. He was wearing faded jeans and a white button-down shirt. He carried a bouquet of white roses.

Nobody said anything. They simply waited for him to arrive. There was no sense in wondering how he knew they were all there today, or whether he'd been invited, or even if he wanted a drink. He'd tell them soon enough.

"All my favorite marine animals in one location," he said, spreading his arms as he came up to them. "What are the chances?"

"Black," Money said, standing up to greet him like a good host. "Can I get you a drink?"

"Beer would be nice," Ian said. "I'll be right back."

He strolled over to where Ella still talked to Quinn and Bailey and handed her the flowers. She smiled and hugged him. Quinn hugged him too. What the hell? And then Bailey hugged him. Well, holy shit, the man was smooth. The other women drifted over and they all smiled and laughed and looked happy while he talked to them.

Dude was smoooooth.

He eventually turned and came back over to the guys. Money handed him the beer and he took a drink.

"I'm assuming you're here for a reason," Viking said.

"It's a party, isn't it?" He set the beer down and let his gaze wander over them. "I thought you might like to hear this one personally... Shan is dead. The Dragon Master ran afoul of Beijing, it seems. He's definitely not a threat to anyone here."

"What happened?" Blade asked.

"Not really sure, other than I had a call from a

contact. But pieces of Shan have been identified, so it's real. He's gone."

Blade wasn't sure how he felt about that. Oh, he didn't mind that the asshole was gone. He just kinda minded he hadn't actually been the one to do it.

"How does this affect Quinn?" he asked, because what if the next master decided to collect outstanding debts?

"I've probed deep into the darkness over there— the mafia, the MSS—and I can tell you she's clear. Shan was obsessive, but his successor saw what happens when you cross Beijing. Nobody is holding her responsible for Halliday."

"The price on her head?"

Ian nodded. "Gone."

Blade was glad he was sitting down because his knees would have given out as the relief flooded him. He'd had niggling doubts in the back of his mind ever since the night they'd defeated Shan—but now it was gone. Shan was dead and the triads didn't care. Beijing and Asia Sun were losers in the information game since Halliday's terminals weren't going to the US military, but they'd just try again. Business as usual, and Quinn wasn't part of it.

Ian lifted his beer. "So I guess you're no longer needed at BDI, Garrison. Black's Bandits releases you back to your natural habitat. Though if any of you ever want to come to work for me…" He eyed them all, took in their expressions of curiosity and hostility and downright stubbornness, and laughed. "I'd be happy to have any one of you. Remember that." He finished the beer and stood. "Later, gators."

"Well, I'll be damned," Dirty slurred after Ian disappeared around the house. "That was beautiful."

Blade couldn't help but snort out a laugh. The rest of his teammates joined him until they were all guffawing and slapping legs and tables. Dirty joined in, though belatedly. Poor guy was drunker than shit. Maybe he was a few more than three whiskeys in.

The day blended into evening, with more food and drink and laughter, until the party finally broke up. Blade put an arm around Quinn and guided her to his SUV. She was animated and flushed, which meant she was slightly tipsy, and she didn't stop talking for even a second. He didn't mind at all. He loved that she was so at ease and happy. Such a contrast to the woman he'd met again that day in Hong Kong.

She leaned against the back of the seat and finally sighed as she ran out of steam. "So what about you, honey? Did you have fun today?"

"I did."

"Are you really going back to work with them now?"

"Yes."

"I'll miss having you around me all day every day, but I guess it's time life moved on, right?"

He glanced at her. "What do you mean?"

"Well, I've been thinking that I need to do something with my life. I inherited all that money from

Hunter—and I want to do what he wouldn't have. I want to help people, you know?"

"You bought Lupe a car. Gave the staff bonuses. And you sent Li-Wu on a cruise with his family."

"I know—and I loved doing it, so I want to help other people. I was thinking of setting up a foundation or something. Ella agrees with me. She's got more money than she knows what to do with, so she wants a cause too. We're going to get together on it and see what we can do. We talked today, and we both want to help women somehow. We think we really can."

"I'm glad, baby. Whatever makes you happy."

She reached out and touched his thigh. Of course his cock leaped to life like he was a horny teenager and not a man who'd had sex with the love of his life just this morning. "You make me happy. I love you."

"I love you too, Quinn."

He eventually pulled up beside the RV and shut off the ignition. Then he got out and went around to open the door for Quinn. She came into his arms willingly when he put them around her and lifted her up. She wrapped her legs around his waist and he walked to the front of the SUV, leaned her back against the grille. Then he tipped his head back to gaze up at the stars above.

"Look at that, baby," he said.

She did. It was dark enough out here in the country to see a few stars, though nothing like he'd seen in some of the places he'd been where the light pollution was negligent to nonexistent.

"It's pretty."

"I'd give you all that if I could. Every single star out there. All the light in the universe. Because that's how important you are to me. You're my light in the darkness. My heart and soul. My everything."

He felt her shudder in his embrace. She put her hands on his face, held him. "When you say things like that, you make me want to cry."

"I don't want to make you cry."

"It's a good cry, I promise."

"I want to make love to you beneath these stars."

"I want that too."

He carried her over to where they had two reclining chaises next to the RV so they could sit outside and have their morning coffee. Then he set her down.

"Hold that thought," he told her as he dragged one of the chairs out from beneath the awning and placed it squarely beneath the night sky. Then he crooked his fingers at her. "Come here, Quinn."

She smiled as she sauntered toward him. "With pleasure, sexy man."

With many kisses and caresses and sighs, he undressed her and lowered her to the chaise. Her pale body was a beacon in the darkness, a beautiful invitation. He stared down at her for a long moment, taking her in.

She was his. Always and only his.

Then, with the full moon rising in the night sky, he joined her and proved why she always would be.

Epilogue

RYAN "DIRTY HARRY" CALLAHAN WOKE TO THE sounds of someone shouting and the beeping of a large truck backing up. His head throbbed as if someone inside chiseled away at his temples. The shouting and beeping continued and he groaned. Where the fuck was he?

He cracked an eye open and pain shot behind his eyeballs. He tried again, slowly. This time he paid attention to his surroundings. He was in his own bed. What the hell had happened?

Then he remembered. The party at Money's place, Ian Black, and a whole lot of drinking and laughing. He'd indulged too much, which wasn't something he ever really did. He usually had an iron will about alcohol and he guarded himself carefully.

But yesterday—shit, yesterday had been different.

Had Neo gotten drunk too? Had they taken an Uber, or had someone brought them home? They shared a house, though they each had their own floor. The kitchen was on his floor, but he didn't smell coffee.

He dragged his hand across his body and reached for his phone. Outside, the shouting and clunking continued. The beeping had stopped, but now the noise was just as bad.

He picked up his phone and squinted. Noon? It was fucking noon?

He dragged his body upright, groaning. Then his gaze landed on the bottle of water and the two horse-sized Motrin sitting beside it. Neo had written a note, which meant Neo hadn't been as drunk as he had.

Gone to the range. Take these, bud. Eat some cereal if you can. Man, you were drunk as shit!

Ryan grabbed the pills and twisted open the water, downing them both. He finished the water and lay back, wishing his head would either split open and kill him or stop pounding. The doorbell rang and shattered whatever peace he was trying to find. He lay there like death warmed over and prayed they'd go away.

Eventually he climbed from the bed, grabbed his Sig, holding it at his side, and stumbled down the hall toward the door. He wished like hell he had the basement floor today, but it wasn't to be.

"Fucking stop pressing that bell," he yelled at whoever was on the other side. And just yelling it made his head threaten to split wide open. He reached the door and peered through the peephole.

A woman stood on the other side, arms crossed, foot tapping as she waited. He jerked the door open and growled at her.

"What do you want?"

Her eyes widened as they climbed from his midsection to his face. Then they widened some more. "Oh. Oh goodness, I am so sorry." She held up both hands as if to ward him off. He squinted at her because the light was killing him, but what he could see looked nice.

Long golden-brown hair, wide eyes, a pretty pink mouth. Her skin was tanned. She wore a loose T-shirt and shorts with flip-flops. Her legs were long, long, long for a small girl. He'd be interested if he wasn't so fucking hungover.

Across the street, a moving van sat kind of cock-eyed in the street. His truck sat next to the curb, right in front of where the van needed to go.

It dawned on him what she wanted. "You want me to move the truck, right?"

She stared hard at his face. "Um, yes? I'm sorry, you clearly look like you're ill or something, but—" She waved a hand behind her, didn't move her eyes from his. "I'm moving in today and the van can't get into the driveway."

He shoved a hand through his hair. "Fine, I'll get the keys."

He turned and went over to the kitchen counter, found the keys and dropped the Sig, and headed back to the door. She was still standing there, back turned as she yelled something at someone across the street. He stepped onto the porch and she turned around again. Squeaked as her gaze dropped, and then she dragged it up to his face once more.

"I, um, oh dear," she said. And then she laughed, throwing her hand over her mouth and giggling in a way that made him frown. Pretty laugh though.

"What?"

"I'm sorry. Really. But, um—" She waved her hand in his general direction. "Shouldn't you put on some pants?"

Ryan stood there, puzzling over her words. Then he looked down—and discovered he was completely and utterly naked. He was standing on the front porch in front of God and everybody, holding his keys, his dick standing at half-mast like a tired old soldier who couldn't quite make it work.

Fucking hell...

Also by Lynn Raye Harris

The Hostile Operations Team Books

Book 10: HOT ADDICTION - Dex & Annabelle

Book 11: HOT VALOR - Mendez & Kat

Book 12: HOT ANGEL - Cade & Brooke

Book 13: HOT SECRETS - Sky & Bliss

––––––––

The HOT SEAL Team Books

Book 1: HOT SEAL - Dane & Ivy

Book 2: HOT SEAL Lover - Remy & Christina

Book 3: HOT SEAL Rescue - Cody & Miranda

Book 4: HOT SEAL BRIDE - Cash & Ella

Book 5: HOT SEAL REDEMPTION - Alex & Bailey

Book 6: HOT SEAL TARGET - Adam & Quinn

The HOT Novella in Liliana Hart's MacKenzie Family Series

HOT WITNESS - Jake & Eva

7 Brides for 7 Brothers

MAX (Book 5) - Max & Ellie

7 Brides for 7 Soldiers

WYATT (Book 4) - Wyatt & Paige

————

Who's HOT?

Alpha Squad
Matt "Richie Rich" Girard (Book 0 & 1)
Sam "Knight Rider" McKnight (Book 2)
Billy "the Kid" Blake (Book 3)
Kev "Big Mac" MacDonald (Book 4)
Jack "Hawk" Hunter (Book 5)
Nick "Brandy" Brandon (Book 6)
Garrett "Iceman" Spencer (Book 7)
Ryan "Flash" Gordon (Book 8)
Chase "Fiddler" Daniels (Book 9)
Dex "Double Dee" Davidson (Book 10)

Commander
John "Viper" Mendez (Book 11)

Deputy Commander
Alex "Ghost" Bishop

Echo Squad
Cade "Saint" Rodgers (Book 12)
Sky "Hacker" Kelley (Book 13)
Malcom "Mal" McCoy
Jake "Harley" Ryan (HOT WITNESS)
Jax "Gem" Stone
Noah "Easy" Cross
Ryder "Muffin" Hanson
Dean "Wolf" Garner

SEAL Team
Dane "Viking" Erikson (Book 1)
Remy "Cage" Marchand (Book 2)
Cody "Cowboy" McCormick (Book 3)
Cash "Money" McQuaid (Book 4)
Alexei "Camel" Kamarov (Book 5)
Adam "Blade" Garrison (Book 6)
Ryan "Dirty Harry" Callahan (Book 7)
Zach "Neo" Anderson (Book 8)

Black's Bandits
Ian Black
Brett Wheeler
Jace Kaiser
Colton Duchaine
Rascal
? Unnamed Team Members

Freelance Contractors

Lucinda "Lucky" San Ramos, now MacDonald (HOT Book 4)

Victoria "Vee" Royal, now Brandon (HOT Book 6)

Emily Royal, now Gordon (HOT Book 8)

Miranda Lockwood, now McCormick (SEAL Team Book 3)

About the Author

Lynn Raye Harris is the *New York Times* and *USA Today* bestselling author of the HOSTILE OPERATIONS TEAM SERIES of military romances as well as twenty books for Harlequin Presents. A former finalist for the Romance Writers of America's Golden Heart Award and the National Readers Choice Award, Lynn lives in Alabama with her handsome former-military husband, two crazy cats, and one spoiled American Saddlebred horse. Lynn's books have been called "exceptional and emotional," "intense," and "sizzling." Lynn's books have sold over three million copies worldwide.

To connect with Lynn online:
www.LynnRayeHarris.com
Lynn@LynnRayeHarris.com

Made in the USA
Monee, IL
30 October 2024